Pharaoh's Forgery

A Karina Cardinal Mystery (Book 4)

By Ellen Butler

A *Karina Cardinal* Novel
K.C.

Power to the Pen

Power to the Pen
PO Box 1474
Woodbridge, VA 22195

Digital ISBN 13: 978-0-9984193-9-8
Print ISBN: 978-1-7343650-0-9

Categories: Fiction, Thriller & Suspense, Mystery, Female Protagonists, Police Procedurals

Cover Art by: SelfPubBookCovers.com/RLSather

Dedication

To Señora Muñoz, for introducing me to *Chichén Itzá*.

Prologue

Flames licked up the walls of the old palace, once the home to the exiled Portuguese royal family in the early nineteenth century. The paint bubbled and popped until, at last, the fire's heat burned through the plaster. The fire didn't stop at the walls; its angry destruction made short work of the dried, mummified remains of ancient Egyptians stored behind plexiglass. Papyrus and shabtis met a similar fate. Butterfly, bug, and arachnid collections disappeared in a matter of seconds as the inferno ripped through their cases. Feathered Incan fans disappeared into smoke, and pottery, wedding accessories from another time in human history, shattered and melted from the intense heat. The angry fire demon tore through dozens of rooms filled with the two hundred-year-old collection of the country's prized artifacts—over twenty million in all. Within hours of the first spark, the roof collapsed, and the fiery fingers no longer simply glowed and snapped from behind the dozens of fragmented windows, instead burst upward, allowing the black, sooty smoke to blend into the inky sky. By morning, only the façade of the exterior shell remained of the palatial structure, and a devastating number of cultural artifacts lay destroyed in a pile of smoldering rubble, slag, and cinders.

Chapter One

"Of course, Jilly. If that's what you want, and you're sure you don't need me to stay?" I fidgeted with the red Swingline stapler on my desk, reminiscent of the movie *Office Space;* I'd scored it at a Yankee Swap gift exchange years ago. It moved with me from job to job and had become a talisman of sorts.

"No, I insist," my sister said through the phone. "Tony is here. Mom's coming out for a few days. I'll be well taken care of." Tony was my sister's *almost* live-in boyfriend, and a paramedic working for Alexandria, Virginia. He was more than capable of helping take care of Jilly during her latest calamity. "I don't want you to lose your vouchers," she continued. "Besides, you need this vacation."

"Yeah, well, so do you. Are you sure the doc won't let you come? I could wheel you around and we can drink piña coladas at the pool," I said, grasping at straws.

"I wish, Rina. Doc says, because of the surgery, blood clots are a factor which increases exponentially if I fly."

I sighed. "I get it. I'm just bummed. You and I were both recovered, and I was looking forward to our relaxing girls' only vacation. I can't believe you're back in the hospital."

"I know, it sucks. It also means that I'll be starting school on crutches. Ugh. Why don't you see if Mike can join you? Even if only for a few days. You guys could use a little hubba-hubba time. Am I right?" If a wink-wink could be heard across the phone lines, Jillian just delivered it.

My sister's suggestion wasn't a bad idea. When we were

together, Mike and I . . . worked. However, in the past few months, a disconnect had developed. He'd been busy with a handful of cases, and I'd been swamped with our legislative docket at the National Health Advocacy Alliance (NHAA), where I worked as director of federal government relations and advocacy; in other words, I was a lobbyist. In addition to the heavy workload, I'd been shoehorning physical therapy sessions into my calendar to recover from a knee injury. We'd simply had less time for each other. With Congress finally adjourning for the month of August, I could breathe. "You're right. I'll see if he can get any time off."

"I've got to go; the doc just came in with a bunch of interns to poke and prod me. Talk later." She hung up before I could say goodbye.

I scrolled through the contacts on my cell phone, stopping at Finnegan, and pressed the little phone icon to dial his number. I know, it was pathetic that I didn't have my boyfriend's phone number memorized. I was terrible with numbers. Mike worked cybercrimes for the FBI and normally locked his personal phone up before entering the inner sanctum of his unit, which is why it surprised me when he answered.

"K.C., what's up?"

"Hey, I didn't expect you to answer. I figured you'd be busy doing special FBI stuff."

"Should I hang up?"

"Ha ha. No, I was wondering if you could take any time off in the next ten days?"

His breath puffed across the line. "Jillian won't be able to go with you?"

"Nope. She can't fly so soon after surgery."

"Well, that sucks."

"So, what about it? Wanna fly down to Cancun and spend some time having fun in the sun with me?" I spun the stapler in a circle.

He didn't respond.

"Wait! Before you answer, let me provide you a full picture of the fabulous adventure that awaits. White sandy beaches, multiple blue sparkling pools with not one, not two, but three, that's right, folks," —I held three fingers in the air— "three swim-up bars. Nightlife includes the famous— or should I say, infamous— Coco Bongo, where it's not just a party, it's an ex-per-i-ence." I reeled off the brochure's highlights in a carnival barker voice, which drew a chuckle from Mike. "*Aaand* in case you haven't been sold by the leisure, we can provide something to stimulate the mind as well. Behind door number one, we have a visit to the Mayan ruins of *Chichén Itzá,* where YOU can visit one of the New Seven Wonders of the World, the famous El Castillo Pyramid. *And* for all you exercise lovers, you can enjoy windsurfing, paddle boarding, and canoeing along the lagoon. So, what say you, Mike Finnegan? Are you up for the adventure of a lifetime with your lover?"

I waited. Nothing. Crickets.

"I'm not talking the whole ten days. I'm thinking just a long weekend. Maybe you could take off a Monday, or Friday?" My voice petered out. "Uh, Mike, are you still there?" I tapped the speaker.

"Yeah, I'm still here." His sigh blew at me. "Ah, jeez. That sounds really great. And I would *absolutely* love to join you. It's not as though I don't have some vacation time coming."

"I hear a 'but' coming. . . ."

"But . . . since this was supposed to be a girls' trip with your sister—which I totally support—I . . . well . . . I took on a new case. I'll be leaving the day before you."

My shoulders deflated and the hopeful smile I'd been wearing slid away. "I get it."

"K.C., I'm so sor—"

"No problem." I cut off his apology. "It's totally last minute. I'd be surprised if you could get away on such short notice."

"Aw, honey, I'm sorry your sister couldn't make it with you. What about your mom? Can she go with you?"

I leaned my forehead against my palm. "No, she's coming here to help Jillian."

"I see. Yeah, that makes sense."

My coworker Rodrigo arrived in my doorway and knocked on the frame.

"Listen, I've got to go," I told Mike.

"Wait, are we still on for dinner tonight?" Mike asked.

"Yes, of course." I tried to infuse some enthusiasm into my tone. "My place. Seven."

"Great. I'll bring the wine and salad. See you then."

I hung up and tossed my phone on the desk with a little more force than necessary. It slid across the surface, knocking aside a pen, and came to a stop hanging half off the edge.

Rodrigo strolled in, pushed the phone firmly back on the desk, took a seat in the guest chair, and crossed his legs. "Trouble with your dashing Fed?"

I glared at Rodrigo, taking in his perfectly ironed, pale pink button-down, black tie with purple polka dots, gray slacks, and a matching gray vest. The pink suited his dark Puerto Rican skin tone.

"That bad?" He smoothed the sharp crease in his pants. "C'mon, now. Tell Rodrigo your problems. Maybe I can help fix them."

I rolled my eyes. "There's nothing wrong with Mike and me. If you want to know, Jillian broke her leg roller skating last night. It was a compound fracture, and they had to put pins in it. She'll be laid up for at least eight weeks. And because she had to have surgery, she can't fly—"

"Because she could get blood clots," Rodrigo finished for me.

"Wait, did you say roller skating?"

I nodded. "The local community theater was having a fundraiser at the roller rink for their fall musical. My sister volunteered to be the costume mistress." I delivered a wry smile. "It's been a long time since my sister's been up on roller skates."

"That stinks."

"Tell me about it." I spun my Swingline in circles. "I asked Mike, to see if he could get away for a day to two, you know, come for a long weekend—"

"He can't."

"No. He took a new case that has him traveling out of town. He took it knowing I'd be away for the week."

Rodrigo shook his head sympathetically. "What about taking your mom?"

"She's coming here to take care of Jilly."

Rodrigo laid a hand atop my spinning stapler and moved it out of my reach. "What about your friend from your old job, you know, the one I met at lunch?"

"Latesha?"

"Yeah, that's the one. She's fun. You two would have a great time."

I cocked my head. "Well, if it's her *was*-band's week with the kids, she *might* be able to get away. With Congress on break, everyone's got a little breathing room. . . ."

"What are you waiting for?" He pushed the cell phone in front of me. I gazed at the blank screen. Rodrigo gave it another nudge my way. "Call her."

"Okay, I will." I didn't need to scroll through my contacts. My old office number was one of the few numbers embedded in my brain. I spun my chair away from Rodrigo to look out my office window. The automated phone tree operator greeted me, and I dialed Latesha's extension.

"Latesha Jones."

"Hey, Latesha, it's Karina."

"Well, hello! Getting excited about your trip to Mexico? When do you leave?"

"That's what I was calling about. Something's happened."

"What's going on, sugar?" she asked with concern in her voice.

"My sister was supposed to go with me, you know, but she broke her leg and the doc says she can't go. So . . . I was wondering, if next week was your week with the kiddos, and if not, would you be interested in spending some time in Cancun?" The last came out in a rush.

"Girl, you know I'd love to go to the beach with you. It *is* my ex's week with the kids. But . . ."

I cringed, waiting for the excuse.

"The week after that, I'm taking the kids to Disney," she wailed.

"Oh, that's right. I remember you mentioned getting tickets last year." I tried to keep my tone upbeat. "So, it's coming up. That sounds like a grand time, Latesha. The kids will love it."

She moaned.

"What? What's wrong with Disney?"

"There is nothing grand about Disney in the summer. It's expensive. A million degrees in Florida. A gajillion people are there, so the lines are hours long. The kids get exhausted. There will be whining and a daily meltdown. They'll bicker about which ride to go on or what souvenir to buy or where to eat. Inevitably, someone will get sick from a ride that I warned them not to go on or because they ate too much junk food. And the throwing up will happen either in the rental car or on my shoes. It's a horror show."

I couldn't help my mirth. "C'mon, it won't be that bad."

"Oh, yes it will," she replied in a deeply serious tone.

"But you'll be making memories with your kids. It'll be

wonderful," I assured her.

"Oh, I know. The lengths we go to in order to make idyllic memories for our children. I swear, I must have been out of my mind to schedule a trip to Disney in August. Especially now that I know I could be sipping mojitos on the beach with you," she cried.

I couldn't help the continued laughter. "I think Disney is compulsory when you have kids. When it's all over, you'll be glad you went."

"Lordy-bee, I hope so."

"When you get back, we'll have lunch and you can regale me with the adventure."

"It's a date," she declared.

I hung up with a grin on my face, in a mildly better mood due to Latesha's comical histrionics.

"So, I gather Latesha's a no?"

I'd forgotten Rodrigo was still in my office, and I rotated around to face him. "She's going to Disney with her kids. Maybe I should just cancel this trip."

"Are your tickets refundable?"

I shook my head. "I used a bunch of points and prepaid for a cheaper room rate. I needed to cancel at least two weeks ahead of time, and even then, they would have charged me a cancellation fee."

Rodrigo crossed his arms and eyed me. "I think you should go. Have you ever been on a vacation like this by yourself?"

"No."

"I read an article in *Cosmo*—" I opened my mouth to say something derogatory, but Rodrigo's open palm stopped me. "I know what you're going to say, but hear me out. The article was talking about all the things you should do before you turn forty. One of the checklist items was taking a vacation by yourself. It talked about going outside your comfort zone and learning to enjoy your own company and doing some introspection."

"I live by myself. I know how to enjoy my own company," I stated drily.

"Yes, but you'll be out of your element." He held up his pointer finger. "You can meet new people. Something you'd be less likely to do with your sister in tow."

"Not necessarily," I said defensively.

"Well, this way, you'll meet new people without a wingman."

"Or I'll be the sad spinster sitting at the pool all by myself."

It was Rodrigo's turn to roll his eyes. "Not if you plan on wearing a bikini. The men will flock. Trust me." He made a flicking motion with his hand, pretending to brush aside long hair. "Your chestnut mane, long legs, and curves will captivate them." With a flourish, he pretended to remove a pair of sunglasses. "Once they see your sea-glass-green eyes, they'll be lost forever."

Embarrassment burned my cheeks, and I delivered a faltering laugh. "Okay. Enough about my trip. What about yours? Aren't you leaving next week to go with Alfonse to his big chef's convention?" Alfonse was Rodrigo's partner, and an executive chef at a five-star French restaurant in downtown D.C.

"Yes." He wouldn't meet my gaze, flicking off a piece of lint from his sleeve instead.

"What's that all about?"

"It's nothing." He uncrossed his legs.

My brows rose at his stonewalling.

"Don't look at me that way." He tsked and held up both hands in surrender. "Fine. This is the fifth time I've gone to this convention. And while it's all rah-rah for Alfonse. It gets . . . old. I haven't done the spouse registration the past two years. The tours start at the most ungodly hours, not taking into account the tastings and drinking that keeps us up late." He shook his head. "That's not a vacation for me. Most spouses don't have time to go all week to the convention. So I end up taking my own tours.

Which, I'll have you know," he said in response to my ironic stare, "I have done and enjoyed. But, it's in Chicago—again." He flopped back in the chair, allowing his arms to hang slack past the armrests and his head to loll back. "And I've done Chicago. I mean D-O-N-E. You have to realize, for Alfonse, it's catching up with friends, meetings, competitions, certification exams" —he ticked off each item with a raised finger— "*and* an awards ceremony, which is a total yawn. He's not up for any awards this year, so I asked if we could skip it, but his friend Jackson is up for some super-duper chef award and he *must* go." Rodrigo said the last in an imitation of Alphonse's French accent, accompanying his statement with an exaggerated eyeroll.

"Then why are you going?"

He shrugged. "It always happens in August, so I figure— since most of the office clears out with Congress—why *not* go? The first time, he was up for an award and I wanted to see him win, which he did. And we've gone to some good places, like Vegas and Miami. Besides, I feel as though I should support him."

"Does he go to our conference with you?"

Rodrigo stared at me for a moment before answering, "No. He can't take the time away from the restaurant."

I shrugged. "I think it's sweet you go to support him. Besides, I'm sure you'll find fun in Chicago."

"I suppose," he mumbled, staring off into space.

The desk phone rang, and my boss's name flashed across the LED. "It's Hasina."

"Catch you later." Rodrigo exited, pulling my door closed behind him.

Chapter Two

I laid the takeout bag of food on the floor and hunted for the condo keys inside my purse.

"Smells delicious. What are you having?"

I jumped and spun around, my heart knocking at a brisk beat. "Mrs. Thundermuffin, I didn't hear you."

My petite neighbor, who lived around the corner and with whom I shared a wall, stood less than six feet away. I must have been far inside my own head not to have noticed her approach. She wore a multi-colored, calf-length patchwork skirt with a pair of purple high-heeled cowboy boots. A bright yellow tunic and matching fascinator atop her neon pink hair finished off the ensemble. To say that Mrs. Thundermuffin's fashion sense was eccentric would be an understatement. I worked very hard to keep my face in a position I termed "interested neutrality," a facial expression I developed during law school. Her outfits were always so outrageous, they made me want to laugh; however, the last thing I ever wanted was to cause embarrassment to such a sweet lady.

"You do seem to be distracted. What is it? Kill off any new congressmen or senators lately?"

I sputtered.

She grinned. "Close your mouth, dear. I know you didn't kill that senator. But you uncovered who did. Didn't you?"

My mouth snapped shut. "I have no idea what you're talking about, Mrs. Thundermuffin."

"It'll be our secret." She winked, and I was stymied for a

response.

She was referencing a recent "adventure"—as I liked to call them, although Mike would argue they were scrapes, plights, or jams—where a sitting senator . . . well, not to beat around the bush . . . basically died at my feet. With the help of Rodrigo, I uncovered a multimillion-dollar conspiracy, but not until two more people were dead and we had been put on the killers' hitlist. A number of people, including some at the FBI, had worked hard to keep my name out of the press.

"It's good to see you back on your feet. Your knee injury all healed?"

I looked down. "Yes. The knee is back to full capacity. Thanks for asking."

Mrs. Thundermuffin sniffed. "Smells like Italian."

"What?"

"Your dinner, dearie. Italian?"

"Oh." I glanced at the bag at my feet. "*Fettuccini Alla Bolognese.* I wasn't up for cooking."

"Is your boyfriend coming over for dinner?"

"As a matter of fact, he is."

"Such a nice fellow. Always so polite when I see him."

I felt like I was getting the approval of a grandmother or aging aunt. "Thank you."

"And so handsome, with all that dark hair and dark brooding eyes." She wiggled her brows. "Looks like one of those handsome superheroes from Hollywood. Like that Doctor Strange fellow, he's one of my favorites." My face must have lost that careful expression of interested neutrality, because she continued, "Oh, don't look so surprised, Karina, dear. I'm up on all that Marvel Universe stuff. Mr. Albert and I like to catch the matinee showings. Only five dollars" —she splayed her hand at me— "with our senior discount."

My fingers closed around the keys. I wanted to get inside, but if I went in, I'd have to invite in Mrs. Thundermuffin. Normally, I would invite her to join me and we'd enjoy a drink together, but tonight, I simply wasn't up for it. "Um, was there something you needed, Mrs. Thundermuffin?"

"As a matter of fact, there is. I have to leave town rather unexpectedly and I was hoping you could pick up my mail," she said.

I stuck the condo key in the lock and twisted. "Well, I can certainly do so for the next few days, but you see, I'm leaving for my own trip on Saturday."

"Then it works out just fine. I've put a stop-mail order in starting on Saturday. But there is a particular package on the way. Would you mind retrieving it from the mailroom when it arrives and holding on to it until we both return?"

"Sure. How long will you be gone?"

"It's unclear." She leaned closer and whispered, "My grandnephew seems to have gotten himself in a bit of a pickle and I'm going down to help him."

"Where are you headed?" I whispered back.

"Mexico." She spoke in her normal voice, so I returned to mine.

"What a surprise. I'm headed to Mexico myself. Cancun. What about you?"

"Mexico City."

I grimaced. "Are you sure you need to go there? I've heard Mexico City can be dangerous."

"Don't worry about me, dearie. I speak many languages, including *Español.*" She flicked her wrist and the half dozen bangles there made a lovely jingling sound.

"I've never asked, Mrs. Thundermuffin, what did you do before you retired?"

"Oh, a bit of this and that, working for the government, you know. Don't we all?" she said in a fadeaway voice. "Well, anyway, thanks for doing me a solid. Isn't that the expression the young people use these days when you perform a favor—doing me a solid?"

I bit my lip to keep from laughing. "That is correct, Mrs. Thundermuffin."

"You needn't laugh."

Chastised, the smile disappeared immediately.

"I like to keep up with social changes, you know," she continued. "The young programmer in 205 put me on the Instagram. He also tried to set me up on Twitter and Facebook, but I refused. 'Only one thing, Jonathan,' I said. I simply don't have enough time to keep up with all the social medias. In the end, we decided on the Instagram." She flashed a set of pearly white dentures. "Not to toot my own horn, but I'm quite popular. I have sixty-six followers at last count. Some of them are gentlemen. Strangers." She winked.

"Good for you. What's your handle?"

"That little 'at' symbol" —she made a circling motion with her pointer finger— "LadyThundermuffin."

I bit the inside of my cheek. With a handle like that, I was surprised she didn't have six thousand followers. "I'll have to follow you."

"Thank you, dear. And I'll follow you back, of course. Now, your dinner is getting cold. Here's my mailbox key." She fumbled in her pocket. "I'm number fifty-nine. Right next to yours."

I took the key. "No problem."

"Be sure to slather up with sunscreen. The sun is quite strong down there, being so much closer to the equator, and your fair skin will burn easily."

"Will do," I said to her retreating back. Her colorful outfit brightened the neutral beige hallway as her cowboy boots clattered down the hall. She did a funny little dance step around the corner, and at that very moment, I decided I wanted to become like Mrs. Thundermuffin when I grew up.

Half an hour later, as I finished plating the takeout, Mike's key rattled in the lock.

"What on earth did you make? It smells delicious." He entered the kitchen and kissed the back of my neck. "I see you started cocktails without me." He referred to the half-empty glass of pinot grigio in my hand.

"*I* didn't make anything. Our favorite Italian restaurant made us some fettucine. My heart wasn't into cooking tonight. It came with salad, so you can stick your bag in the fridge for another time. Would you like a glass of this white, or do you want to open the red?" I indicated the bottle he pulled out of his grocery bag.

"White is fine with me." He tossed the bag of salad in the fridge and watched me as I poured him a glass of the pinot grigio and put it on the kitchen island next to his plate.

"You seem rather . . . melancholy. Is it the wine, or the trip?"

I climbed onto a stool and sighed, placing my chin in my hand. "It's the trip. My mom can't come because she's taking care of Jilly. I tried Latesha, but she's already taking time off the following week. *You* can't come. There's really no one else I can think to call who could take off time so last minute. It just sucks."

Mike sat on the stool next to mine and stared at me for a beat before giving a snort. "First world problems."

I delivered him a side-eye.

"Don't give me that look. It's too bad that Jillian can't go with you, but you're spending ten days at a beautiful resort in paradise. You listed a dozen different activities that you can do while you are there. And" —he O'd his mouth and put a hand up— "you could actually, you know, relax. Read a book. Sit by the pool and sip daiquiris. Get a tan."

"All right, smartass, I get it. Don't look a gift horse and all that. Rodrigo basically told me the same thing."

He gave me a hard stare. "I think you need this trip. You've been working ninety-to-nothing, even while recovering from your knee injury. You could use some down time."

"Right back atcha."

"Actually, my workload has been normal. Yours has been off the charts. When was the last time you got a full eight hours of sleep?" He gently touched the bags beneath my eyes—bags I'd had to hide with more and more makeup lately. His dark gaze was alert and caring. In the past two weeks, my own had become droopy and bloodshot. I'd even developed a stress twitch in the corner of my left eye, which wiggled on and off throughout the day, driving me crazy. "You've had a helluva time lately. Are you afraid to go alone? Or to be alone without work to bury yourself in order to occupy your mind?"

He was right. Of course.

"Neither," I lied, throwing back the last of my wine. "It would just be nice to have company on my vacation."

"K.C., have you contacted the psychologist I recommended?"

I snorted. "When would I have time for that? Between work, appointments, and physical therapy, there is no time to add any more doctors into my schedule. Besides, I'm just fine."

His gaze became pointed. I didn't need ESP to know what was on his mind. "You need a break. You're worn out and cranky. Something's changed." He tilted his head. "You haven't been the same since your sister—"

Mentally pulling up my big girl panties, I held up a hand to stop him. "You needn't go on. You're right. This trip will be good for me. A full night's sleep and some R&R will be beneficial. I'm sure when I return, I'll be back to my jolly old self."

Mike looked as though he wanted to say more.

I glanced away and scooped up a pile of salad. "Anything interesting happen at work?" I asked.

After a moment of excruciating silence, Mike must have accepted my change of subject. "As a matter of fact . . ."

Chapter Three

Tuesday morning, the alarm blasted me out of a deep sleep. I slammed the button and rolled over—to an empty bed. Mike hadn't spent the night. I recalled crawling into bed around nine, laptop in hand, with plans to clean out some email. Glancing over, I found the laptop closed, sitting on my bedside table with a sticky note attached to it.

Mike's bold handwriting scribbled across the paper.

Have an early meeting. Gone home to let you sleep. Text you later.
Love, M

Gee, I'm a fun date. I crumpled the note and tossed it in the general direction of the wastebasket next to my dresser. It dropped into the metal receptacle with a quiet thunk.

"Huh." Figuring it was a good omen for the day, I got out of bed, slightly more cheerful than I had been in . . . well, let's just say it'd been awhile since I'd gotten out of bed with anything resembling a spring in my step.

An hour later, the smell of coffee and cinnamon toast filled my two-bedroom condo as I trotted around in my pantsuit and high heels, methodically gathering the day's necessities. With my to-go cup of java in one hand, I placed my laptop bag by the front door next to my purse. Then I packed a gym bag with sneakers, shorts, and a T-shirt.

Last week, the doctor and my physical therapist had given me a clean bill of health and encouraged me to return fully to my normal physical activities. That same afternoon I made arrangements to get in a self-defense class at Silverthorne Security before heading out on vacation.

Silverthorne was a private security firm in Washington, D.C. The staff, or at least the few staff members I'd met, was comprised of former military special operations guys. They provided security for foreign diplomats in Washington and a variety of other services, including private investigation. They also worked overseas. Mike once told me that when you wanted to generate a small country coup d'état, you called Silverthorne. I'm fairly sure they performed black op missions for the CIA, though I'd never received confirmation when I asked. I'd stumbled across Silverthorne when, unbeknownst to me, they'd been hired to protect me from a mafia threat that I'd been blissfully unaware of until one of said mafia thugs attacked me in the back stairwell of my building. Ever since that incident, I'd been taking private self-defense classes from one or another of the Silverthorne guys.

Mike was not thrilled about my relationship with Silverthorne. He thought they worked in the gray areas of the law, and he might have had a better idea of what they did than I. However, back in May something happened that may have altered his feelings, because when I told him I had arranged a self-defense class, he hadn't delivered his usual disapproving face. Instead, he'd nodded approvingly and said, "Good!"

So, after a relatively slow day at work, I was ready to get back into fighting mode. I'd always found a workout with one of the boys helped release the frustrations of the day, something I'd come to miss over the past few months as I healed.

As I parked in front of the large, nondescript warehouse, the front door opened, revealing a figure I knew well. A little over six feet tall, Rick, the head of Silverthorne Security, nicely filled out his worn jeans and black polo. The muscular biceps were noticeable and firm, but not obscenely bulging. His BMI probably ranged within the zone of perfection.

I waved, pulling my bag from the trunk of my beat-up Honda. "How's it going, Rick? Haven't seen you in a while."

A small grin spread across his face as he strolled out to meet me. "What happened to Batman?"

I'd nicknamed him Batman because of the way he swooped in and out of my life—more often than not, getting me out of hot water. "Hmm." I put a finger to my lips and cocked my head. "I don't know if I can continue with that moniker. Now that I know your last name, it's like the mystery is gone."

He took the pink-and-white striped duffle from my grasp and hung it on his shoulder. "You don't know where I live."

I slammed my trunk closed. It didn't catch the first time and I tried again. "Do you live in a cave?" I teased.

"No." Together we slammed the trunk shut and it finally caught. "Cardinal, when are you going to get a new car?" he asked as he pointed to the fist-sized dent in my rear bumper.

"Never. I'm taking a page out of your book. I plan to hold on to it until it becomes a classic." I winked. Rick sometimes drove a 1970 Ford Torino Cobra Jet, a badass muscle car.

Those slate gray eyes shot me a disbelieving stare. "It's a Honda Accord. It'll never be a classic."

"Shh, you're ruining my delusions of grandeur." I sighed. "Seriously, I'm waiting until I hit the jackpot."

He gave me a hard stare.

"Ugh. I know what you're going to say, but there's *no way* I could've taken that money. Besides, considering everything you did to help me in May, I'm fairly certain I've run through quite a bit of my retainer."

He grunted, opening the door for me. "Not even close."

My brows rose in surprise, but I didn't probe deeper. "So, who's on the list to toss me around today? Jin? Josh? Some unwitting newbie? Wait." I halted. "This is new."

The long beige hallway had been painted a soft teal, and the old brown carpet replaced with a rustic gray wood laminate, but the biggest change was the addition of a reception area with a desk and pair of black lounge chairs. A wall had been knocked down to create the new area. The desk was currently unmanned.

Rick paused midstride, glancing back over his shoulder. "It's been a while since you've been here. Things change."

I rolled my eyes and mumbled, "Some things don't." Like good ol' Rick, a man of few words. "It looks nice. Very professional."

As I trotted after Rick down the hallway toward the elevator, the door into the gym opened, and Joshua popped his head out.

"I thought I heard a voice I knew. Good to see you, Karina." Joshua stepped out and gave me a side hug. I was grateful he didn't go in for a full-on hug; sweat dripped down his temples and he smelled like the gym—sweat socks and Pine Sol. Joshua, a retired medic and Navy SEAL, towered above my five-foot-nine-inch frame, and, with his bulgy muscles, made Rick look slim. "We've missed you. Jin hasn't cracked a smile since you've been gone."

"It's good to see you too, Josh. I wanted to thank you for the chocolates and encouraging emails you sent during my recovery. It was very kind of you."

He blushed and squeezed me again.

"You stopped visiting in June." I looked him up and down. "And you're very tan. Your blond hair is almost white. Where have you been? No, let me guess. You've recently shaved off a beard, so I'm going to say . . . somewhere in the middle east. Afghanistan? Iraq? Iran? Israel? Jordan? Syria?" Joshua just grinned at me as we played our game where I reeled off countries and he neither denied nor acknowledged my attempts. However, I noticed his nostrils flare when I mentioned Syria. "Syria? Really?

Seems kind of dangerous."

Joshua said nothing, while Rick shook his head. Their missions and clients were kept confidential, and I knew I'd get nothing further from either one of them.

"So am I working with you today, then?" I directed at my favorite sweaty blond bear.

"Not today," Rick answered. "We're trying something new."

I shrugged. "Guess we'll catch up another time."

"Take care." Josh disappeared back into the gym, while I followed Rick to the elevator.

He swiped his card, entered his code on the keypad, and when the elevator arrived, he pressed *B2*.

"*B2*? I've never been to the sublevels. What goes on down there? Is that where the waterboarding happens?"

"You have a very vivid imagination." Rick pursed his lips. "How did you know Joshua had just shaved a beard? Did you see him yesterday?"

"Same way I know you just shaved one too."

Rick's granite gaze speared me.

"Tan lines. The lower part of your face isn't as dark as the upper. Not a lot, but enough. I assume that means you were also in Syria with Josh."

Rick didn't respond, and the elevator opened to another lengthy hallway. This one, however, could best be described as utilitarian. My heels clacked on the concrete, and the white walls were in need of a new paint job. One of the exposed pipes above me gurgled and hissed.

"Love what you've done with the place. Are you sure this isn't the waterboarding level?" I commented. "No? Perhaps waterboarding is on *B1*?"

Rick stopped in front of a door and handed me my duffle. "You can change in there."

A piece of white paper was duct taped to the wall, and written in black marker were the words UNISEX BATHROOM.

My pink lacquered nail tapped the sign. "Did you put this up this morning?"

All the times I'd been in the building, I'd never met any women, and the only ladies' room I'd ever used was housed on the second floor. Yup, I had to have someone escort me to the elevator to go pee at Silverthorne. When I once asked Joshua about this phenomenon, he told me they contracted with a handful of women, depending on the job. Knowing there were some badass women out there perfectly capable of doing the type of work Silverthorne did, I'd planned to discuss it with Rick, but I'd never gotten around to it. Really, they were lucky they hadn't had an EEOC lawsuit slapped on them.

Rick cleared his throat. "Why do you ask?"

"Seeing as I've *never* seen another woman in this building, I'm fairly sure *all* the bathrooms, except the one on the second floor, are men's rooms." I believe I saw the tiniest hint of a flush around his neck.

"As a matter of fact, we've recently hired two new women and are rectifying the . . . uh . . ." He coughed. ". . . bathroom situation."

"Hallelujah," I said drily as I turned the knob and entered the most utilitarian bathroom I'd ever seen. "Well, at least it's clean."

Ten minutes later, I stood with Rick in front of a two-lane gun range and a table splayed with half a dozen handguns. The range consisted of white-washed concrete side walls with an angled black rubber wall at the end for trapping the bullets.

"I guess this means you're teaching me how to handle a gun." I stared at the weapons, which both repulsed and fascinated me.

"What's that look for? A few months ago, you expressed regret when you didn't know how to use a handgun."

I shuddered. "I know, but with all of the gun violence in our nation—I'm not sure I want to be a part of it."

"What about this past May?"

"Oh, I doubt *that* will happen again." My scoff held a snappish tone.

Rick's brows rose and those flinty eyes glared at me. "Of course it won't. But you seem to find trouble as easily as a bee finds nectar. It homes in on you like a pigeon returning to its roost," he said with exasperation. "Don't tell me you didn't want that Ruger" —he pointed to the compact gun at the far right— "tucked into your utility belt when the shit hit the fan with Jillian. I've been trying to get you to learn how to use it ever since the Rivkin incident."

My spirits and any sort of amity I'd felt from returning to Silverthorne deflated, exiting with an audible whoosh as though I'd been sucker punched. Tears pricked the back of my eyes. I crossed my arms, locked my jaw, and looked away from Rick to stare down the empty range.

"Shit," he grumbled, "Jin was right." He cleared his throat and softened his tone. "Karina, look at me."

I refused, mashing my lips together and desperately trying to keep the tears at bay.

He stepped into my line of vision. "It wasn't your fault."

I sniffed and shifted my gaze to the toe of my bright blue sneaker.

"It wasn't your fault," he repeated.

I shook my head.

"It wasn't your fault."

Holding my head down wasn't helping the crying situation. My nose started to fill, and one tear broke the surface. Surreptitiously, I wiped it away.

"Ah, Karina, your sister's kidnapping was not your fault," Rick crooned. It was my undoing. If he'd barked those same words at me, I would have bucked up and shouted back at him. "It wasn't your fault," he whispered.

The dam broke loose. Rick gathered me into his arms as the sobbing commenced. Mortification at crying in front of this man slipped in under the feelings of guilt I'd been carrying around since May. I am not an attractive crier. My eyes and nose turn clown red and my sobs come out in heaving gasps. Rick rubbed my back and continued his monologue about how it wasn't my fault and I needed to stop blaming myself for what happened, blah, blah, blah. After a bit, the storm finally wound down.

I drew out of his embrace, still staring down, and mumbled, "Bathroom." I made a hasty retreat from the gun range, retracing my steps to the bathroom. Things didn't look much better in the mirror than I'd imagined, but at least I could wipe my face and splash cold water on my Bozo nose.

Rick was leaning against the wall across from the bathroom when I came out of it. If he hadn't been there, I might have tried to sneak away, knowing full well I never would have made it because I didn't have a security card and code for the damn elevator. I suppose his presence stopped me from making even more a fool of myself.

"All done?"

I cleared my throat and nodded, staring at the baseball-sized wet stain on his black shirt.

"Feel better?"

Taking a deep breath, I assessed. Actually, I did kind of feel better. The crying had been cathartic. "What did you mean when you said, 'Jin was right'?"

"Jin mentioned you'd changed . . . become brittle and that darkness followed you."

My eyes widened. Jin, another Silverthorne guy, had popped into my office or stopped by my condo once a week to "check on me." I thought I'd done a better job hiding my troubles from him. I should have known. Jin "saw" things others didn't.

"Is that the first time you came to terms or acknowledged the trauma?" Rick asked quietly.

I rolled my lips inward and nodded again.

His slate gaze softened. "I'm surprised your Fed didn't send you to a shrink."

"He did. I didn't go."

Rick shook his head. "Listen, you've been through some pretty rough stuff. I've seen a man three times your size and better trained mentally crippled by less. If you keep sweeping that shit under the rug, you'll reach a breaking point. And it might not be in a safe place like here."

My brows rose and I crossed my arms. "*Is* this a safe place?"

His head jerked back in surprise at my words.

"I mean, I know every inch of this building is monitored." I pointed at one of the black cameras on the ceiling. "Is my waterworks display going to get around to the other guys?"

His brows crunched together. "Hell no. And even if it did, no one would think less of you, or give you crap for it. Trust me, the guys respect you." He shook his head. "I think when you nailed that gangbanger with the van, you reached pinnacle heights. They high-fived over it for weeks."

A half-smile crept up my cheek. "You should have put me on coms."

"Don't remind me." He grunted and pushed his shoulders off the wall. "Every man in this building has had to face his own demons. If shrinks aren't your bag, there's a group that meets here on the first and third Tuesdays at 8:00 p.m. It can help."

I chewed my lip. "Thanks. I'll think about it."

"You know what else might help?"

"What?"

"Don't cancel. Go on your vacation and get some rest. You look like hell."

One of my brows rose. "You sure do know how to sweettalk a girl. How did you know about my vacation plans?"

"Mike called me."

I was so shocked by that, a mouse's sneeze could have knocked me down.

"Pick up your jaw. He's worried and thought I might be able to talk some sense into you." He rolled his eyes. "I have no idea where he got the impression that you'd listen to me."

Wow. Mike must be desperate to have reached out to Rick.

"You know what else we can do to help your situation?" Rick asked.

I shook my head.

"Learning how to handle a gun. C'mon," —he motioned his head toward the range— "get your butt in there."

So I did.

Rick pointed to each weapon and gave me a rundown on the specs. When he got to a black 9mm Glock, I picked it up, dropped the mag, popped out the bullet in the chamber, caught it handily, and laid them all back down on the table.

Rick's mouth turned into a fine line. "I see you're familiar with the Glock."

"It's Mike's service weapon. I can't count how many times I've seen him perform the same routine after work. He showed me how to do it one day, but that's all I know. Frankly, it feels bulky and heavy to me. I like the compactness of the Ruger. Like you said, it conforms to a woman's hand. If this lecture is to help me decide on a weapon, I'm going to go with the Ruger." I pointed at the snub-nosed gun. "Nine-millimeter with a seven round single stack magazine," I reeled off, remembering the first time Rick offered it to me.

"The Ruger it is." He picked up the weapon and gave me a short lecture on the history of the Ruger company and this particular weapon.

"Does it come in pink?" I asked cheekily.

One brow went up. "As a matter of fact, I believe it does."

Rick lectured me about gun safety, then taught me how to load and unload the weapon. I must have done it a dozen times before he took me over to one of the lanes. He handed me a pair of noise-cancelling earmuffs and clear safety glasses, then hooked up a paper outline of a man and sent it about twenty yards down the lane. That's when we got into the fun stuff. A weapon gripping, aiming, and firing demonstration went on for another ten minutes before he placed the fully loaded Ruger in my hand.

My first shot hit the target dead center of the head.

"Hey, that's fantastic, Cardinal." Rick smiled and patted my shoulder. "But it's better to aim for center mass, especially if the target is moving." He adjusted my aim downward.

The next shots were nothing less than pathetic. We reloaded once, and of the thirteen other shots, one went in the shoulder, one pinked the neck, three hit the paper outside of the target, five didn't even hit the target, one hit below the belt—which made Rick cringe—and two made it to a location near center mass, if you're being generous. Which I was.

I put the Ruger on the platform in front of me, and we removed the earmuffs. Rick wheeled the paper in and, with confusion writ across his features, evaluated the destruction. Finally, he asked, "What were you aiming at on the first shot?" He pointed to the direct hit between the eyes.

"Center mass." I couldn't help the smirk that spread across my face.

He strained to hold back a strong emotion. Our eyes locked, a chortle crept out between my lips, and that was it. Both of us busted up laughing.

"You're a lousy shot," he declared through his amusement.

"You should have seen the confusion on your face after that first one." I folded in half, slapping at my knee. "You thought I was some sort of sharpshooter."

Full on laughter, in a way I'd never seen from him, shook his entire body. "After your handling of the Glock, I thought Mike may have taught you, and you were just messing with me."

Righting myself, I put a hand on his shoulder and tried to speak. It didn't work. I stumbled away, and just shook my head in the negative as I sought to calm the howling.

"Oh, God." I laid a hand on my stomach. "It hurts." Tears of merriment squeezed through my eyes.

Drawing deep breaths, we both slowed the laughter, though it was hard because when one of us seemed to get it under control, the other would bust out with another whoop. Finally, *finally*, as I leaned against the far wall and Rick against the lane divider, our amusement dissipated, and our breathing returned to normal.

"Oh, hell, that felt good." I put a hand to my heart. "I can't remember the last time I laughed that hard."

"I don't know if I've ever laughed that hard," Rick admitted.

Our gazes met. And lingered. The moment drew out. Electricity sparked down my spine all the way to my toes, my stomach fluttered, and my heart sped up.

Holy shit.

I broke the connection. "Well, you have your work cut out for you. However," I said as I glanced at my watch, "I've taken up more than an hour of your time. We should call it a night." I turned away from the lane, looking anywhere but directly at Rick. "Do you need me to help you with the weapons?"

"No, I'll take care of them."

"Okay." I slung my purse over my shoulder and scooped up my duffle. "I'm going to hit the head before I leave. Meet you at the elevator." I scrambled out of the range.

Once in the bathroom, I stared at myself in the mirror. *What the hell? Where did that come from?*

Don't get me wrong, Rick was hot. He had washboard abs, fascinating eyes, a strong jawline, and close cut hair with a bit of silver at his temples. I'd known him for almost a year and never felt that . . . zing before.

Maybe it's that transference crap shrinks were always talking about. Rick had gotten me to finally allow that pressure pot of guilt to pour out. Or maybe it was the endorphins that comes from laughter like the kind we just shared. If I'd done it in front of Josh, it would've been the same. Wouldn't it?

"Get your head on straight," I hissed.

After a few more minutes of convincing myself that little zing was nothing, I washed my hands and met Rick at the elevator.

The elevator closed. Rick's shoulder brushed mine as he pressed the button to the ground floor, and that damn zing shot through my shoulder, flooding my entire body.

What the hell!!

I refused to react and held my breath the entire way up. It was the longest elevator ride. Ever. The doors opened and I breathed a sigh of relief.

"When do you leave?" Rick asked.

"What?" I stumbled over the elevator door track, but he caught me before I could fall down.

"You okay?"

"Fine." I pulled my arm out of his grasp. "What did you say?"

His hand dropped to his side and he scrutinized me. "Your vacation? When do you leave?"

"Oh, on Saturday."

"Cut loose. Get some rest. Have some fun. When you get back, set up another lesson."

"Yes, sir." I gave him a snappy salute and took off down the hall.

"*Cardinal.*"

I jumped and spun around.

He stood with his hand on the doorknob to the gym. "Tuesday night, after you return. Think about it."

"I will." No zing or tingle affected my body and a small sigh of relief escaped. *Must have been an aberration.*

Chapter Four

"What are you doing?" Rodrigo, wearing a black suit, a blue French dress shirt, and red tie, strolled in and plopped down in my guest chair.

I swallowed the bite of grilled chicken salad that I'd been chewing. "Eating lunch and shopping for sundresses. There's a green flowered print I'm eyeing. What do you think?" I turned my laptop around for him to see.

Rodrigo nodded. "Very nice. It'll look fab on you. Is that for your trip to Mexico?"

"Yes." I swung the laptop back. "It's got two-day shipping, so I should get it by Friday—just in time to take it with me. When I dressed this morning, I thumbed through my closet, and realized all my outfits are too" —I scrunched my nose— "work-ish. Nothing shouted beachy resort. So I'm also putting a peach flowered sundress, a swimsuit with matching sarong, and two frilly tops that will go with my white shorts into my cart."

"Great. It sounds like you're finally getting into the swing of things."

I smiled. "I am. You were right—everyone was right, I need this trip. You know, get some time to relax. I've even scheduled a massage the day I arrive."

"So you don't mind going alone anymore?" Rodrigo asked.

"Well, it's not my first choice, but I'm not giving it up. I've stocked my tablet full of books, and after work I plan to swing by the store to get sunscreen and a new pair of sunglasses. I'm actually looking forward to it now." I clicked the mouse, adding the green sundress to my cart. "What about you? Starting to look forward to your trip to the big Expo?"

"Actually . . ." Rodrigo dragged out the word, and I glanced up from the computer. "I've had a change of plans."

"Really?" I put my chin in my hand. "Do tell."

He closed my office door with a flick of his wrist and replied nonchalantly, "Well . . . a friend of mine is going through a hard time right now, and I told Alfonse that I needed to provide support to my friend, instead of going to Chicago with him."

"Oh, I'm sorry to hear that. What happened? Is it someone I know?"

He leaned forward with excitement on his face. "It's you!"

I took a few beats. "I don't get it. You told Alfonse you needed to stay here in D.C. to be with me? Are you telling me I'm your cover story to get out of the Chicago trip?"

"It's not a cover story, and I'm not staying here."

I didn't like the sound of that. "Rodrigo—"

"I'm going to *Cancun with you!*" He let out a whoop and pumped his fist.

"Wait. What?"

"I changed my plane ticket and got a room at your hotel. I figured, what's the next best thing to going with your best girlfriend?"

I put my palms up in confusion.

"Going with your best gay friend! I found a great last-minute deal at your resort and booked it!"

"Let me get this straight, you're ditching your significant other to go with me?" I pointed to my chest. "To Cancun?"

"Well, I wouldn't put it that way. I'm going to provide moral support, and help you get around. You've not been yourself lately, and I'm worried about you. Secondly, your Spanish is pathetic." He shook his head in despair.

"My Spanish is just fine. *Donde está la biblioteca?*" I said with a flourish.

"Oh, that's wonderful." He gave a condescending clap. "I'm sure identifying the location of the library will be one of the first items to tick off on your vacation 'To Do List.'"

"I know more than that," I replied defensively.

"Oh, yeah?"

"Yeah. *Cerveza, piña colada, mojito, vino,* and the most important one, *el baño,*" I indicated with my fingers.

"Well, at least you're able to ask for directions to the bathroom after drinking your *cervezas* and *mojitos.* But will you be able to understand the directions when they are given in Spanish?"

"I'm going to rely upon the universal directional language of finger pointing."

Rodrigo frowned. "I don't know, there are all sorts of nefarious characters prowling these beach resorts that could take advantage of a single, young thing like you."

I raised a brow. "Laying it on a bit thick, don't you think?"

His face fell. "What? Don't you want me to come?"

I sat back, pinching my lower lip in thought. Having Rodrigo with me *would* have its advantages. His fluent Spanish would definitely come in handy. Additionally, Rodrigo's personality usually ran on the upbeat scale; he was fun to hang out with, and I could use some of his enthusiasm. The separate rooms would also give us space when we needed it, so his presence wouldn't be smothering. The only issue that caused hesitation was the fact that he was a coworker.

I closed the laptop and leaned over it. "Okay, you can come. But" —I held up a finger, causing Rodrigo to halt mid-cheer— "there are conditions. First, what happens in Cancun, stays in Cancun. If one of us gets blitzed and makes an ass of his- or herself, we don't speak of it outside of Cancun."

His head bounced in agreement as I listed the rules.

"Second, if one of us needs time alone, the other will understand, and not feel hurt. Third, no speedos."

He frowned in disgust. "Good gawd."

"Finally, we do not leave each other stranded at a bar to go off with another guy."

"I am in a committed relationship. I would never . . . !"

"That's fine. It's kind of a girl code that we don't leave each other behind, especially when there is drinking going on. I don't mean to be offensive, but I've known a guy to walk away from his crew if he thinks he's—you know—getting some. I don't know what the . . . uh . . . gay code is. . . ."

"Well, I know my code is to leave with the person you arrived with. No matter what. You can count on that."

"Great! Then you're welcome to join me in Cancun. When do you arrive?" I steepled my fingers.

"I couldn't get a flight out until Sunday afternoon. I land sometime after seven, and I check out on Friday morning."

"Okay then. Welcome to Rodrigo and Karina's Cancun adventure." We fist-bumped. I placed my order, then we discussed some of Rodrigo's wardrobe plans until my lunch hour came to an end.

****

They say you learn something new every day, and that evening, I learned Mrs. Thundermuffin's first name was Mildred. When I went to check the mail, the package she'd been expecting had arrived. It hadn't weathered the shipping very well. The box was approximately twenty inches square and about ten inches thick. One end was mashed, and a corner torn. Some of the shredded paper packing material stuck out through the hole, and there was a rattling sound when I picked it up. The front displayed no return address, and the smeared postage identifier didn't reveal its initial shipping location, but the word, *FRÁGIL* was stamped across the front and back in red. I didn't have to know Spanish to realize the word meant fragile. I wasn't sure which postal carrier damaged the box, but I hoped whatever was inside had been insured, because I was fairly certain the fragile item was now a broken one.

Poor Mrs. Thundermuffin. I hated when the postal carriers trashed my stuff. I left the box on my front hall table and thought no more about it.

Thursday, work at the office was uneventful, except for Rodrigo, who texted every fifteen minutes to ask my opinion on everything from wardrobe choices, to activities we should do while in Cancun, to my personal alcoholic beverage choices. He was more excited about this trip than a four-year-old on Christmas morning. Luckily, Hasina, our boss, left for vacation on Wednesday, and things were kind of slow around the office. So I didn't begrudge Rodrigo's enthusiasm.

After work, Mike and I had dinner at his place. We ate at the coffee table while the news played in the background. I told him about my embarrassing meltdown at Silverthorne. "Rick invited me to attend the group meetings that his guys hold twice month. It's on Tuesday nights. What do you think?" I rounded out the story and waited, unsure of his reaction.

He turned off the TV and asked in a completely neutral tone, "Do you think it would help?" Concern tightened around his eyes.

I'd waffled on that question myself, and I didn't want to start a fight with Mike tonight, so I shrugged and delivered nonchalantly, "It might. I don't think it could hurt."

He released a breath and his shoulders relaxed. "Then you should absolutely go."

"Seriously? You don't mind?"

He reached across and pulled me to his chest. "Anything that can help you, I'm all for it. You haven't been in a great place for a while. If this will help . . ."

"I thought, since it was Silverthorne . . ."

"No, I don't mind." He stroked my hair and pulled me tighter.

Mike had a crack-o-morning flight the next day, and I left around nine. The ringing of my home phone greeted me as I walked through my front door. I didn't recognize the phone number. It looked like an international number, and I figured it was just another scammer, so I let it go to voice mail. A moment later, my cell phone rang, displaying the same number.

"Hmm, that's strange." I dumped my computer bag and purse on the couch, then pressed the answer button. "Hello?"

"Karina, is that you?"

The connection was scratchy, but I thought I recognized the voice. "Mrs. Thundermuffin?"

"Yes, dearie, it's me. I'm so glad I caught you."

"Where are you?"

"In Mexico. Didn't—" Her voice faded out.

"What? I can't hear you." I checked to make sure the volume on my phone was up all the way. "Hello?"

"I said . . . Mexico."

"What?"

The connection cleared as she spoke again. "I'm in Mexico. Didn't I tell you that's where I'd be?"

"Yes, you did. I'm surprised you're calling. Is something the matter?"

"I'm not sure. Did you get that package yet?"

"Yes, as a matter of fact, it came in yesterday." I winced. "Only, I hate to tell you, I'm afraid it's been damaged."

"What? Did you say the item was damaged?"

"Well, I'm not sure about what's inside, but the outer box was partially crushed, and there is a tear. Also, when I picked it up, there was a rattling sound."

"Oh, boy." She seemed to turn away from the phone to speak to someone else. Faintly, I heard, "She says the package is damaged. I don't know, I'll ask." Her voice came back on the line at full strength. "Karina, would you do me a favor and check it out for me?"

"You want me to open the box?"

"Yes, and tell me what the contents look like."

"Okay." I retrieved the box from the front hall and brought it to the kitchen. "Let me put you on speaker." Placing the phone on the counter, I sliced into the end that was not crushed.

"Okay, there's a good bit of packing material." I pulled out a bunch of the brown shredded paper. "We have a manila envelope, about four-by-eight, and scrawled across the center— 'To Aunt Milly for your stamp collection.' I didn't know you were a stamp collector." I put the unsealed envelope aside.

"I collect all sorts of things."

Half a dozen loose coins fell out, clanking their way across the counter. "And there are some coins in here. Maybe that's what was making the noise. They say *centavos* on one side, and the other—oh, I see, they're from Brazil." Someone spoke in a foreign language in the background, really more like bellowed in short, demanding sentences. I couldn't catch what he was saying, but the tone didn't sound nice. "Are you okay, Mrs. Thundermuffin?"

"Just fine, dear. My grandnephew sends me coins from the places he's visited. Now about the case inside the box, has it been damaged?"

I gave the box a shake, and a hard, black plastic case, about twelve-by-ten inches, slid into my hand. "The case looks undamaged, and it feels fairly sturdy. Should I open it?"

"No, I don't think that's necessary. As long as the case is undamaged, I'm sure it's fine."

"Okay. Then it'll be here when you get back." I laid it down.

"Actually, dear, I was hoping you could do me the favor of bringing it with you when you come to Mexico."

"Um, I suppose I can do that. But I'm headed to Cancun, I don't think that's very close to Mexico City at all."

"I'm no longer in Mexico City. I'm on my way to Mérida. It's on the Yucatan Peninsula, not far from Cancun. I can arrange to get it after you arrive," she explained.

"Well, I suppose that would work." Someone shouted in the background and the line went dead. "Mrs. Thundermuffin? Hello?"

I hung up and waited for a few minutes to see if she would call back. When she didn't, I dialed the number on my caller ID. It went straight to voice mail. Or at least I assume it was voice mail; there wasn't any message, simply a long beep. "Mrs. Thundermuffin, it's Karina. I think we got cut off. I'm a little concerned about you. Can you please call or text or private message me through Instagram to let me know you're all right?" I hung up and studied the black box on my counter.

You know when you're at an airport and the overhead announcements come on telling you to keep track of your stuff and warning you not to carry items that aren't yours? Well, Mrs. Thundermuffin just asked me to carry an item that wasn't mine, and I had no idea what was inside. Of course, my overactive imagination jumped to drugs. While I didn't believe Mrs. T. would ask me to bring something illegal into a foreign country, I knew nothing about this illusive grandnephew of hers. I couldn't even imagine what Mike would say about this new development. Nothing good, I'm sure.

You are an idiot if you bring this into a foreign country with no knowledge of what is inside.

That nasty little voice continued to bang around in my head while I went about my business and tried to ignore the package.

At quarter past eleven, I opened the case.

Inside was a mask, packed securely in molded foam. The face was painted a bronzy golden color. It had large black eyes with shadowing details reminiscent of Egypt during Cleopatra's time. Beautiful turquoise detailing with stripes of blue, red, and cream on the headpiece rose above the brows. Tilting the box up, I could see a scarab design decorating the top of the crown. Cracks and breaks riddled the mask, and I dared not touch the piece with my bare hands. It looked old. Like ancient Egyptian old. I didn't even want to breathe around it.

A sick knot began to tighten in my stomach. Gently, I closed the box. I'd dealt with a stolen painting in my past and wondered if I'd stumbled across something similar. And what, if anything, did Mrs. Thundermuffin have to do with it?

I had one person in my past who might be able to tell me more about the golden mask. I just didn't know if I had the guts to pay him a visit.

In the morning, I found a text from Mrs. T.

Karina, I am fine. Please bring the box. It's of great importance. Don't fail me.

Her text did nothing to ease that little voice in my head.

At lunch later that day, I stood outside a downtown D.C. office building and began to question my sanity. I pivoted and turned away, only to pivot back again and stall ten feet from the front door. While the debate raged in my head, the decision was taken out of my hands.

"Karina, is that you?" asked Martin Dunne, the father of a man to whom I was once engaged. He wore a perfectly tailored, storm gray business suit, with a white shirt and yellow tie. He had a few more wrinkles, but overall, he hadn't changed since I'd seen him last year. I'd forgotten how much he and his son resembled each other. Martin's dark hair was almost fully gray, and he may have been slightly taller than Patrick's six feet, but the jaw and brow lines were similar, and the tentative smile mirrored his son's. I no longer held strong emotions for Patrick, but it didn't lessen the uncanny feelings I experienced standing in front of his father.

I realized Martin was waiting for me to stop staring and answer him. "Hello, Martin. How have you been?"

"Fine, and you?"

"Fine. Fine." I chewed my lip, trying to decide what to say.

"Is there something I can help you with?"

"As a matter of fact, yes, there is. Could we go up to your office?"

His face remained placid and kind. "Of course."

Martin escorted me through the building lobby and onto the elevator. Lucky for me, two more people boarded after us, so I felt no need to make small talk on our way up. Once we got into his luxurious office at Dunne and Jenkins Building and Real Estate, I took a seat on the uber-modern black leather couch, slid the oversized green tote off my shoulder, and placed it at my feet.

"Can I offer you something to drink?" Martin asked.

"No, thank you."

He folded himself into the club chair across from me and waited expectantly.

"How are things at the FBI?" I asked.

His face shuttered, and his mouth turned down. Immediately, I regretted my words. After the painting incident, Martin's lawyer negotiated a deal with the FBI's Art Crimes division, which basically made him a confidential informant on black market items that came to his attention. I needed his help. Putting his back up was not a great way to start the conversation. "That was tactless of me."

His expression didn't change. "Did you come to speak to me about FBI business?" he asked in a chilly voice.

Embarrassed, I glanced away. "No, I didn't. I apologize. I don't know why I opened with that." I fidgeted with my necklace. "Small talk seems to be eluding me at the moment."

He softened. "Why don't you tell me why you're here today?"

"Right then, down to the brass tacks." I pulled the black case out of the bag and placed it on the glass coffee table between us. "I'm hoping you can tell me something about this piece."

Martin leaned forward, flicked open the clasps, and lifted the lid. Drawing in a breath, he frowned and pulled a pair of reading glasses out of his coat pocket to scrutinize the beautiful golden mask.

"I'm guessing it's Egyptian," I said.

"You would be correct."

"It reminded me of Cleopatra's time."

"Very good. It's definitely late period, Hellenistic or Ptolemaic Dynasty." He shifted the box left and right. "The face is more rounded. I see Macedonian and Greek influence. It doesn't have the long facial features of earlier Egyptian Pharaohs like Akhenaten or Tut. But I'm not sure it's from Cleopatra's time, maybe two or three-hundred B.C., I would guess."

"But what is it? Some sort of Egyptian decoration?"

He shook his head. "It's a funerary mask. Placed over the face upon burial. You've probably seen pictures of the famous golden one found in Tut's tomb. It lives in the Egyptian Museum of Cairo."

Good lord, of course I have! Who hasn't? "I have," I replied calmly. "You're saying this a Pharaoh's death mask?"

He tilted his head and his brows drew together in thought. "Not a pharaoh. Not intricate enough. There is quite a bit of gold leaf. I would say, more likely a nobleman's mask."

He stood and carried the box over to his desk. I followed him. From the top middle drawer, he withdrew a pair of white cotton gloves and donned them. Then he swung the arm of an elbow lamp directly above the mask and flicked on the bright LED light. He leaned down and sniffed it, then spent many minutes in silence examining the paint work, before he picked it up with his gloved hands. Inwardly, I cringed because the mask looked so old and fragile. However, well aware of his affinity for art and antiquities, I trusted him not to damage it.

He turned the piece over and held it inches from his eyeballs as he examined the backside. "Ah, I see." I waited for him to clarify that comment. Finally, he said, "It's a beautiful reproduction. How the artist was able to capture the detailing in the gold leaf and aging technique is intriguing."

I opened and closed my mouth twice before I was able to speak, "You're sure it's a replica?"

"Undoubtedly," he said with assurance.

"How? Is there something in the workmanship that stands out? Gives it away? I mean, it looks like an Ancient Egyptian artifact to me."

"A number of things give it away. First, funerary masks were created from a variety of different mediums—gold or silver, like Tutankhamen's mask; plaster; and this technique of gilded cartonnage. It's a technique similar to papier mâché, using papyrus and resin. This artist also used papyrus, however, he used new papyrus that he aged with modern day techniques."

"Okay, I'll bite, how did he age the papyrus?"

"Here, smell." He held the mask out for me.

I took a whiff. "It smells ... earthy." Shrugging, I said, "Wouldn't you expect that smell from something that was buried for a long time?"

"Desert sand smells different from soil. But it's not that. Take another whiff. Smell anything else?"

This time I sucked in a deep breath and smelled another aroma near and dear to my heart. "Uh, this sounds weird, but ... I think I smell ... coffee?"

He nodded. "Very good. Aging techniques include staining with coffee or tea."

"Okay, but why does it smell like dirt?"

"He probably buried it in the garden for a month or two to

continue the aging process. He also didn't use resin to shape and adhere the papyrus. Resin has a distinct piney scent, like balsam. Think fresh Christmas tree."

"Okay."

"Add a hint of mustiness to that scent, and you've got the smell of ninety percent of ancient Egyptian artifacts that used resin or rested inside a sarcophagus. It's quite distinctive."

"Huh. I've seen a number of Egyptian pieces, but they are always behind museum glass. I never thought about how it smelled. I would have thought it smelled rotten. So, if the artist didn't use resin, what did he use?"

"My guess—Elmer's glue."

I burst out laughing. "You're joking."

He shook his head. "It's an excellent adherent for the medium and it's water solvent."

Sobering, I asked, "Okay, what else gave it away? When you turned it over—there was an . . . 'aha' moment."

"I suspect the artist created the piece to sit on a shelf and never be observed from the back. There is no finishing work on the backside. No cartouche, which, for a nobleman's mask, I would expect. Additionally, the aging process wasn't as detailed, and right here, you see that?"

"Yes, it's a blop of something."

"That little blop is the glue I mentioned. He didn't finish dissolving it, here and here. As I said, the artwork is beautifully done. However, there is one other reason I know it's a reproduction." He placed the mask back in its mold, took off the gloves, and moved to his computer keyboard. After quickly typing something, he pivoted the monitor to face me. "Read this."

Across the top, the article read, "Fire Devastates Brazil's National Museum in Rio." The photo below the headline showed a stately white palace with every window ablaze and flames shooting through the roof into the sky. I scrolled down, scanning the article. The fire destroyed the museum and twenty million artifacts on the night of September 2, 2018. "This is terrible, but what does it have to do with the mask?"

Martin swiveled the monitor back and typed some more. "It took me a while to realize where I'd seen it before. But then it suddenly came to me in a flash of insight."

The monitor flipped back around for my perusal. He'd gone to the destroyed museum's website and brought up a page of Egyptian artifacts. Dead center, at the top, was the golden Egyptian funerary mask.

I blew out a breath. "So it burned in the fire?"

"Yes. Scientists, students, and staff members combed through the rubble for months in an effort to recover what they could. Millionaires have pledged monies for rebuilding. Before you ask, there is no way the mask would have survived such a devastating fire. As a matter of fact, the entire Egyptian collection was destroyed. A tragedy, considering it was the largest collection in South America."

I chewed my lip, wondering why Mrs. Thundermuffin so desperately needed the mask. Did she know it was fake? "Do you think a buyer would notice the things you mentioned?"

"If he was worth his salt, a savvy buyer would."

I continued scrutinizing the golden mask, wondering. Wondering. Wondering. Too many thoughts whirled around in there to solidify into a solid notion.

"Is it for sale?" Martin's quiet question pierced my contemplation.

"No, it's not."

He took my sharp reply in stride. "Can I ask how you came by it?"

Finally, I transferred my gaze to his. "I'm holding on to it for a friend."

His eyes widened with understanding. "Ah, let me guess, you

couldn't resist opening it, and once you got a gander, you thought you'd run across another stolen masterpiece."

My face blazed at his accurate assessment.

"You may rest easy, Karina, you're not wrapped up in another art heist. Any art collector would have the piece analyzed or have the skills to do it himself. This reproduction isn't going to get past someone who knows what they are doing."

"I see. Thank you, Martin. You've relieved my mind."

He scrutinized me. "You look like it gave you a sleepless night."

Clearing my throat, I replied, "It did."

"I wonder if I know this friend of yours."

"Petite." I held my hand up to my chest. "Retiree, with a flair for fashion and multi-colored hair."

He shook his head. "Doesn't ring a bell."

I drew in a relieved breath. "Tell me, Martin, if it were for sale, what would you pay for this?"

He rubbed his chin in thought. "Hmm, like I said, there are noticeable flaws in the replication, but they don't detract from the artistry and beauty of the piece. Maybe three thousand before the fire. Since the original is gone, it might increase the price."

"How much?"

He shrugged. "To a private buyer, maybe five to ten grand."

"Ten grand?!"

"Some of that depends upon the artist's reputation in the field. Maybe more, if it got some press and excitement surrounding its connection to the original that burned. The Brazilian National Museum might be interested in getting its hands on a replica like this to replace the one destroyed. Right now, I don't see it being sold for much more than a few thousand." Martin closed the box and pushed it toward me.

Curiosity had me asking, "Let's say the real funerary mask wasn't destroyed and was up for sale. What would it bring?"

"Hmm, let me look on some of the auction sites and see what I can find." He spent a few minutes surfing the internet. "Looking at Christie auctions over the past few years, prices of Egyptian funerary masks range from three to upward of eighty-five thousand. But this one, I would guess, might go for something in the twenty to twenty-five thousand range. Its age and medium aren't as desirable as some of the older dynasties."

I retrieved the case and replaced it in my tote. "Thank you, Martin. I appreciate your help."

"Anytime." He led me over to the door. Placing his hand on the knob, he paused before opening it for me. "Karina?"

"Yes?"

"I never properly apologized for putting you in danger or thanked you for what you did for me." His voice softened so low I could barely hear it. "I know you could have handled things very differently, and had you done so, we'd be talking through a set of bars."

Eyeing him, I replied, "Or six feet under."

He visibly swallowed. "I'm sorry."

He seemed to be waiting for me to say something, perhaps "no problem," or "it's okay." I couldn't. It's not that I was still angry, but Martin's monkey business couldn't be easily forgiven. Instead, I replied, "Give my best to your wife, Molly."

****

My curiosity, having been piqued by Martin's information, led me down an internet rabbit hole on ancient Egyptian artifacts, Dynasties, and belief systems. Thankful again for the slow week with my boss out of the office, I spent the afternoon deep in research. I found that the Egyptians were obsessed with death. Upon reaching adulthood, an Egyptian spent the rest of his life planning for death—at least the kings and noblemen did. Perhaps the common man didn't have quite as much time on his hands to spend planning for the afterlife, but some thought was definitely put into it. Not only did one have to build a tomb, but also plan for body preservation through mummification, and arrangements for family members afterward.

The funerary mask was an important part of this plan. Ancient Egyptians believed that a person had two spirits or souls that continued to live on once the physical body was mummified. The Ba spirit would remain near the family to watch over them. The Ka spirit flew off to the Land of Two Fields, ancient Egypt's idea of heaven. However, at night, both the Ka and Ba would return to the dead person's tomb to rest until the next day. It was this reason that Egyptians spent years of their life building for their death. Death masks, in particular, were not meant to be seen publicly, and the purpose of the mask was to give the dead a face in his afterlife. Funerary masks would also help the Ba and Ka return to the proper tomb. If something happened to the preserved body, or your name was stricken from the walls of your burial tomb, then the Ba and Ka would not be able to find their home, and your spirit would be lost forever. This is why cartouches would be carved into a coffin, and why Pharaohs would have their names carved or painted into their tombs and every building erected during their reign. In this manner, your name would also live on in the history books.

Some Pharaohs who took the throne by force, or despised their predecessors, would remove all traces of the former ruler in order to banish him or her. It is believed that Horemheb so despised his predecessor, Ay, that he destroyed Ay's tomb, smashing the sarcophagus and chiseling his name from the walls. Furthermore, the reign of Akhenaten—the 'Heretic King'— caused strife and unrest in Egypt. Akhenaten sought to change the religious landscape during his time in power, forcing the people to believe in a single deity, Aten, rather than their previous polytheistic beliefs. Horemheb, in an effort to calm the unrest that had arisen from Akhenaten's rule and reinforce the old ways, set out to destroy Akhenaten's city of Armana and did his best to wipe out all mention of the heretic Pharaoh and his beautiful queen, Nefertiti.

Another effort to erase a Pharaoh's name from the history books came from Thutmose III, stepson to Hatshepsut, the chief wife of Thutmose II. Thutmose III was an infant when his father died, and Hatshepsut took on the role as regent. However, as Thutmose III grew up, Hatshepsut became one of the most powerful queens to rule Egypt, and before his age of maturity, she had herself declared Pharaoh in order to maintain her power. Officially, the two ruled as co-regents, but texts indicated that Hatshepsut clearly overshadowed her stepson in both power and popularity among the people, and during her rule, Egypt enjoyed peace and prosperity. When she passed and Thutmose III finally rose to become the sole regent, he had her temples defaced and her name stripped from the list of kings. It wasn't until 1903, when archeologists found her tomb and deciphered hieroglyphics from Deir el Bahri, that her legacy was restored.

Unfortunately, for as long as there were Pharaohs building tombs, there were grave robbers who came along behind to steal the expensive goods buried with them. Noble men, queens, and Pharaohs were buried with the items they lived with, including precious amulets, golden coffins, and jewelry of gold and silver. Over five thousand objects alone were buried with Tutankhamun. Since grave robbing was so prevalent in ancient Egypt, it is considered a miracle that Howard Carter found Tutankhamun's tomb still intact.

Just before the end of the day, Rodrigo swaggered into my office, startling me out of a daydream where I was a trusted advisor on Cleopatra's court, and asked, "Have you packed yet?"

"No, I've been procrastinating. I'll get it done tonight," I answered him, making myself busy with removing the junk mail in my spam account.

"Are you checking a bag?"

"Probably. I'm a terrible packer. I always overpack and only wear half the stuff I bring. I'll never be able to get everything into one small enough to carry onboard. What about you?" I glanced at his skinny black jeans, wine-red button-down, and royal blue vest. "I can't imagine you'll be able to get all your accoutrements into a carry-on."

"I am an excellent packer." He surveyed his nails. "Why don't I pick up Chinese and come over tonight to help you pack? I bet I can get your pretty new clothes into one suitcase that will fit in the overhead compartment."

"Fifty bucks says you can't!" I threw down.

"You're on!" he exclaimed, and we shook on it.

Chapter Five

"Damn it, if you didn't need to take this big-ass box, we'd be able to fit everything into your roll aboard suitcase and backpack." Rodrigo pointed to the death mask box with distaste. "Really, are you sure you have to take it?" His question turned into a whine at the end.

"I'm sure. Pay up, buster." I held out my palm.

Standing in the center of my bedroom with his hands on his hips, he childishly kicked aside a pair of sandals he'd talked me out of packing.

I laughed. Granted, I hadn't told Rodrigo about the bulky box that needed to fit in the luggage when we made the bet.

"Are you sure you need two pairs of flip-flops?"

"Yes," I stated. "Besides, one pair of flip-flops will not make enough space for the box."

"Wait. I've got it." He snapped his fingers. "Why don't *I* bring it with me?"

I gave him the side-eye.

"No, listen, I only need to pack for five days. I'll have loads of room in my roll aboard."

"Is this a ploy to get the fifty bucks out of me?"

He swished his hand. "Forget the fifty bucks, it's yours. I just think it's safer and easier if you have your luggage with you at all times. Especially when traveling to a foreign country."

I didn't disagree with Rodrigo's assessment. "Let's forget the bet. I'll agree to letting you carry the black box, but you can't flake out on me, Rodrigo. The box *has* to get to Mexico with you. Mrs.

Thundermuffin is counting on me."

"Yeah, yeah." He flipped the suitcase closed.

I took ahold of his elbow and he paused. "I'm not kidding."

"I get it, Karina. The box will arrive with me. I promise." He pulled out of my grip and drew a big X across his chest with his finger.

Reluctantly, I allowed him to leave with the golden mask. That night I slept like crap, imagining all the ways the mask could be damaged or lost on its way to Mexico with Rodrigo. I never should have agreed to let him take it.

****

I once read that an Ethiopian goatherder from the ninth century discovered coffee. If that goatherder had walked past me this morning, I would have kissed his feet. Those dark beans got me to the airport properly clothed, with all my stuff, and relatively alert. The morning improved when I received a pleasant surprise. Checking in for my flight, I found out Mike had gotten me upgraded to first class. I texted him as soon as I found out.

You are the best boyfriend. Ever! Thanks for the upgrade.

I sent him a kissy emoji. First class provided a free drink, real food, and excellent space for napping.

Chapter Six

Every moment I spent in Mexico got better and better.

Upon arrival, I was met by the shuttle driver for the resort. Handing me an ice-cold bottle of water, he relieved me of my luggage and escorted me to the air-conditioned bus, where two couples were also waiting to be taken to the resort. The water and air conditioning provided a relief from the steamy tropical heat that didn't mix well with the combined scent of jet fuel and exhaust from the waiting taxis and busses.

The smell greatly improved at the resort, where ocean breezes sent the palm trees swaying, and the fragrance of sand and salt enveloped me. Even though I arrived at noon, my room was ready, and a porter carried my luggage as he escorted me to it. After unpacking, I ate a delicious lunch of ceviche in their five-star restaurant, then changed and headed to the pool for a few hours to soak up some rays and drink some rum. At the swim-up bar, I met a friendly couple from Spain, and a foursome of twenty-something party boys from Cincinnati who tried to talk me into doing tequila shots with them. I declined, sticking with my piña colada. I enjoyed an afternoon of harmless flirtation with the crew.

At four, I headed over to the spa for my massage. An hour later, I came out loose as a spaghetti noodle, and took a nap. Refreshed from the relaxing day, I donned my new peach sundress and headed down to the lounge for a drink, where I found the couple from Spain, Marietta and Adrian. They kindly invited me to join them for dinner. We shared an appetizer of calamari, then I ate fish tacos, and Marietta and I splurged on flan. Afterward, we hung out in the disco, dancing and drinking mojitos. Around eleven, I pleaded fatigue and headed upstairs.

Arriving in my room, I kicked aside my wedge-heeled sandals and flopped onto my luxurious pillow-topped king-sized bed, tired but happy. Everyone was right, I needed this trip. My cell phone rang, and I pulled it from the little beaded handbag lying beside me.

"Hello."

"Karina? It's Mildred Thundermuffin."

The lethargy from my happy little buzz disappeared, and I bolted upright. "Hi, Mrs. Thundermuffin. It's good to hear from you."

"I hope it's not too late to be calling. I tried reaching you earlier, but I kept getting your voice mail." Mrs. Thundermuffin sounded much calmer and less harried than the last time we spoke. There was no background noise, and our connection quite clear.

"I'm sorry, I was at a disco. I must not have heard the phone ringing over the music."

"I figured you might be out enjoying the nightlife." She paused. "Did you bring the box?"

Uh, no. "Yup."

"You didn't have any problems in customs?"

This would have been the moment to cut bait and tell her the truth about Rodrigo. I have no idea why I continued the obfuscation. "No problems. Why? Were you expecting there to be?"

"One never knows in this country," she said cryptically.

"Well, they didn't check my luggage." And I now silently prayed they wouldn't check Rodrigo's luggage either. "When do you want to meet up?" If she said tomorrow, I already had a lie planned out and would suggest another day—after Rodrigo arrived.

"Well, I thought, since you're here, we could meet at a wonderful tourist spot. Have you ever heard of the famous Mayan ruins of *Chichén Itzá*?"

"Yes, of course. I'd been planning to take one of the resort excursions there. I went with my parents when I was little, I can barely remember it. I know my friend Rodrigo, who is arriving tomorrow, would love to see it. He mentioned it was on his bucket list."

"Then you won't mind visiting it again? Good. How about Monday?"

Silently, I let out a sigh of relief. "Monday is perfect." Monday would also relieve me of this little albatross around my neck earlier in my trip, allowing me to stop worrying about it.

"I'll send a driver to pick you up at your hotel at eight. You and your friend can explore the grounds first, then we'll meet at the base of the Castillo at twelve-thirty. We can go to lunch at the *Casa de Chichen*, a lovely little café. If you haven't finished exploring the grounds, you can return after we eat. How does that sound?"

"Quite lovely. How will I know the car?"

"He'll have a sign with your name. But I will also give him a letter written by me. Do not get in the car until you read the letter. In it you will find the phrase, 'Don't forget your white hat and sunscreen.' If there is no letter, or you receive a letter without that phrase, do not get in the car. Understand?"

Mrs. Thundermuffin sounded a wee bit paranoid, but I supposed bad things did happen to unsuspecting tourists. On the flight, I'd read an article about the rise of kidnappings in Mexico. The State Department had travel warnings on practically every providence in the country. I had no interest in foolishly getting into a car with a kidnapper, so I supposed her letter made sense.

"Yes, I get it. Anything else?"

"I don't think so, dearie. I look forward to seeing you on Monday."

"If I need to reach you beforehand, is this the number I should contact?"

"Yes, this number should be working until then. Remember the code. 'Don't forget your white hat and sunscreen.'"

"White hat. Sunscreen. Gotcha. See you soon."

The line went dead, and while Mrs. Thundermuffin's—I simply couldn't think of her as Mildred—demeanor over the phone seemed tranquil, I couldn't determine if her concerns were for me or the package I carried for her.

Had I not been filled with a bellyful of mojitos, I probably would have stayed up half the night fretting over that question. Instead, the booze worked its charm. After checking my messages—three from Mrs. T., and a text from Mike wishing me well and sending his love—I tossed the phone on the bedside table, changed into my jammies, and zonked out.

I woke around seven with a mild headache—probably due to dehydration more than the booze.

Okay, it might have been the booze.

I sucked down one of the complimentary bottled waters the hotel kindly left in the little bar area and decided to order room service. Sometime in the night, a kind soul had slipped the resort's newsletter under my door. Activities included water volleyball, a sandcastle contest, poolside trivia, and other games throughout the day. One activity caught my eye; at nine, they had yoga on the beach. I changed into a tank top and shorts, and after my continental breakfast of yogurt, fruit, coffee, and croissant, I headed to the beach for some stretching.

An hour and a half later, I returned to my room and almost dropped my freshly squeezed orange juice as I stood in the doorway.

Chapter Seven

"What the hell?"

My clothes littered the floor, the mattress lay half off the bed, and both it and the box spring sported the jagged wounds of a knife. The dresser drawers weren't just taken out, they'd been ripped apart, and the minifridge pulled out from its cubby hole. The room had been trashed. I picked up one of my frilly tops, price tag still attached. One of its little poufy sleeves was torn and hung by a thread. A sliding door to the closet had been pulled off and left on the ground. The green dress still hung straight on its hanger, the only piece of clothing I'd brought that hadn't been touched. They'd drilled the safe open, and I got down on my knees to see if they'd taken the few bits of jewelry that I'd put in there. I found the black silk bag on the closet floor beneath the safe and unrolled it to find nothing had been taken. Luckily, my passport and wallet—with my pesos, credit cards, and traveler's checks—had been with me at yoga, in the beach bag that still hung on my shoulder.

It didn't seem to be a burglary, but rather vandalism. I picked up the hotel phone from the floor and dialed 0.

A woman answered and spoke first in Spanish and then English. "Front desk, how may I help you?"

"Hello, my name is Karina Cardinal in room 521. Someone broke into my room. Please send security up here immediately."

"I'm so sorry. I'm sending someone up now."

Hanging up, I sniffed and smelled the faintest scent of a spicy aftershave. Five minutes later, there was a sharp rapping on my door.

"Security!"

Opening it, I found a man of around fifty, of average height, a bit on the hefty side, wearing a black suit and tie, and a nametag that read Ortiz-Marin.

His rounded features were drawn into a frown. "You called about a break-in?"

"Are you security?" I asked.

"I am."

"Can I see some ID?"

Those dark eyes didn't flinch. "Of course." He pulled a badge out of his front pocket and held it out for me.

The badge had the name of the hotel across the top and a washed-out photo of the man in front of me. His name was David Ortiz-Marin, and at the bottom I could identify the words *Director de Seguridad*. I pushed the door wide and stood back to allow him in.

He prowled the room, taking in the mess, saying nothing, while I remained standing in the doorway watching him.

"Pardon me," a voice said.

I glanced over my shoulder to find a woman in a beautiful royal blue suit, red stilettos, and with the most gorgeous mane of black hair I'd ever seen outside of a magazine.

"I am Rosa Moreno, Director of Guest Relations. I understand—"

I moved aside so she could see inside the room.

"*Dios mio!*" she muttered, stepping over the threshold. She and David began speaking in Spanish far too quickly for me to follow.

At one point, David dialed someone on his speaker phone, so there were three in on the conversation. The discussion continued for so long, I thought they might have forgotten me, so I walked up behind them and cleared my throat to remind them of my presence.

Rosa spun around, her dark eyes sympathetic as she spoke. "I apologize for our rudeness. You don't speak Spanish?"

"Not fluently." I crossed my arms.

David ended the call.

"We are so sorry this happened to you, and we are doing everything to fix the situation," she assured me, gently patting my shoulder. "Have you checked the room?"

"Can you tell us what is missing?" David asked.

"From what I can tell—nothing. As you can see, they got into the safe" —I pointed over my shoulder in the general direction of the closet— "but left my jewelry behind. Admittedly, I didn't bring much with me, but there are a pair of gold earrings and a gold necklace. I'm wearing my sapphire ring, the only other piece of jewelry that isn't costume."

"What about cash or your passport?" David prompted.

I shook my head and pointed to the beach bag still on my shoulder. "I had it with me."

"*Bueno*, that is good." Rosa nodded. "Unfortunately, there have been break-ins just like this in the area. Last week the *policía federal* arrested a ring of criminals selling stolen passports that they believe were perpetrating the thefts." She stumbled with the word "perpetrating", but for the most part, her English was flawless.

"So this has happened here before?"

"Here? Only once. About a month ago." David put his hands on his hips. "For the safety of our guests, we stepped up security, and after the arrests, we didn't think it would be an issue."

"It looks like they didn't get the whole gang," I replied.

David gazed around the room, assessing the destruction, and muttered something in Spanish that I don't think I was meant to understand. It was a foolish assumption on his part. I may not know the language well, but high schoolers always learned the dirty words.

"My thoughts precisely, David," I agreed.

His head whipped up at me and he frowned. "Pardon my—"

"Language?" I finished for him, then waved my hand in dismissal. "Forget it. My problem is . . . what am I to do now? My clothes are ripped," —I picked up and dropped my new top— "my luggage trashed," —I pointed to the black suitcase, which had been slashed to ribbons— "and I certainly can't remain in this room. I'm not even sure I feel safe enough to remain in the resort. Although, you mentioned it has happened at other hotels. I don't know what to do." I slumped against the wall and pressed my fingertips to my eyes. "I just wanted a relaxing vacation."

"Don't worry, Ms. Cardinal. I am fixing it as we speak," Rosa said with the confidence of a woman used to being in charge and getting things done. "My assistant, Lorna, is bringing you a new suitcase from our resort shop, *La Salamandra*, so you may collect your things to move to another room. I will be issuing you a five-hundred-dollar gift card, which you can use anywhere in the resort, including our shopping plaza, to replace your damaged clothes. We can look through your things, and anything that isn't torn and only needs cleaning and pressing will be taken care of and returned to you by this evening,"

"Well, that certainly will go a long way toward fixing the damage, but as for my security . . . I just don't know." From what Rosa and David explained, I'm sure the break-in was random, but there was such a sense of violation. And the destruction seemed so . . . unnecessary for a simple burglary.

David and Rosa exchanged a quick conversation in Spanish, then she turned to me. "I will move you to a room on our concierge level. There are more cameras, a concierge on duty from six in the morning until ten at night, and you must have a keycard to get to that level."

"It is undoubtedly our safest floor," David added.

I'd seen the instructions for the tenth floor in the elevator. If you pressed the button, it wouldn't light up unless you stuck your keycard in a slot on the panel. I know this because I tried it once, just for the heck of it.

Rosa's proposal held appeal. Being on the concierge level would definitely give me more peace of mind. The five hundred would undoubtedly replace the damaged items of clothing. Yesterday, after lunch, I'd taken a moment to browse through the four shops that made up the shopping plaza. *La Salamandra* sold beautiful, high-end resort clothing, and there was a gorgeous sea-green beach cover-up that I'd been thinking about purchasing. There was also a jewelry store, and a general store that sold food items and the usual souvenirs. The last store was more of a gallery with Mayan jewelry, figurines, paintings, and other pottery from local artisans.

"Will my room face the ocean up on the concierge level?" I'd paid extra to get an ocean view; I didn't want to lose that no matter where they put me.

"Of course. I am upgrading you to a suite." Rosa's phone beeped, and she checked it. "Lorna is here with your luggage and the keys to your new room. I cannot force you to stay, but I will do anything in my power to make sure the rest of your stay with us is superb." She cocked her head, waiting for me to answer.

I sighed, brushing a stray hair away from my face. "Yes, I suppose that will be fine. Thank you."

"Good." Rosa strode over to open the door.

Lorna, a petite blonde wearing the resort uniform of khaki pants and a hot pink blouse, handed Rosa a turquoise suitcase and a small envelope that held room keys. They spoke briefly in low tones, then Rosa shut the door. "I hope this will be acceptable to replace your bag. It also comes in red, if you prefer."

I adored the color, and the designer label indicated this

suitcase was certainly more high-end than the one the burglars had vandalized. "It's fine. Thank you."

She handed it to me. "The *policía* have arrived. David, if you will go down to speak with them, I will help Mrs. Cardinal pack her things and take her to her new room."

"Are we allowed to move my stuff? Aren't the police going to want to see the crime scene?" I asked.

"Since nothing was stolen, it is a simple vandalism. The police will look at the damage and write up a report." David shrugged. "There is not much more they will do."

"What about fingerprints?"

"There are probably a hundred fingerprints around this room." He made a sweeping motion with his arm. "They'd be here for days trying to collect them all. I doubt they will bother for simple vandalism. Besides, the thieves haven't left any behind in the past. Gloves." He held up his fingers and wiggled them.

"Yes, I see." I guess I'd gotten so used to dealing with major crimes, I'd kind of forgotten that this was a simple case of property damage. No one was hurt. My clothes could be replaced, and the hotel room fixed. To them, it was nothing more than a minor inconvenience and a need to placate an injured guest. "Will I need to speak with the police?"

"Goodness, that won't be necessary. We have no wish to inconvenience you further and take up more of your vacation time dealing with this dirty business," Rosa stated. "David can take your statement and relay it to them."

I looked to see if David disagreed with this plan. He didn't contradict Rosa. Frankly, I didn't have anything helpful for the police, and Rosa was certainly going out of her way to make up for the trouble. I reminded myself that this was a foreign country, and they did things differently. I shrugged and went with it. David took my brief and useless statement, then left to go deal with the police.

Rosa stayed behind to help me pack. We ended up throwing away five clothing pieces and a torn pair of flip-flops. I silently patted myself on the back for insisting on packing the second pair of flip-flops. Although—with my five hundred bucks, I could easily invest in another pair. Rosa set aside the clothes that needed cleaning, and we packed the items that weren't ruined. In the bathroom, they'd basically swept all my makeup products into the sink. Luckily, nothing had broken except for the blush case, which could be fixed with tape or a rubber band. Except for dumping out the contents of my backpack, they'd done nothing else to damage it.

When Rosa opened the door, we found Lorna lounging against the opposite wall, playing on her phone. Apparently, she'd been waiting the entire time. She straightened up and, at Rosa's direction, took my suitcase. The three of us trooped to the elevators in a row. The children's song "The Ants Go Marching In" came to mind as we walked the lengthy hallway, and I had to bite my lip to keep from allowing inappropriate laughter to sneak out.

On the tenth floor, Rosa introduced me to the concierge on duty, Pedro. He manned the lounge near the elevator bank. She explained to me that in the morning, coffee and pastries would be available, and iced tea, sodas, fruit plates, and cookies throughout the afternoon and evening. From four to six, a bartender would be serving cocktails. Pedro was there to help me in any way. Rosa handed my dirty clothes to the concierge and directed him to have them cleaned and returned to my room by five.

She then led our little troupe around the corner to the end of the hall. As she opened the door, she told me, "This is our Lady of Tikal suite, named after the queen of the Mayan city of Tikal."

My new suite wasn't just a bigger room with more seating, as I'd expected. The "room" was bigger than my condo. The circular entry was decorated with marble floors and a large, round table in the center with a bouquet of beautiful island flowers. A half bath lay to the left; on the right, a small coat closet. Past the foyer, we walked into a living room large enough to hold three different seating areas and a baby grand piano so shiny I could see my reflection. The main seating area faced a wall of windows overlooking the ocean. To the left of the living area was a galley style kitchen, complete with stainless steel appliances and granite countertops. To the right of the living room was the first bedroom with two double beds and windows that faced the golf course. It had an attached bathroom. On the other side of the living room was the master bedroom. An enormous four-poster king-sized bed centered the room and faced the view of the ocean. The master bathroom couldn't have been more luxurious—a glassed-in shower, jetted tub built for two, and a separate room with a toilet and bidet. All the furniture ran along neutral tones, with bright colors on the walls and in the accessories—many of which were decorated with Mayan symbols.

In my head, I ooh'd and ahh'd, while externally, I retained an approving but nonchalant façade as Rosa took me through each room.

When the tour finished, she turned to me and asked, "Would you like Lorna to unpack for you?"

Lorna, who had remained in the foyer with my new luggage while Rosa and I reviewed the apartment, perked up at the mention of her name.

"No, I don't think that will be necessary. Thank you, Rosa. This is a beautiful room and I appreciate everything you have done for me."

"Of course." She handed me the keys for the room, along with her business card. "Please contact me if you need anything further." She and Lorna exited, and I was finally left alone.

I spun in a slow circle, marveling at my luck. Really, I could almost thank my intruder. Almost. I grabbed my new suitcase, wheeled it into the master bedroom, and ran myself a bath.

Around lunchtime, Rodrigo texted.

Packed and ready to roll. Mexico, here I come!

See you soon!

Thankfully, my bikini hadn't been damaged, so my afternoon consisted of reading Judith Gonda's latest mystery, *Murder in the Secret Maze,* and drinking margaritas, while intermittently wandering in and out of the ocean to cool off. Tension from the break-in ebbed as the afternoon, and the drinking, progressed. One of the water activity instructors stopped by my lounger and offered to teach me how to kite surf. By this time, I'd downed a few margaritas and couldn't muster up the energy to leave my chair and suggested another day. The man good-naturedly tried to change my mind, but eventually gave up with a dimpled grin and moved on to the next set of lounge lizards.

A waiter trotted out with a fresh pitcher of margarita, and I waved my empty glass at him. He trotted my way, and I sighed with contentment. *A girl could get used to this.*

****

I took a nap before dinner, and then stuffed myself with lobster and shrimp tacos to try and soak up some of the booze. It occurred to me, if I kept eating and drinking like this, I'd outgrow my brand-new clothes.

Around nine, I received another text from Rodrigo.

Hip hooray, I'm here! Where are you?

What room?

507. Where are you?

On the 10th floor. I'll come down.

I took the elevator back down to the fifth floor, finding Rodrigo's room not far from my recently vacated one. Rodrigo whipped open the door with a massive grin on his face. "Can you believe this place? It's fabulous! A million times better than Chicago. I'm in heaven. Come in!" He grabbed my hand and dragged me into what the resort labeled as a "Deluxe Double room"—a replica of the one I'd originally occupied. It housed two double beds, a pair of chairs, a desk with a charging station, and little bar area. "Check this out. They left me chocolates and flowers." He pointed to a small box and vase of three purple roses with baby's breath sitting on the desk, and then he pulled me out to the balcony. "Check it, I've got a view of the golf course. What about you?"

"I have an ocean view." I rested my hands on the railing and gazed down at the solar lights glowing at the tee boxes.

"Maybe I should have paid for an ocean view. Do you think it's worth it? Should I go down and upgrade?" He tapped a finger against his chin.

"Nah, the golf course is beautiful in a different way. It's actually quieter on this side of the building."

He shrugged. "Then I'll stay. If we want ocean, we'll go to your place. What have you seen or done?"

I chuckled. "Not much. I got a massage and have lazed around the pool and ocean. Oh, and I've drunk *a lot* of booze. You need to be careful. I wouldn't have thought an all-inclusive would be so generous with the booze, but they are. I've asked them to halve it. Otherwise, I'd be passed out before cocktail hour." Okay, maybe I wasn't exactly napping before dinner. I'd kind of passed out in my room for two hours. Tomorrow, I'd do a better job monitoring my intake.

"What should we do now? Go out? Stay in? Should I change?" He indicated his khaki shorts, blue madras shirt, and navy boat shoes.

"Let's stay in. You don't need to change. Why don't you come up to my room and I'll give you the run down on tomorrow's plans? Then we can go down to the bar."

"Lead the way."

"First, where is the box?" I held my breath.

"Oh, stop. Of course I brought the box." He tsked, stepping back into the room. "How can you doubt me? It's over here on the bedside table. See?" He held it out to me.

With relief, I took the black plastic square. "Thanks, Rodrigo. I appreciate it."

"No problem. Now I have space in my luggage for gifts."

"C'mon, I have a surprise for you."

A few minutes later Rodrigo stood in my suite with his jaw on the ground. "Damn, girl. Who did you have to sleep with to get this upgrade?"

Chapter Eight

I joined Rodrigo for breakfast at one of the poolside patios. After filling our bellies with huevos rancheros, fresh squeezed orange juice, and toast, we wandered out to the front portico to wait for our ride to the pyramid. But Mrs. Thundermuffin's promised ride did not materialize, and, by nine, Rodrigo became restless. He wandered over to chat with a group of American hotel guests standing together like a flock of sheep.

A few minutes later, he returned to where I stood by the valet stand. "Hey, that group has a bus taking them out to *Chichén Itzá*. Why don't we tag along with them? They said it was eight hundred pesos. How much is that?"

"A little more than forty bucks." I chewed my lip and considered his suggestion.

It seemed like Mrs. Thundermuffin's driver was a no show. There could be a million reasons for it. I'd already inquired on prices for a taxi to take us out to the ruins, and it was substantially more than forty dollars. I'd also tried to reach Mrs. Thundermuffin on her cell number. It rang twice, then gave me a busy signal. I didn't know if there were dead zones in Mexico. Granted, Mrs. T. had been a little squirrelly about the phone number.

A green-and-white bus rolled up the circular driveway, and the sheep shuffled closer to the curb.

Rodrigo looked back and forth between me and the bus. "Karina, what do you want to do?"

It'd gotten to the point where I simply wanted to get rid of the death mask residing in my backpack. I shivered thinking about it—somehow, I doubted carrying around such a grim item did anything for my karma. When you got down to it, a death mask was a creepy thing to have in one's carryall. "I think it doesn't matter how we get there. Just that we do get there. Let's see if we can join the group."

It turned out the bus driver was very flexible and had a "more the merrier" attitude. Not only did *we* join the bus, paying our eight hundred pesos, three others climbed on after us. I left word with the valet desk about our change of plans, just in case Mrs. Thundermuffin's delinquent driver showed. Rodrigo and I found seats halfway back and hunkered in for the two-hour drive out to the Mayan ruins.

The bus arrived at quarter after eleven, dropping us off at the end of a large line of tourists waiting to purchase tickets. Knowing our time was limited, since we'd arrived so much later than expected, Rodrigo and I declined an invitation to join the regular tour with the rest of the American sheeple that exited the bus, and instead got in line to purchase individual tickets. While we waited, I slathered on sunscreen and adjusted my big floppy white hat. That may have been Mrs. T.'s code, but she was right, sunscreen and a hat was a must. Being so far inland, we'd lost our ocean breezes, and the heat of the August day was already upon us, it would only get hotter as the day progressed. We'd both worn sneakers, lightweight T-shirts, and shorts, but I could already feel the sweat pooling between my shoulder blades. An enterprising vendor had set up next to the line and was offering cold sodas and bottles of water. Rodrigo and I each purchased water.

Chichén Itzá is an archeological site of a Mayan civilization dating to between 750 and 1200 A.D. It became a UNESCO world heritage site in 1988. The main attraction is the Castillo, the giant pyramid dedicated to the Kukulkan, or the Plumed Serpent. Much like the Egyptian pyramids of Giza, the Castillo was built with astronomical precision, and every year on the spring and autumnal equinox the sun strikes the side of the building in such a manner that the shadows and light appears as a snake along the steps of the magnificent building. When I came as a child, tourists were still allowed to climb the pyramid and look out upon the vast city from the top temple where ancient sacrifices were made to the gods. In 2005, following a misstep that led to the tragic death of a tourist, the owners of the site stopped allowing visitors to climb the Castillo.

After taking our fill of photos at the pyramid, Rodrigo and I wandered over to the Great Ball Court and the Jaguar temples. At 545 feet in length and 225 feet in width, the Ball Court was quite magnificent. Each end had a raised temple area for the royalty to watch the games. After the Ball Court, we wandered over to the Platform of Venus.

At twelve-thirty, we were back at the base of the Castillo with our eyes peeled for Mrs. T. Even though the place was crowded with tourists, I figured it wouldn't be that difficult to spot my pink-haired neighbor. By twelve-forty-five, worry set in.

"Phew, it is *hot*." Rodrigo took off his straw fedora and began fanning himself. "Do you want to walk around again to see if she's waiting on the other side?"

"We might as well. I feel like a broiled lobster." I swiped the sweat from my upper lip and shook off one of the rucksack straps to allow some fresh air on my soaking wet back.

My turquoise sneakers were grimy from the hard-baked dirt, and our shoes left dusty imprints as we walked one more time around the Castillo. We rounded the final corner when I heard my name.

A young man in tan linen slacks and a light blue designer polo, with his long brown hair pulled back into a low ponytail, waved at me. "Excuse me, are you Karina Cardinal?"

"I am. Who are you?"

"I'm Craig, Mildred's nephew." He held out his hand and delivered a toothy smile.

He had fine, long fingers, and a sweaty palm. I ended the shake as quickly as possible, surreptitiously wiping the wetness on my shorts as I introduced Rodrigo. "This is my friend Rodrigo."

"Where is your aunt?" Rodrigo must have noticed my hand wiping because he knuckled up and forced Craig into a fist bump.

"Aunt Mildred did not sleep well last night. Sent me instead. Said you would understand."

"I'm sorry to hear that. Where is she now?" I asked.

"Staying in . . . uh, Campeche . . . with friends."

Call it women's intuition—there was something off about this guy. He enunciated every word a little too clearly. Almost as though English was not his native tongue. Also, I could see no resemblance to Mrs. T. That unto itself meant nothing, but she had a mantel full of family photos, and for the life of me, I couldn't remember seeing this fellow among the framed pictures.

"I assume you have it?" Craig asked, leaning to the side, eyeing my backpack.

"Have what?" I replied, shifting it out of his line of sight.

Those dark brows furrowed over his big doe eyes. "The mask, of course."

Well, he knew I had a mask at least. "Oh, that. Yes." I tapped the shoulder strap. "It's all right and tight."

The jocular smile returned to his thick lips.

"Mrs. Thundermuffin said there was some place we could eat lunch." Rodrigo stepped forward, waving his hat faster. "Do you know where that is? I'm getting hungry, and I'm sure we all could use a drink."

"Ah, yes. There is a restaurant by the front entrance that she suggested. Why don't we walk that way?"

Rodrigo replaced his hat with a frown. Craig's loping walk fell into step with me, and when his arm brushed mine, I crowded closer to Rodrigo.

Surveying the slender man on my right, I asked, "I was wondering if the cat sitter was able to reach your aunt?"

"Cat sitter?" He looked confused.

"Yes, the woman taking care of her cat, Smokey. She said she had to take the cat to the vet."

"Oh, Smokey." He forced a laugh that made me shiver. "I had forgotten about that beast. I do not know if she has spoken to the cat sitter."

I stopped short. The two men walked a few more steps before turning around. "Mrs. Thundermuffin's cat isn't named Smokey," I said, squint-eyed. "Who are you?"

The jocular smile disappeared, and, in a nanosecond, those long fine fingers gripped the strap on my shoulder and yanked. "Give me the mask!" He growled something else in a foreign language—not Spanish, but I'm fairly sure he cursed me.

The strap got as far as my elbow, which I bent, bringing my hand to my chest to keep him from jerking it off. I stepped back, pulling hard, and yelled, "*Security!*"

Rodrigo jumped forward, planted a hand against the guy's shoulder, and shoved. "Get off!"

The man calling himself Craig stumbled but retained an iron grip on the strap, and nearly took me down with him.

Rodrigo grabbed my assailant's wrist and squeezed while calling, "*Policía, policía, ladrón, ladrón!*"

I bent my neck forward, got hold of a bony finger and bit down hard. The impersonator shouted and released his grip. We'd garnered attention from other tourists, and I heard a woman yelling, "He's trying to steal her bag. Thief! Pickpocket!" I faltered backward but managed to stay upright. Rodrigo grabbed the guy's ponytail and stuck out his foot, tripping him backward. Fake Craig went down in a poof of brown dust. Rodrigo grabbed my hand and we took off.

I did not dare to look back. Instead, I focused only on keeping in step with my swift-footed friend as we fled toward the front entrance.

Two men wearing navy blue uniforms with guns at their hips and batons in hand came jogging toward us. Rodrigo pointed and yelled something in Spanish. The guards' faces turned fierce and their jog turned into a sprint. We burst out of the entry gates, startling a large group of Asian tourists gathered around a tour guide who was holding up a Japanese flag placard.

I tugged Rodrigo's hand, and we slowed to a trot. Busses filled the front driveway two-deep, and I glanced over my shoulder to make sure our assailant hadn't gotten past security. I didn't see our ponytailed friend, but as my gaze swept the area, it connected with a blond man wearing dirty khaki chinos and a red-checked shirt, exiting the men's room about thirty yards away. Recognition dawned across his sunburnt features. He opened his mouth; I turned away, yanking on Rodrigo's hand. One of the busses pulled out and I didn't hear whatever the blond man called above the noisy engine.

"The taxi stand is across the way. Hurry!" Rodrigo shouted as he hauled me in front of a bus lurching forward. We dodged around it and were met with an angry blare of the horn. I didn't blame the driver; our little stunt probably gave him a minor heart attack. Gaining the curb of the taxi median, Rodrigo raised his arm and called, "TAXI!"

A white Cadillac slid to a quiet stop in front of us and the passenger window rolled down. I leaned over to look inside.

"Karina Cardinal? Is that you?" The man stretched across the center console.

I began backing away.

"I'm so sorry I missed you at the hotel. I have the letter, here." He held a folded white paper toward me.

Rodrigo snatched it from his hand and passed it to me.

"Hurry up. The last bus is pulling away."

I skimmed the contents for her secret code.

"He's coming!" Rodrigo bellowed, whipping open the back door of the Caddy. "Do we get in?"

Sure enough—white hat, sunscreen—listed at the end of the communique and signed, Mildred Thundermuffin. I shoved him, hollering, "Get in, get in."

We fell across the seat in a tumble of arms and legs with Rodrigo yelling in my ear, "Go, go, go!"

Chapter Nine

The Cadillac zipped forward, and the door slammed shut with the momentum. I pushed up to look out the back window and witnessed the blond manically waving his arms and chasing behind the vehicle's dust.

"Karina, your hand," Rodrigo wheezed.

Looking down, I found my hand pressed against his windpipe. "Oh, sorry." I rolled off him onto the floorboards. After we rearranged ourselves into a proper sitting position, I leaned forward and addressed our driver, who had taken our frantic entrance into his vehicle in a surprisingly unflappable manner, "Who are you?"

"I am Marcellus Oceano." He put his right hand over his shoulder toward me.

I gave his hand a two-fingered shake. "Karina Cardinal, and this is my friend Rodrigo Alvarez."

"What happened to you this morning?" Rodrigo asked.

"I am very sorry. A flat tire. By the time I got to the hotel, you had already left. The valet gave me your message, and I followed you here."

"Do you know where Mrs. Thundermuffin is?" I asked.

"She did not show up?" Marcellus frowned with concern, coming to a halt at a red light.

"No. We were accosted by a man claiming to be her nephew."

"I will be honest, Missus Karina," —he pronounced it mee-sus, and enunciated each syllable of my name— "I was not able to contact her when I found the flat tire this morning. I have known her for a long time, and it is unusual for her to miss a meeting."

This entire mess is unusual. "Call me Karina, and I agree with you, Marcellus. I'm afraid she is in trouble. We were supposed to go to a restaurant called *Casa de Chichen*. Do you know where that is?"

"We passed it. Should I go back?"

"I think we should. Just to cover our bases."

"What bases?" At the intersection, Marcellus slowed and made a U-turn, his thick fingers expertly spinning the steering wheel hand over hand.

"It's an American expression," Rodrigo said, and translated into Spanish.

"How long have you known Mildred?" I asked.

Marcellus pondered a moment. "A very long time. Since I was a child."

"And she's, what, a friend of the family?"

"She is more than a friend. She saved my life and that of my sister. I would do anything for her." Marcellus made another turn, rolled into the parking lot of the *Casa de Chichen*—a building with pink adobe walls and Spanish tiled roof—and pulled to a halt at the front door. He placed his arm across the passenger seat and turned to face us. "Shall I go in and look for her?"

Rodrigo and I exchanged glances. "Yes, I think that would be best. We're both too recognizable," he said.

"I will return." Marcellus got out of the car and adjusted the gray button-down over his pouch of gut.

Thankfully, he left the blessed air conditioning running. My clothing cooled, goose bumps popped out on my arms, and I could feel the salt from the drying sweat tightening around my hairline. It felt wonderful.

"Do you think we can trust him?" Rodrigo asked.

"Lord, I hope so. I do believe this letter was written by Mrs.

T." I waved the paper in the air. "And we've got to trust someone. He doesn't give me the creeps like the guy back at the ruins."

"Yeah, I thought that fellow was a little squirrelly before you tripped him up with the cat question."

I removed my hat and lifted my wet ponytail off the back of my neck. "How did you know?"

"I didn't. But he didn't know we were supposed to have lunch at *Casa de Chichen*. It's actually a rather well-known restaurant to visit when you're at *Chichén Itzá*. When did you figure it out?"

"I don't know, his speech pattern was off. He called her Aunt Mildred, when the letter in the package called her Milly. He also didn't speak in contractions. What twenty-something doesn't use contractions in their speech?"

Rodrigo's mouth turned down. "Someone whose native tongue is something other than English."

"Yeah."

Marcellus's stocky body pushed through the glass door.

"How does he wear black pants in this heat?" I asked.

"As a native, I suspect he's grown accustomed to it. He doesn't look happy."

Marcellus slid into the driver's seat and shifted into gear. "She was not there."

I leaned between the front seats. "You're sure? What about the ladies' room?"

"No one remembered seeing an older woman with pink hair."

Disappointed, I slumped back into the luxurious beige velvet seat.

"We can do nothing more here," he said, pulling back onto the main road. "I am returning you to the resort."

Since I could see no other alternative, I didn't argue.

"I'm thirsty and hungry. Is there somewhere we can stop on the way?" Rodrigo asked.

I cleared my dusty throat and echoed Rodrigo's need for a

drink.

Marcellus reached over to the passenger seat and retrieved a small blue cooler. "Cold drinks and cheese."

"Thank you." Rodrigo placed the cooler between the two of us and we each took a bottle of water.

I gulped so fast it ran down my chin and dripped between my breasts. I didn't bother to wipe it away. The cheese was shaped into a ball the size of my fist with the words Oaxaca on the wrapper. Rodrigo opened the package and pulled off a hunk. I found it could be peeled apart much like American string cheese. Rodrigo, apparently famished, gobbled his first bite like a starving hyena, so when he offered another chunk my way, I declined, allowing him to finish the package. Once he finished, I decided we needed to make a plan.

While the Caddy produced a nice, quiet ride, the air vents continued blasting out the cool air, and I raised my voice to be heard over the whooshing. "Marcellus, when and where did you last see Mrs. T.?"

"She came to my home in Mérida Saturday morning," he answered succinctly, keeping his eyes ahead on the road.

"And what did she tell you?"

"She said she needed someone she could trust to drive her friend; of course, she thought of me."

"That's it? Nothing more? Did you ask her why she was in Mexico?"

"No, I do not pry. She asks. I do." He tapped his chest.

Rodrigo leaned forward. "You said she saved your life, and obviously you are a trusted friend. Who is Mrs. Thundermuffin to you?"

Marcellus drew in a breath and paused, before letting it come out as a gusty sigh. "My father grew up in Nicaragua. I was born there. My sister was born there. It was a poor country, but one way to make money was working for the drug cartels. So that is what my father did. He began working for them at the age of fourteen. When he was twenty-two, he met my mother. She went by Solidad—and she worked for the CIA. She convinced my father to help her, and then they both worked for the American government, feeding them information about the cartel. But the cartel, they find out. . . ."

Rodrigo and I drew in a collective breath, waiting for what we knew would be coming next.

"They tortured and killed both of them. As soon as my mother went missing, the woman who I had known as *tia* Maria realized something was wrong. She picked up my sister and me from school and told us that our parents had been killed in an auto accident, and that distant relatives in Mexico were going to take care of us. The following forty-eight hours were a blur. At the end of it, we flew out of Nicaragua on a cargo plane with new names, new clothes, and a new set of foster parents waiting for us at the other end. My sister was five. I was seven." He spoke in a monotone, delivering each nugget of information as if he was telling us a story he'd read in the news. Sometimes he switched to Spanish, and Rodrigo quietly translated for me. "We got postcards from foreign lands, and Christmas presents, every year. But I did not see *tia* Maria again until I turned eighteen. She came to visit the farm where I grew up, and she told me the truth about my parents. That was the first time she told me her real name. She said, 'Call me Milly.' She was a coworker and good friend of my mother."

"Jesus," I breathed. My brain scrambled in many directions at Marcellus's revelations.

"Milly told me there is a star on the wall, at the CIA building in Washington, D.C., for my mother," Marcellus said with pride.

"What happened to your sister?" I asked.

"She married a banker and lives in Mérida with her three children. Her oldest daughter is named Solidad," he said with a poignant smile.

"Wow," I whispered. "I'm sorry, Marcellus. I didn't mean to bring back such terrible memories."

"It is okay. The past, it is past." He made a flicking motion with his hand as if throwing those memories behind him. "The couple she placed us with were good, loving people."

Rodrigo shifted forward.

"Are you still in touch with your foster parents?"

"Tito and Lita? Of course, they are my parents. You see, they could not have children of their own, and when Milly brought us . . . they saw it as a sign from God. We became their children. Ten years ago, they sold the farm and bought an apartment in the city to be closer to me and my sister."

"Wait, wait, my brain is still trying to catch up." Rodrigo put the flats of his palms against his forehead. "You said Mrs. Thundermuffin, the woman with the bright pink hair, worked for the CIA?"

Marcellus grunted an affirmative. "When I knew her, she had brown hair, and then later, blonde."

Rodrigo's hands made exploding motions. "Mind blown. Did you know this?" He zeroed in on me.

I shook my head and drew my shoulders upward. "She once told me she worked for the government, but I figured she was a paper pusher for, like, the Department of Transportation. I never would have guessed the CIA."

"Do you think this entire thing is some sort of CIA op?" Rodrigo asked.

I chewed my lip for a moment. "No, she's around seventy. She's got to be retired by now."

"Oh, ho!" Rodrigo wiggled his pointer finger at me. "The CIA is like the Hotel California, you can never leave, and you take your secrets to the grave."

My colleague had a point. However, I couldn't imagine her

pulling me into a government op. It just didn't ring true. "No, I think her grandnephew is in trouble and she came down to help. Maybe it was more trouble than he let on. Maybe she's trying to use some of her old contacts to get him out of it."

"Marcellus, what do you think?" Rodrigo asked.

Marcellus shook his head. "Like I said, I don't ask questions. I do not know about Milly's life in America. I do not know this nephew you speak of. She is very capable. I trusted her to know what she is doing."

Marcellus had more faith in Milly than I. Not that I thought she was stupid—there was always something "knowing" about her—but a mastermind of espionage was far from the Mildred Thundermuffin that I knew. Clearly, she'd become proficient at living the double life.

"But now," Marcellus continued, "I do not know. It is not normal for her to miss a meeting."

Rodrigo turned to me. "Are we going to talk about the elephant in the room—or should I say, the car?"

My eyes widened in confusion.

"The golden mask in the box." Rodrigo tapped my backpack, which lay on the floor between us, with his foot.

"You looked?" I said in an accusatory manner.

"You didn't?"

"Of course I did."

Rodrigo crossed his arms. "Care to explain?"

My coworker deserved an explanation. I pressed fingers to my eyes, trying to figure out where to start the story. "It began on Monday, after my sister bailed on this trip. . . ." I gave Rodrigo and Marcellus the run-down of events leading up to today's attack.

"And you're sure this art expert knows it's a fake?" Rodrigo asked, skeptical.

"Yes, he pointed out the telltale signs, and there *is* the fact that the building *burned down* in 2018. I searched. Nothing indicated the item was stolen before the fire."

"So, who was that guy and why did he want the mask? What's so important about it?" Marcellus asked the obvious question.

I sighed. "I have a theory, but you're not going to like it."

"Lay it on us," Rodrigo encouraged.

"What if Mrs. Thundermuffin's grandnephew is trying to sell this off as the real thing? What if he is involved in some sort of black market for antiquities, and he made a deal that's gone sideways?"

"What kind of people are involved in black market antiquities?" Rodrigo asked.

"Drug dealers," Marcellus supplied.

"Do you think that guy back there was a drug dealer?"

"I don't know." I stared hard at the backpack. "All I know is he wanted the mask and lied to me about Mrs. Thundermuffin."

"Now what do we do?" Rodrigo asked.

During our conversation, a niggling feeling had been working its way into full blown anxiety over Mrs. Thundermuffin's safety and whereabouts. Even though she'd been a trained spy, she wasn't as spry as she used to be, and whatever this was, she may have gotten in over her head. "Marcellus, where did Mildred stay when she came to see you in Mérida? With you?"

"No. My sister and I both offered, but she insisted on staying at a hotel."

"Since Mérida was the last known location of Mildred, I think we need to start there. Marcellus, can you start making subtle inquiries? Maybe we can determine when and how she left the hotel."

"What is this, 'subtle'?"

Rodrigo translated.

Marcellus nodded. "Yes, yes, I am most subtle. I own a tour company. I know people all over Mérida. I have a police friend.

A little *dinero*" —he rubbed his thumb and forefinger together— "and he will subtle help me."

"Wonderful."

"Okay, Marcellus has a job. What are we going to do?" Rodrigo asked, eager as a beagle.

"Well, I might know someone who has some contacts at the CIA." I stared hard at Rodrigo, mentally trying to get him to keep his mouth shut.

"You mean—"

Ever so slightly, I shook my head. Rodrigo clammed up.

Marcellus turned into the long driveway that led up to our hotel. As he pulled to a stop in front of the resort, I gripped the passenger side headrest and sat forward. "Marcellus, would you like to come inside? Rodrigo and I need to eat, and so do you, undoubtedly. Why don't you join us?"

"Thank you, but I must decline. I think you are right to be worried about Milly. I shall return to Mérida, contact my police friend, and begin our subtle questions."

"Very well. Thank you for finding us at the ruins."

Rodrigo echoed my thanks.

"It was my pleasure. Again, I apologize for missing you this morning."

Before getting out of the car, we took a moment to exchange phone numbers. Breathing in the salty air, my shoulders loosened. Though the anxiety didn't exit my body completely, it certainly eased. There was something about the relaxing qualities of the beach.

We shook hands with Marcellus and parted ways.

"So what shall we eat?" Rodrigo drew the large glass door open for me.

"I don't care, as long as it's fast. I'm starving."

Chapter Ten

It turns out, the only thing open at three in the afternoon, besides room service, was the snack bar at the pool. The other restaurants didn't reopen until four-thirty. The good news, our quesadillas and French fries were ready quickly. Rodrigo ordered a beer. I, needing something a little more substantial, ordered a mojito.

"Why didn't you want Marcellus to know about your Silverthorne pals? I assume that's who you are planning to get in touch with. Don't you trust him?" He took a pull on his *cerveza*.

I stared off into the distance. "I trust Marcellus. I don't know why I didn't want you to bring them up. Maybe it's my own history, but I kind of feel like things need to stay . . . compartmentalized."

Rodrigo paused with the bottle halfway to his lips and burst out laughing. "Geez, are you sure you don't work for the CIA?"

"*Rodrigo!*" I hissed.

He shook his head, still smiling, and sipped.

"There you are! I've been searching all over this place for you!"

I almost choked on the bite of quesadilla in my mouth. Rodrigo spat out his beer, spraying the bedraggled blond from the ruins who had chased us out of the parking lot.

The blond grabbed a napkin off our table and wiped his face. "Sorry, didn't mean to startle you."

"Who the hell are you? And how the hell did you find us?" I snapped, pushing my feet closer together to tighten their hold on the backpack, with its Egyptian treasure, between my legs.

He pushed his stringy bangs off his face, glanced around, and pulled up a chair from a neighboring table. "I'm Aunt Milly's grandnephew, Craig. I tried to get to *Chichén Itzá* to meet you, but Adolfo got there first."

I sat back and crossed my arms, giving "Craig" a disbelieving glare. "Okay, 'Craig.'" I made finger quotes. "What is the name of Mrs. Thundermuffin's dog?"

"She doesn't have a dog. You mean her black cat? It's Mr. Tibbs. She named him after Sidney Poitier's character from *The Heat of the Night,* one of her favorite actors. You know she once met him at the Kennedy Center," he mused, flagging down a waiter. "*Una cerveza, por favor.*"

I scrutinized this character, hating to admit there was a slight family resemblance to Mrs. T. Something around the eyes and nose that seemed similar, and I did recall a photo of a blond, high-school-aged student on her mantel that might be this guy. His sweat-stained polo and pants were wrinkled and dirty, he'd moved a few days past a five o'clock shadow, and there was the faintest yellowing of a healing bruise around his left eye, but he could be the guy on the mantel.

I tested him again. "Where does your aunt live?"

He rattled off the building address and apartment number.

"Um-hm. And how are you related?"

"She is my grandmother's sister. What is all this? We need to stop fooling around with the twenty questions. Aunt Milly is in trouble," he said, exasperated.

Rodrigo bent closer to Craig and delivered, in a rather menacing manner, "The twenty questions are because your friend Adolfo told us *he* was Craig, just before he attacked Karina."

"Adolfo? Attacked you?" Craig let out a shout of laughter. "That effeminate twit. I don't imagine he was successful. No? You saw through him? Thank God you're as smart as my aunt said you were. All the same, it's a good thing it wasn't one of his brothers."

"Brothers? There are more of them?" Rodrigo squinted.

"Yes, a pair. They are rather hefty fellows. Probably playing guard over Aunt Milly. Oh, great, thanks." The last he said to the waitress as she passed him the beer. Then he said something in Spanish that made her blush and giggle. Rodrigo's frown deepened. Craig gulped down half of the bottle before taking a breath.

"You mind explaining that comment about your aunt?" I drawled.

"Yes, but not here." He swiped his mouth with the back of his hand and glanced around furtively. "Finish up and we'll go someplace quieter, where we can talk."

I crossed my arms and leaned them on the table. "Look, pal, I don't know you, and I have no plans to go anywhere outside of the public eye until you convince me you are who you say you are."

"Oh, for heaven's sake—here!" He reached into his back pocket and pulled out a wallet. "This is my ID, and here is a picture of me and Grandma and Aunt Milly at my college graduation."

Taking one in each hand, I scrutinized the New York driver's license first. It had one of those ghastly, pale-faced, blank stare photos that the DMV was so skilled at taking. The ID put Craig Mettler at the tender age of twenty-six. The other photo was indeed Mrs. T., back when she was still coloring her hair an ashy blond. The other woman was slightly taller, a little heavier, with mostly gray hair, wearing a frumpy black flowered dress. Between the two ladies stood a smiling Craig in a black cap and gown. I held up the photo, comparing the bedraggled man in front of me to the clean-cut graduate. They were one and the same.

"May I?" He snatched a fry off my plate before I could answer and chowed down. "I haven't eaten since yesterday." He took another fry.

Rodrigo scrunched his face and glared at Craig as if he were a distasteful cockroach.

A quarter of quesadilla and a pile of fries remained on my plate. I tossed the ID and photo down and shoved the plate at Craig. "Help yourself."

Rodrigo, on the other hand, pulled his plate further away from Craig's grabby fingers. "You better start talking, pal. And it better be the truth because, right now, I don't like what I'm hearing."

In between bites, Craig began his explanation in undertones. "You see, there are people who . . . need things. I help them with their needs."

"What kind of things?" Rodrigo asked.

"All sorts of things."

"Let me guess, you're in the import export business," I said, repeating a euphemism another thief once used on me.

Craig pointed a fry at me. "Exactly, a perfect way to explain it."

"What do you import export?" Rodrigo, still clueless, pursued his line of questioning.

"He's a thief." I sipped my mojito. "Or is it a fence?"

Craig's face fell for a moment before the smile slipped back in place and he turned on the charm. "Such a crude term. No, no, I'm more of a—"

"I don't care what it is. We know the mask is a fake," I stated baldly. "Were you trying to sell it, they caught on to you, and you dragged your poor aunt into this business? Hmm? Did it go something like that?"

Craig stopped mid-chew and needed to take a drink from his beer to get the bite down. "You don't understand," he said, trying again.

I could tell Craig was used to charming his way out of tricky spots. I'd worked too long on the Hill to be fooled by charisma and doubletalk. "Cut the crap. I understand very well. What I don't know—where is your aunt?"

The façade fell, and his face turned to misery as he gazed at the remaining two fries on the plate. "They have her."

I sucked wind.

Rodrigo's beer slammed down onto the table.

Craig glanced up with pleading eyes and whispered, "I need the mask to get her back."

Rodrigo gripped Craig's elbow, rather tightly from what I could tell, and rose, bringing Craig to his feet. "You're right, it's time we found some place more private."

We ended up in Rodrigo's room, in part because I didn't want Craig to find out which room I was in, and also because I didn't want him stinking up my lovely suite. I wasn't sure when the man had taken a shower last, but once we got in the elevator, the smell, no longer being blown off by the beachfront breezes, thickened and filled the space. If B.O. was a color, the elevator would have been filled with a green fog.

"Boy! You reek." Rodrigo did not mince words as he shut the door to his room behind us.

"I know," Craig replied miserably. "I've been in these clothes for days."

"Well, I can't concentrate through the haze of stench. Take a shower, and then we'll talk." He pulled out a pair of shorts and a T-shirt from his open suitcase and practically shoved Craig into the bathroom. "Don't come out until you're clean!" Rodrigo yelled at the closed bathroom door. Then he strode across the room and threw open the slider onto his balcony.

I waited until the shower started before joining Rodrigo.

He didn't look happy. "Want to tell me why we didn't go up to your fancy suite?"

"I don't trust him. Period."

Rodrigo stared morosely at the empty fairway below. "You don't think he's the grandnephew?"

"Oh, I believe he's the grandnephew. But he's either a thief or a fence or a forger, and I don't trust him to make the exchange for his aunt if he sees some sort of con can be made. I also believe that my room, being on the concierge level, is more secure than yours. And I plan to keep the mask with me, in my room."

Rodrigo rubbed his chin. "You could put it in the hotel safe."

"I already looked into that. You have to declare whatever valuables you're putting into their safe. It's for their insurance purposes. The fewer people who know we have this thing, the better." I indicated the backpack now safely strapped onto my shoulders.

"So what are we going to do?"

"First, I want to find out what he knows, and where they are holding Mrs. T. Second, if there is some sort of exchange to be made, I want to make sure *we* are there to make it."

Rodrigo nodded. "Agreed."

I heard the shower turn off and suggested we move inside. We took our seats in the two wingback chairs, and I tucked the backpack in the corner behind mine just as Craig opened the bathroom door. The black shorts were tight, but Craig had been able to zip them up. He pulled at the hem of the white T-shirt, glancing down at the rainbow and letters "UBU" across his chest. He hadn't shaved, but his hair was combed back, and he looked rather handsome in a swashbuckling pirate manner. He carried his dirty clothes in a ball.

"What should I do with these?" he asked.

Rodrigo rolled his eyes and sighed. "There's a plastic bag hanging in the closet. Put them in there, and for the love of Pete, tie it closed."

"Thanks for the clothes. I owe you one." He dumped the

dirty laundry in the bag and pulled it tight.

"Alright, enough chit-chat. Craig, have a seat." With one foot, Rodrigo shoved the wheeled desk chair at him.

"And tell us about the mask," I added.

Craig crossed his arms and frowned as he rolled closer to Rodrigo and me. "Speaking of the mask," he drawled, "I believe you were told not to look in the box. I'm not happy that you've been blabbing about it all around town."

My feet, resting on the coffee table, slammed to the floor, and I jammed my pointer finger at him. "Listen up, you little crap weasel, your aunt asked me to carry an object into a foreign country. Of course I'm going to look in the damn box. And you can eliminate your self-righteous indignity. I want answers, and if you want the mask, you'll give them to me. You got that?"

Craig, duly chastised, gave a sharp nod.

"Now, the mask *is* a fake. Am I right?" I asked, because I hadn't put it out of the realm of possibility that Martin had been mistaken.

Craig nodded. "Yes, it's fake."

"Does Adolfo and his pals know it's a fake?"

"Of course. Adolfo made it."

"Adolfo made it?" Rodrigo got into the inquisition. "What do you mean he made it? Is he part of your scheme? Is he trying to double cross you? Or did you double cross him?"

Craig crunched his eyes shut for a few moments. "Adolfo is an artist." He said the word "artist" with a note of disdain.

"Is he famous? Should we know him?" I asked.

"No, he cleans and restores paintings and artifacts for a living. Occasionally, art enthusiasts hire him to make copies of well-known masterpieces so they can hang them in their homes. He is excellent at reproductions."

"Does he create his own art?" Rodrigo asked.

Craig nodded. "Of course, Adolfo fancies himself an abstract impressionist."

Rodrigo didn't look impressed. "Has he had showings of his own work?"

"Yes. Twice. Both splendid failures."

"I see." I tapped a finger to my chin. "Always the bridesmaid, never the bride."

"So you understand." Craig's mouth pinched.

"Why did he make the mask?"

Craig shifted uncomfortably.

"Craig . . . why did he make the mask?"

"Because I asked him to," he mumbled.

"Care to elaborate?"

"I had a buyer for the real one."

I waited to see if Craig would say more. He didn't, so I prompted, "Did Adolfo know you planned to steal the real one?"

"He did."

"And . . . ?"

"Adolfo created the mask on credit."

"On credit. You mean, he was to be paid—when? After you stole the one from the Brazilian museum and sold it to your dirty collector?" Rodrigo asked.

"Something like that." Craig stared down and played with the hem of his T-shirt.

I was getting tired of Craig's hedging. I'll admit my tone may have been a little snappish when I asked, "What happened?"

"The museum burned down before I could . . . uh . . . obtain the original."

"The museum burned last year." I gritted my teeth. "Why do they want the mask back now?"

Craig gulped and delivered big blue puppy dog eyes. "I-I don't know," he said tragically.

"Enough!" Rodrigo banged his fist on the coffee table.

Craig jumped and the pound puppy look disappeared.

"Enough of this subterfuge and dribbling out information. Listen to me, you little—what did you call him?" Rodrigo glanced at me.

"A crap weasel."

"You little crap weasel. I'm sick of you jerking us around." Rodrigo grabbed a hunk of shirt in his fist and tried to shake Craig. Unfortunately, the shirt was so stretchy, all Rodrigo managed to do was wrinkle the front. However, the fierceness in which he delivered his next sentence kept us all from laughing. "You'd better start talking, or I'm going to call security and tell them that the man who broke into Karina's room yesterday just broke into mine. You got me?"

Craig's gaze flew up to us, wide-eyed with anxiety. "Someone broke into your room?"

I put my feet back up on the coffee table and tilted my head. "On Sunday morning."

"But they didn't find it, did they?" His voice pitched.

I took a few moments to examine Craig. "If you're speaking of the mask. No. *They* did not."

Craig's posture physically deflated with relief and he blew out the breath he must have been holding.

"Now, as Rodrigo said, it's time for you to start talking. Tell us why Adolfo and his brothers want the mask. I'm assuming they are the ones that trashed my room."

"I'm not positive, but it wouldn't surprise me." He paused, and my brow rose. "Okay, okay, I'll tell you. Adolfo borrowed money from his brothers and expected to pay them off with the money from the sale of the mask. The entire plan went belly up when the museum burned down. So, we were both out the payday. I was trying other avenues to . . . uh . . . acquire the money, and Adolfo assured me he could hold off his brothers until I made some cash for us. However, it seems they wanted their money sooner and decided to take an active hand in the situation. They left Milan with Adolfo, and came to Mexico to find me."

"Are these brothers . . . 'family men?'" I used my finger quotes.

Craig caught on immediately and shook his head. "No, no. More like nickel-and-dime thugs."

Rodrigo snorted. "You keep delightful company, Craig."

Getting back to the point, I asked, "Why didn't you just give it back to Adolfo?"

"The brothers got it in their head that I could sell the fake to my buyer."

Rodrigo and I took a moment to process that information.

"What the—Are you kidding?" I stuttered.

"Right?" He tsked. "Those two aren't the brightest bulbs on the Christmas tree. When I told them that my buyer knew the original burned with the museum, they started putting out their own feelers to find some other sucker to sell it to."

"Again, why didn't you just give it to them?" I asked with irritation.

"Well . . ." Craig pondered his answer for a moment. "I figured if they did find a buyer, then I should act as the fence. After all, why shouldn't I get a cut? I convinced them they needed me. However, Adolfo's brothers are bungling idiots when it comes to antiquities, and their inquiries started making waves, and suddenly someone from Interpol's Arts and Antiquities Bureau turned up asking questions in Mexico City. I barely had time to ship the mask off to my aunt and get the hell out of there. When I got settled in Escondido, I called Aunt Milly to tell her what was coming and ask her if she could reach out to some of her contacts to see what Interpol knew. Only instead of getting the information, she came down to Mexico. Unfortunately, Dumb and Dumber tracked me down and weren't too pleased when I told them I'd 'moved' the mask for safekeeping." He touched the bruised left eye. "It got worse when Aunt Milly showed up, because then they knew they had leverage. First, they hid me in a storage warehouse and told her to bring the mask or they'd kill me. Somehow, she found out who and where they were, and made a deal to trade herself for me. She told me to make contact with you, get the mask, and make the trade. And that's where we stand right now."

It took a moment for my brain to catch up with this guy's story.

Rodrigo must have processed faster than I, because he asked an important question. "Why was Adolfo at the meet today?"

Craig ran a hand through his damp hair and glanced out the window. "I have no idea. Adolfo sometimes dances to the beat of his own drum. For all I know, he may have his own lead on a buyer and plans to cut us all out."

"Would he do that?" I asked.

Craig pondered for a moment. "I wouldn't have thought so, but the last time I saw him, he was acting rather strange."

Rodrigo opened his mouth, but I didn't want to go off on an Adolfo tangent, so I cut off whatever he was about to say. "Where are they holding your aunt?"

"I don't know. They didn't put her in the warehouse in Villahermosa where they were holding me."

"Do you know if she's okay?"

"As far as I know, she is fine." He went back to twisting the hem of his T-shirt. "I'm supposed to contact them when I get the mask, and we will set up a meet in Mérida."

"Where in Mérida?" Rodrigo jumped in.

Craig shrugged. "I don't know. Probably some back alley, if I know these two clowns."

I didn't like the sound of that. "Forget Mérida and the back alley. If they want to make the exchange, we do it at a public venue, during the day. They bring your aunt. We bring the mask."

"They're not going to like it."

"I don't care what Dumb and Dumber like. If they want the mask, they'll make it work." Rodrigo snipped.

I nodded in agreement with Rodrigo. "Now make your phone call. Tell them you want proof-of-life before you decide on a place to meet."

"What kind of proof do you want?" Craig asked.

I wasn't a kidnap and ransom professional, but I'd seen the movies. "Tell them to text you a photo of your aunt holding today's paper. If they are as dumb as you say, we'll get twofer. Knowing your aunt is alive and well, and her location."

Craig retrieved his phone from the bathroom, went to the sliding glass door, and pushed it open.

"What are you doing?" Rodrigo stood up.

"I'm doing what we discussed, calling Adolfo's brothers. I thought I'd just step out on the deck."

"You can do it here. In front of us." I pointed to the rolling chair.

Craig shrugged, plopped into the chair, and dialed. Someone on the other end must have answered. "It's Craig," he told them.

He might as well have gone out on the balcony, because he started speaking in a foreign language. Even though he didn't put it on speaker phone, we could hear some sharp responses, and halfway through the conversation, they must have threatened him or his aunt, because he burst out in English, "Don't you dare threaten me!" before gabbling angrily in the foreign language. Eventually, they seemed to come to an understanding. Craig finished with, "I'm waiting," tossed the phone on the coffee table, and commenced pacing about the room.

My own phone binged with a text from my sister Jillian.

Hey, Rina! Checking in to see how your trip is going. I

haven't heard from you since Saturday, and there are no new posts on social media lately. I bet it's because you're tanning by the pool with a drink in your hand and a flock of admirers. Are you drunk by noon every day? I'm doing okay. This cast is itchy, and Mom is driving me a bit cray-cray, but I'm glad she's here because this cast is a pain in my ass. By the end of the day my poor toes are swollen to the size of fat sausages. Throw me a bone and send a pic soon. Say hi to Rodrigo for me.

I burst out laughing at my sister's presumptions.

"What? What's so funny?" Rodrigo asked.

"My sister. She's assuming I'm so busy flirting with random strangers by the pool and drinking myself into a stupor that I don't have time to post on social media." I rolled my eyes.

"How is she doing?"

"Apparently, Mom is driving her nuts, her cast is itchy, and she's probably in more pain than she's letting on. Overall, I think she's pretty miserable." I could only thank my lucky stars that she hadn't come and wasn't involved in this mess. "Oh, and she said to say hello."

"Tell her I say hi, and I hope she feels better," Rodrigo replied.

"I'm not going to reply!"

"What happened to her?" Craig cut in. We both glanced at him and saw he had halted his pacing to stare out the sliding glass door.

"I beg your pardon?" I asked.

He turned to me. "Your sister. She's in a cast. What happened?"

"She broke her leg roller skating. She was supposed to be on this trip, instead of Rodrigo. Right now, I'm rather glad she isn't,"

I said in clipped tones.

Craig's gaze returned to the outdoor vista.

After a moment, Rodrigo filled in the awkward gap. "You have to reply. If you don't, she'll keep pestering you. There are too many bad stories about tourists these days. If she doesn't hear from you, she'll start to believe the worst."

She wouldn't be far from wrong. "I wouldn't know what to text."

"Tell her you're fine. Having fun in the sun. You've been leaving your phone in the room for safekeeping, and that's why you haven't posted photos."

"So, I should just make up a pack of lies?"

"It's better than the truth. Here, do you want me to do it?" Rodrigo held out his hand, but I pulled the phone protectively to my chest.

"Your friend is right. You should tell her you're fine." Craig added his two cents in monotone.

I stood up and huffed. "Fine. Excuse me while I go out on the balcony to text Jillian a bunch of BS."

Craig chivalrously opened the door. I took the handle and did my best to slam it shut. It closed in a very unsatisfying whoosh and click. I debated all the things I could write. In the end, I stayed as close to the truth as possible, telling her about our trip to *Chichén Itzá* . . . at least, the part before we were attacked by Adolfo. I attached a picture Rodrigo had taken of me in front of the Castillo, pressed send, and prayed Jillian would leave me alone for another day or two. Surely, by then, this situation would be resolved, and I could start taking poolside pics to satisfy my sister's curiosity.

Rodrigo stuck his head out. "Proof of life came in."

We received a photo of Mrs. Thundermuffin in a large-brimmed hat and a brightly colored beach cover-up sitting on a lounger by a pool and holding today's *Wall Street Journal.* To my relief, she looked hale and hearty. However, the pair of thugs must have been smarter than Craig thought, because the *Wall Street Journal* did not tell us anything of her whereabouts.

I rose from my chair. "Tell him we'll text him the meeting location soon."

"What are you thinking?" Craig asked while his thumbs tapped out the message.

"I'm not sure yet. I'm going up to my room to shower and change. We'll meet back here in an hour. Rodrigo, walk me to the elevator." I pulled my backpack out from behind my chair. Craig's gaze zeroed in on it and followed me as I exited with Rodrigo.

"Do you think it's safe to leave him alone in my room?" he asked as we strode down the hallway.

"What's he going to do? Steal your underwear? Run away? No, he'll stick close to us until he gets the mask. He knows I have it in the backpack. I can see his weaselly little brain trying to figure out how he's going to retrieve it. Did you catch any of the phone conversation? It sounded like he was speaking Italian."

"Yes, he was. There are some similarities to Spanish, but I could only catch words here and there. At some point, I think they wanted to know where he was and he refused to tell them. I'm also fairly certain he told them he had the mask in his possession."

"I'm not surprised." We arrived at the elevator bank and I held out my hand. "I need the key I gave you to my room."

Rodrigo blinked. "Why?"

"Because I have a feeling ol' Craig's skills extend to pick-pocketing. I don't need him getting ahold of that key. When I get up to my room, I'll find a place to hide the mask, and then I'll call Silverthorne to see if they have any suggestions for a meeting place for the exchange."

"Good idea." Rodrigo pulled out his wallet and handed over the keycard to my room.

The elevator arrived. "See you in an hour," I told him.

Chapter Eleven

The shower may have refreshed my body, but it did nothing for my state of mind. I stared at my phone, trying to decide which of my Silverthorne contacts I should call. Did I go straight to the head honcho and call Rick, or go a little further down the line and call Joshua? Joshua would certainly give me good advice, and it's not as though I hadn't dragged him into my past troubles. It would be old hat to Josh. On the other hand, maybe I should try Jin. He respected my instincts and, where Josh might give me a hard time, Jin was more likely to deal with the situation matter-of-factly. *Yup. Jin it is.*

I dialed.

It went to voice mail. *Damn.*

I didn't have time for voice mail, so I fell back to Joshua.

"Go for Joshua."

"Hey, Josh. How are you doing?"

"Karina Cardinal! Aren't you supposed to be on vacation?"

"As a matter of fact, I am in Mexico."

"Well, what can I do for you? Is this a jailhouse call? Did you get drunk and disorderly down there in Mexico? Are you calling for bail money?" he said in a breezy, tongue-in-cheek manner. "Hey, Jin," he called on his end, raising his voice, "guess who's on the phone? Cardinal, she's calling from jail."

I didn't hear Jin's response. "Joshua," I said in a warning tone, "I am *not* in jail."

"Never mind, she says she's not in jail."

"And ask Jin why didn't he answer my call?"

"Jin, she wants to know why you didn't answer her call." Josh chuckled. "He's checking his pants pockets. Nope, not there. Looks like he left it in his locker. He's off to go find it. So, why did you call Jin first? I thought I was your favorite."

I coughed. "Josh, you are my favorite. Jin's number came up first on my contacts list."

"Considering you're calling around the Silverthorne house, it must mean you're in trouble. Lay it on me. What's happened now? You stir up a drug cartel down there? Cause an international incident? Do I need to contact the State Department or send in the Marines?" Josh ribbed me.

"Cripes. Is Jin still around?"

"Nope. I'm all you've got."

I blew up my bangs. "Okay, so, if you needed to make an exchange, what kind of venue would you choose?"

"What are you exchanging?" The joking tone disappeared.

"A person for an item."

"Drugs?"

"No. Antiquity."

"Who is the person?"

I debated what I should reveal.

"Wait, Rick just walked in, I'm putting you on speaker."

"Crap," I muttered.

"Karina, are you okay?" Rick's concerned voice came over the lines.

"Yes, yes, I'm fine." I stared out my sliding door at the majestic view of ocean waves washing upon the shore and suddenly I wished I'd never met Mildred Thundermuffin. "Do you remember my kooky neighbor, Mrs. Thundermuffin?"

"I do," Josh said.

"No," Rick said at the same time.

There was a whispered conversation, then Rick came back on. "Yes, Josh refreshed my memory. What's it got to do with her?"

"She's been kidnapped. Well, they didn't actually kidnap her, it sounds like she went willingly in exchange for her crap weasel of a grandnephew. Anyway, they're holding her until we turn over a fake Egyptian death mask. We need to make a time and place for the exchange, and . . . I figured you might have done something like this. I'd . . . uh . . . like to get your thoughts on a good place to do that." My explanations met silence. "Hello? Rick? Josh?"

"We're still here," Josh said.

"Cardinal, aren't you on vacation in Mexico?" Rick asked.

I licked my lips. "Um, yes." I couldn't see or hear Rick's reaction, but I had a feeling he was running frustrated hands through his hair.

"Ok-kay, K-Karina." Josh choked on barely contained laughter. "Why don't you read us in. Tell us the story from the beginning."

I collapsed on my lovely white couch, grabbed a pillow to hug, and poured out the story.

"Are you saying that you were involved in this mess even before you left D.C.?" Rick asked accusingly.

"No. I had no way of knowing this would happen. I thought I was just a messenger, delivering a package to my neighbor," I defended.

"Hm, well, your instincts were correct. You need to make the exchange in a public location. Preferably somewhere with a bunch of tourists." There was no humor or frustration in Rick's voice. We were back to business. "What do you know about these brothers?"

"Not much. Craig said they are nickel-and-dime thugs. I'm not really clear on what he meant by that. Considering Mrs. T. is sitting poolside, I don't really believe we're dealing with hardened criminals here. Even Craig didn't look too bad. He's got the hint of a healing black eye, but that's it. The rub marks on his wrists from being tied up are barely visible. I don't get the impression they are violent. Craig does seem to think they aren't too bright."

"Well, they weren't so foolish as to give you a location with the newspaper. Either they had the newspaper on hand, or they are close enough to a shopping district to get one quickly," Josh pointed out.

"True, and city centers tend to carry international newspapers like the *Wall Street Journal*." I tapped a finger to my chin. "Come to think of it, I can get *USA Today* here at the hotel. Perhaps they are in a hotel district."

"Possibly. My best advice is to meet at one of the tourist destinations at the height of capacity. When do you need to get back to the kidnappers?" Rick asked.

"Soon. I want to wrap this up as quickly as possible, get Mrs. T. on a plane home, and get back to my vacation. If I can make it happen, I want the exchange to go tomorrow."

"I need to do some research. Josh or I will get back to you within the hour."

"Thanks, Rick. I'm sorry to have to call you, but I didn't really know where to turn. I've heard too many stories about corrupt cops down here. And to be honest, I don't trust Craig. I'm afraid if we contact the cops, Craig will be in the wind, leaving us no way to contact the kidnappers, and Mrs. T. high and dry."

"It's fine. Call you soon." Rick hung up, and I hugged the pillow tighter.

It was only ten minutes later when Josh called back, but I'd lapped the suite a dozen times. "We've decided the best place to make the exchange is *Chichén Itzá*."

"What? No. Really? I've already been. Why not make it closer to Cancun? Like in a marketplace or restaurant?"

"Too many variables. We like the idea of wide-open areas that still have tourists around."

"What about a different set of ruins closer to Cancun? I think

Tulum is nearby. I haven't been there yet."

"You've been to *Chichén Itzá*. It's one of the reasons we want the exchange to happen there. You're familiar with the layout. The terrain. The exits. You'll meet at the south side of the Platform of Venus. It supplies a bit more privacy than at the Castillo, but you'll still be in sight line to the big pyramid. Arrange the exchange at 3:00 p.m."

"Fine," I huffed. "*Chichén Itzá* it is. I'll call Marcellus to see if he can come back and drive us there."

"Forget Marcellus. Rick is arranging transportation as we speak. Someone will text or call to let you know the final arrangements." He hung up before I could say anything more.

When I got back down to Rodrigo's room, I found the guys sitting around the coffee table, which was piled with food from room service—fish tacos, enchiladas, chips and salsa, a bucket of beer bottles, and a blue drink with a cherry, orange slice, and pink straw.

"What are you two doing? We just ate an hour ago." I stood over them like a clucking hen.

"Two hours ago." Rodrigo crunched on a chip.

"Yes, and I was still hungry. I only got to eat a few fries and a bite of quesadilla." Craig swallowed a gulp of beer. "Look—" He picked up to the blue drink. "We got you a drink too. It's called a Blue Salamander. We thought you might like it."

"Fine." I took a sip as I sat on the bed. "Not bad. By the way, Craig, I noticed you got a wristband. Where did you get it?" The resort had varying levels of inclusivity. Rodrigo and I had red wristbands, which allowed us to eat food at any of the restaurants, and it included alcoholic beverages. However, it didn't include top shelf booze, nor any of the spa services. I'd paid extra for my massage. Craig wore a black wristband, which included everything the red band did, along with the top shelf liquor and a handful of spa services.

He glanced away and took another swig of beer before answering. "I took it off a lady sleeping on the beach."

Rodrigo stopped chewing his noisy chip.

It was what I'd expected, but I still rolled my eyes and grunted, "Uh-huh."

"What? I was desperate, and I needed to get in the hotel to find you," he cried.

"Forget it." I sipped my blue drink, which was heavy on the rum. "Now, before we get sloshed, let's discuss the plan to get your aunt returned." I ran down Rick and Josh's plan.

"Back to *Chichén Itzá*?" Rodrigo said in a plaintive tone. Probably similar to the one I used when Joshua suggested it.

I made the same explanations Josh did. When Rodrigo seemed ready to argue the point, I shook my head. "Forget your objections. This is what we are doing. Considering Adolfo was there this morning, I think they are holding Mrs. T. not far from *Chichén Itzá*, so they will probably be amenable. Craig, text them the time and place. Let's see what they have to say."

Craig wiped his hands with the pristine white linen napkin, leaving behind a blood-red stain of enchilada sauce before picking up his phone. I don't know why, but it gave me an unexpected shiver.

He received an immediate message in return. "They want to meet at a market in Valladolid."

"Forget it. Market places are to their advantage, not ours. We also know nothing of Valladolid. No. We stick with *Chichén Itzá*."

"What if they threaten to hurt Mrs. Thundermuffin?" Rodrigo cautioned.

I looked at Craig. "Do you think they will get nasty? How badly do they want the mask?"

He mused for a moment as he popped open another bottle of beer. "The brothers are definitely capable of bodily harm.

However, there seems to be a deep-seated respect for their elders, so I'm not sure they would willingly hurt her. I also know Adolfo wants the mask back and he's less likely to allow those two to beat up an old lady."

"But can he stop them?" Rodrigo shifted forward, leaning his elbows on his knees.

Craig shrugged and continued drinking the beer.

I chewed a hangnail for a moment. "Why don't you contact Adolfo directly. Tell him it's *Chichén Itzá* at three. We won't meet anywhere that we're not familiar with. If she gets hurt, so does the mask. I don't imagine Adolfo wants to see his masterpiece destroyed. No?"

Craig nodded and sent the text. "By the way," he said with nonchalance, "I sent my aunt a letter in the package—"

"For her stamp collection," I interrupted, "along with some coins. It's one of the reasons I knew Adolfo was lying."

Craig stopped tapping on his phone and glanced questioningly at me.

"You wrote Aunt Milly on the envelope." I gave a wan smile. "He called her Aunt Mildred. Do you call her Aunt Mildred?"

"Good God, no. I couldn't imagine." He finished the text. "And what did you do with the coins and note?"

I hesitated a moment before answering. I'd meant to leave them with Mr. Albert to put in Mrs. T.'s apartment the next time he checked on the cat. But right at this moment, I couldn't recall what happened to them. I remembered putting the coins in the envelope and using the silver brad to seal it shut. Past that . . . my mind was a blank. The last time I saw the envelope, it was sitting on my kitchen counter. Was it still there or did I give it to Mr. Albert? Craig continued to watch me while Rodrigo watched him.

"I left them on your aunt's kitchen table, along with the rest of her mail. Why?" I don't know why I lied. Probably because I didn't want to look like a bad caretaker of someone else's mail.

Also, something I couldn't put my finger on nagged at me.

He shrugged and checked his phone. "No reason. You'd said the box had been damaged, I wondered if anything had fallen out."

"Oh. No, I think everything was still inside." I stuck my toe in the shallow end to test the waters. "Are the coins worth a lot?"

He shook his head. "No more than five or six bucks. No big deal."

There seemed to be no subterfuge in his response, and I relaxed. "The packing material was the only thing coming out of the box."

Craig seemed unconcerned and dropped the subject. The conversation died. We sat in tense silence waiting for a response. Rodrigo finished his beer and opened another. Eventually, nerves got to me; I couldn't sit still. Unfolding myself from the bed, I paced around the room. If Craig read the situation incorrectly, bodily harm or death to Mrs. T. would be my fault. I cursed my neighbor for voluntarily putting herself in this position. Mindlessly, I grabbed a chip and chewed. It held little taste for me, and I washed it down with my fluffy blue drink. I'd imbibed about half of it by now, and the rum had started to kick in. The slight buzz did wonders for my nerves; however, I didn't want to get too inebriated before the issue was settled. I needed to keep my head on straight. I set the drink aside and opened a bottle of water.

"Do you think Adolfo has his phone with him?" I asked no one in particular.

Craig, who didn't seem to be having any qualms about the situation, chowed down on a soft taco. "Mmrrebbon."

"Say what?" Rodrigo scrutinized Craig.

He swallowed and wiped his mouth. "He had it on him the last time we met. They are probably arguing. Just wait." Sure enough, Craig's phone dinged. "Okay, they'll meet at *Chichén*

Itzá. But not at three. He says there is some sort of laser light show at night. They let tourists back in at eight. We'll make the exchange at eight-thirty, at the Jaguar Temple. East side."

I wasn't thrilled about the change of location or the timing, but this thing needed to be done. Cover of night was their compromise. "Fine."

With relief, Craig texted our response and jammed the phone in his back pocket. "Now that's taken care of, what should we do tonight? Head out on the town?"

I eyed him, a little confused by his outward lack of concern. When he'd approached Rodrigo and me on the pool deck, there'd been a healthy amount of panic regarding his aunt. Was it the booze? Or was there something else going on? Rodrigo too stared disbelievingly at Craig.

"What?" Craig held his arms open. "There is nothing we can do right now. Going out will take our minds off of tomorrow."

He had a point.

Rodrigo clearly disapproved. "I think we should stay in tonight."

"Fine, there is a disco here at the resort. Let's go dancing." Craig hopped up and did an impression of a bad shimmy-shake. "Got to drain the lizard. Be right back."

Rodrigo and I stared at each other in confusion as Craig loped off to the bathroom. Maybe he'd been under so much stress the past few days, seeing the end of the line caused a bit of euphoria.

"How many beers did he have?" I whispered.

"That's his third."

It didn't seem like much to me. "Maybe he doesn't have a head for alcohol."

Rodrigo snorted with disdain. "I think he doesn't have a head, period. What happened to his concern over Aunt Milly?"

"I've been wondering the same," I murmured. "Maybe he's relieved that it's coming to an end."

"Well, we haven't got her back yet," he snapped.

"I know."

"You know what?" Craig asked as he exited the bathroom.

"I know that I'm going to need a good night's sleep. Why don't we hit the bar for a bit, then get to bed early? You've had a rough couple of days, Craig. Aren't you looking forward to a decent night's sleep on a comfy bed?" I indicated the one I currently sat on. "We should stop at the shops and get you some clothes for tomorrow."

Craig seemed amenable to the idea and we cleared out of the room.

On the way down to the lobby level, Rodrigo kept shooting me looks. I knew he wanted to have a word, and as soon as he'd loaded Craig up with a dozen outfits to try on and practically shoved him into the dressing rooms, Rodrigo dragged me to the front of the shop. "What the hell is going on?" he hissed.

"Well, I didn't think you'd want Craig wearing all your clothes. This seemed to be best."

"That's not what I'm talking about. Why are we going down to the bar? Shouldn't we be in the room making plans for the exchange since it's not going to happen at three in the afternoon? Are we going to be ready if they start some shenanigans?"

"Look, Rick and Josh are on it. I plan to call them as soon as I get back to my room."

"Good idea." He grabbed my elbow. "Let's abandon Craig and get back there now."

Gently, I drew away. "First, I want to get Craig so liquored up that I don't have to worry about him sneaking up to my room to try and steal the mask."

Rodrigo studied me with a frown. "You pointed out that he couldn't get to your room."

"On the elevator, yes. But I don't underestimate that little crap weasel. If he's truly a thief, he'd probably scale the walls, or come up through the elevator shafts. Or simply bribe one of the staff with his charm. If we get him drunk as a skunk, he won't be able to pull any sort of shenanigans. Get it?"

The lightbulb went on in Rodrigo's head as I spoke. "Okay, I get you."

"Good. Because we need to get him drinking more than beer. Let's get him some shots, and hard liquor."

Craig came out of the dressing room wearing a pair of red Bermuda shorts and a black polo. He turned in a circle. "What do you think?"

We both gave it a thumbs up, and Craig retreated to the dressing room.

Rodrigo stared after him with narrowed eyes. "Commence Operation Get Craig Shit Faced."

Chapter Twelve

"Oof, he's heavier than I thought." I staggered under Craig's dead weight. While he'd stumbled into the elevator with the help of Rodrigo and I, by the time we'd reached the fifth floor, Craig had passed out, and we had to haul him down the hall.

"Hey, this was your idea." Rodrigo shoved the keycard into the lock.

"Mission accomplished." I pulled Craig's limp arm a little tighter around my shoulder, and we lurched through the doorway into the room. When we reached the closest bed, we unceremoniously dumped him face first. He flopped over, folded half-on, half-off the bed. "We'd better pull him up. Grab an arm." Together we dragged him to the pillow, and I removed his shoes. "You might want to get a wastebasket to put next to his head."

Rodrigo made a disgusted face but followed my suggestion. "Tell me again, why he can't sleep in your room?"

"Forget it. I'm not dragging him up to my place now. Besides, look at him, sleeping like a baby." I pointed at Craig. The left side of his face was smooshed into the pillow, but the half we could see was set in a drunken grin.

"Yeah, let's hope he stays that way," Rodrigo grumped.

"I'm sure you two will be just fine." I patted my colleague on the shoulder. "Although I'm not sure how *you're* still standing." I scrutinized my all-too-sober friend. "You look barely buzzed. Didn't the pair of you do four shots of tequila apiece?"

"Correction—Craig did four shots, and the plant sitting next to me did four shots." He grinned. "That poor fern's gonna have a hell of a hangover tomorrow."

A bark of laughter escaped, and I held a hand to my stomach. "Classic." Once we finished chuckling, I paced away from Rodrigo, rubbing the back of my head where a low-grade headache had developed during the last hour in the bar. "Listen, I'm sorry about all of this. Tomorrow we'll get Mrs. T. back, we'll send her home with Craig, and then we'll get on with our vacation. Okay?"

Rodrigo toed off his boat shoes. "Well, I have to say this for you, Karina, life is never boring when you're around."

"Hey, I want to point out, none of this is my fault." I put a hand on his shoulder. "But I'm glad you're here helping me."

"Anytime, girl." He pulled me in for a hug.

I really was glad Rodrigo had come. Not only did his presence provide some relief from the anxiety of the situation, his knowledge of the language had become invaluable. "Well, I'm going to get some shut eye. Call me in the morning, and we'll make a plan."

A gentle snore rose from Craig.

Rodrigo slit his eyes at him and grumbled, "Karina."

I rolled my lips inward to keep from laughing. "Okay, bye now." Quick as a cricket, I skipped out the door.

"This isn't funny!" Rodrigo hollered down the hallway. "You're going to owe me one."

"Turn him on his side," I called over my shoulder. The door slammed shut and I could finally release my amusement.

The clock on the microwave in my room read quarter past ten. I hadn't received any texts or phone calls from my friends at Silverthorne, which surprised me. Josh had said Rick was taking care of our transportation tomorrow. I texted the pair of them.

What's the transpo plan for tomorrow? Call me.

After texting, I realized I hadn't let them in on the change of plans from three to eight-thirty. I'd gotten so wrapped up in Operation Get Craig Shit Faced, I'd completely forgotten to reach out to Silverthorne.

Should I call them? I shrugged and decided to break the news when they reached out. Besides, we had all day tomorrow to make our plans.

While I hadn't heard from Silverthorne, I had heard from Marcellus. He'd texted at half past nine that he'd had no luck finding Milly but would continue to look. I didn't feel like texting all of the events that had happened in the past seven hours, and simply replied:

Don't worry, we have a lead. I'll call you in the morning. Get some rest.

****

I lay in my giant king-sized bed with the lights off, munching a half can of Pringles while watching an action film. The doorbell rang—yes, my suite had its own doorbell—startling me. The chips went flying everywhere. I'd be finding little pieces in my bed for days. I don't know why I reacted in such a manner. The doorbell had a nice sing-song triple chime. Perhaps it had to do with the fact the bedside clock read half past twelve, and with all the crazy things happening, I might have been just a little bit on edge.

I should've drunk more at the bar.

Turning lights on as I went, I swept through the living room and into the foyer. "Who is it?" I asked, pressing myself against the door to peek out the peephole. A round faced, stocky man with black hair and brown eyes, wearing black jeans and a black T-shirt stood on the other side of the door. I didn't hesitate to whip it open. "Hernandez? What on earth are you doing here?"

"Rick sent me. Said you were in some trouble."

"Come in, come in." I closed the door behind his black suitcase. "How did you get on this floor? You need to have a keycard."

He stared at me, deadpan. I shouldn't have been surprised. Though I didn't know Hernandez as well as Josh or Jin, I'd worked with him recently and was just as impressed with his skills. I figured Rick had picked him up somewhere along the way during one of his tours. Hernandez projected a bearing that had ex-military written all over him, like the rest of the Silverthorne guys I'd met.

"Never mind. Why don't you have a seat?" I led the way into the living room. "Can I get you something to drink? Eat?"

"I'm fine." He dropped onto the couch, spreading his arms across the back and putting his feet up on the coffee table. "Nice digs, Cardinal. I'm impressed." His head bobbed as he took in the splendor.

"Thanks, I upgraded just for you." I couldn't withhold the sarcasm that came out.

"So, I hear we are making an exchange tomorrow afternoon. An Incan shrunken head for some old lady."

"An Egyptian death mask for my neighbor," I corrected. "And the time was changed to eight-thirty."

His feet dropped to the floor and his brows crunched together. "What happened to three?"

"The kidnappers wouldn't go for it. There is some sort of laser light show in the evening. I assume they wanted the cover of darkness. There should still be plenty of people around. I was worried they were going to hurt Mrs. T. We had to go with it. Why? Is that a problem?"

His brows remained tilted downward. "It's an unexpected complication."

"I'm assuming you are our transportation out to the site?"

"Correct."

"And you'll be providing some sort of back up."

"Correct."

I waited.

Silence.

With a sigh, I curled up on one of the slipper chairs next to the couch. "You want to expand on that? Exactly why did Rick send you down? I didn't ask him to."

"I speak the language, and I have contacts in the area who can help. He also wanted to make sure nothing goes sideways with this op. It was supposed to be an in-and-out for me. With the later time tomorrow, I'll need to let Rick know I'll be staying another night." He pulled out his phone and began tapping out a text.

"Don't sweat it," I said drily, indicating the door to his right, "I've got a spare bedroom you can use."

"I may take you up on that." He continued tapping on his phone.

Though I'd never say it out loud, internally, I was relieved Rick sent someone down. I wasn't overly worried about Adolfo and his brothers, but what Craig would do when it came to the sticking point had me concerned. I just couldn't trust that little crap weasel, and knowing we had someone with better skills than Rodrigo and I was a great relief. It also might make Craig think twice before doing something stupid that might jeopardize his aunt.

"Where is this mask?" Hernandez asked absently, still focused on his cell.

"Hidden."

"Hidden in the room safe?"

"No, at the bottom of the fake ficus tree in the corner."

Hernandez glanced up from the phone and followed my pointed finger to the plant. "That's rather clever. What's wrong with the safe?"

"Craig is a thief. I imagine if he wanted to get into the safe, he would. Just like you."

A single dimple peeped at me. "Who's Craig?"

I sighed and crossed one leg over the other. "I guess I'd better read you in on the situation."

Chapter Thirteen

The trilling cell phone at my ear woke me out of a stress dream where I'd been running through a maze of tunnels searching for Rodrigo while something chased me. My subconscious was about as subtle as a brick bat.

"Hello?" I groaned.

"Karina? It is Marcellus."

"What time is it?" I rolled over and saw a shaft of bright sunlight striped across the bed where the drapes didn't quite close all the way.

"Seven-thirty. You said we would speak in the morning. Did I wake you?"

I yawned. "Yes, but it's fine."

"Did you find Milly?"

"Not exactly, but she should be back in our possession by tonight." Sitting up, I rubbed my eyes.

"I do not understand. What do you mean?"

"Let me call you back. I need coffee in order to be coherent. We'll talk at eight."

Opening my bedroom door, I was hit with a most welcome scent of brewing coffee. Hernandez, who had slept in the spare bedroom, was up, showered, and dressed in all black—again—and sipping from one of the disposable coffee cups provided by the hotel.

He took one look at me. "Coffee?"

"Yes, please, cream and sugar," I grunted, knotting the belt to the hotel's complimentary white terrycloth robe.

"Rough night?"

Flopping down on the couch, I put fingers to my temples and rubbed. "How'd you guess?"

"I've never seen your hair styled in quite that manner."

"Uh-huh. I call it *á la* rat's nest. It's the latest fashion." I think Hernandez snickered, but I couldn't be sure, because I was resting my eyes. A moment later, the scent of coffee grew stronger and I could feel Hernandez's presence looming over me.

"Coffee's ready."

I opened my eyes and heaved myself into a sitting position. Hernandez left the cup on the table and took one of the side chairs. We didn't speak again until I'd drunk three quarters of the life-giving beverage. "I see you are ready and raring to go. What time did you get up?"

"Six. I went for a swim and then took a shower."

"Uh-huh. So what's our game plan for today?" I pushed a hank of hair out of my face.

"I want to meet the rest of the crew."

"We'd better wait a few hours. If you think I'm moving a little slow this morning, I'm fairly certain Craig will be moving at glacial speed."

Hernandez's brows went up.

I gave a sly grin and rose from the couch. "Four tequila shots and two margaritas. Order us some breakfast. I'm going to call Marcellus back and get cleaned up. Then we'll invade Rodrigo's room."

****

"What are you doing up so early?" Rodrigo yawned and scratched his head. He wore a plain blue T-shirt and pajama bottoms.

"It's after nine o'clock." I squeezed past him. "Rodrigo, you remember Hernandez."

"How's it going? Didn't know Karina had called in the big

guns." The two shook hands.

"I didn't. Batman sent him down." I stood at the foot of Craig's bed and raised my voice. "How we doing this morning, Sleeping Beauty?"

Not a peep from Craig.

Rodrigo came next to me and crossed his arms. "He hasn't moved since last night."

"He's not dead, is he?" I took hold of a foot and shook.

"Nope, been snoring on and off all night," Rodrigo grumbled.

Hernandez swept open the curtains, allowing light to flood the room.

Still Craig didn't budge.

"Hey! Craig! Wakey, wakey, hands off snaky!" I yelled.

Nothing.

Hernandez picked up the ice bucket from the coffee table. *Splash!* The ice had melted, but I'm fairly certain the water was still cold. Craig leapt up off the bed, banged his head on the overhead lamp, then turned and whacked his knee on the bedside table. He stumbled around for a moment before tripping over a shoe and landing face first on the opposite bed. I don't believe a Hollywood director could have staged a more entertaining pratfall. If I'd been in the mood I would've cackled with laughter. I think Rodrigo and I were too stunned to do anything but watch in disbelief.

Craig, now awake, rolled to his side, cursing and rubbing his knee and back of his head at the same time. "What the fuck, man?"

"Quit screwing around. It's time to get up," Hernandez replied sharply.

Craig stared confused. "Who are you?"

"That's Hernandez. He's here to make sure this affair doesn't turn into a shit show." Taking pity on the poor fool, I walked over to the coffeemaker. "I'll make you a cup of joe. We have things to discuss."

Rodrigo took a quick shower while the coffee percolated, and I stripped the wet bedding off, leaving it in a pile on the floor. I made a mental note to leave a nice tip for the maid. Craig sat in the rolling chair, hunched over with his head between his hands. Hernandez hung out on the balcony, enjoying the view. After Craig finished his first cup of coffee, he seemed coherent enough to answer questions.

Hernandez started with, "When was the last time you got a proof-of-life?"

"Yesterday afternoon," Rodrigo supplied, relaxing on his bed with his own morning brew. He found Craig's phone on the bedside table and tossed it to Hernandez. "They sent a text."

Craig didn't even flinch when Hernandez held the phone out to him and demanded, "Unlock it and show me the text." Craig tapped-tapped-tapped, then handed it back. "Why is she smiling and giving the peace sign?" Hernandez looked perplexed.

"Mrs. Thundermuffin is a little . . . quirky." I crossed my legs and cozied further back into the chair, slowly sipping my own cup of java.

"What do you know about the people holding her?" Hernandez directed at Craig.

He scratched his growing beard. "Well . . . they're not exactly Einsteins."

"You know, you keep saying that, Craig. Yet they managed to find you" —I pointed at him— "twice, in a foreign country. First, they kidnapped and ransomed you, and now they have your aunt. So, while you're not giving them a lot of credit, they've come this far and have you dancing to their tune."

Craig blushed.

"You said they are from Italy. Are they old enough to have served compulsory military service?" Hernandez asked.

"I'm not sure. When did Italy end compulsory service?"

"2005," Hernandez supplied.

"Let me think. They are from Adolfo's father's first marriage, he said they are ten years older, he's twenty-nine. . . ." The wheels in Craig's head turned as he counted. "Yes, I suppose they did. So what?"

"In other words," Rodrigo drawled, staring at the ceiling, "they've been trained in firearms, you twit."

Hernandez didn't seem to like what he heard. Rising abruptly, he pulled his cell out of his back pocket and dialed.

"In other words," I growled, "they are smarter than you've been giving them credit for, and your aunt is probably in bigger danger than you've let on."

Craig rolled his eyes. "Pfft. They want the mask. Why would they hurt her?"

I didn't answer. Hernandez started speaking into the phone in rapid Spanish while pacing the room. Rodrigo and Craig watched Hernandez, while I watched Rodrigo. At a pause on Hernandez's end, I leaned toward my coworker and whispered, "What's going on? Who's he talking to?"

"He's getting reinforcements," Rodrigo answered. "And it sounds like we'll be getting to *Chichén Itzá* early."

"How early?" I asked.

Hernandez hung up. "We're leaving now. You two," —he pointed to Craig and Rodrigo— "get yourselves together and meet us in the lobby in twenty minutes. Karina, you come with me."

I didn't hesitate to follow his demands. It was clear Hernandez just called in some favors. I waited until we were back in the elevator going up to my room. "So what's the deal? Who did you call?"

"Some of my contacts in the area. I don't like the time change or the fact that these guys have been military trained. I need to get some equipment before we head out to the site." He looked me up and down. "Do you have anything lighter? White shirt? Shorts?"

I glanced down at my navy-colored shorts and wine-colored top. "I've got some khaki shorts that are clean, and I think I have a white T-shirt. Why?"

"Change into them. I want you to be visible tonight."

"Huh. Total opposite of what I was expecting."

****

The black SUV rolled to a stop outside an iron gate. I rode up front with Hernandez, while Rodrigo and Craig sat in the back. The mask, once again in my backpack, lay securely between my feet. Through the gated bars, I could see a large stone and stucco Spanish style estate, surrounded by a creamy stucco privacy wall. A brass plaque next to the gate read *Estudios Históricos de Bibliotecas Españolas*.

"Historical Spanish Library Studies?" Craig snorted, and said with sarcasm, "How are a bunch of librarians going to help us?"

Nobody bothered to answer. The gate swung open, and Hernandez drove past the front circular drive, around to the back of the building, where there was a small, covered parking area. He pulled up next to a shiny, blue El Camino, in pristine shape with a tri-fold cover on the bed. Four people came out of the back door to meet us. A blond head towering above the others had me hopping out of the front seat.

"Joshua?" I trotted up to him and we hugged. "What are you doing here?"

"I volunteered." Josh nodded at Hernandez who opened up the back liftgate of our SUV.

"Good lord, why?" I laughed.

"Didn't think Hernandez could handle your mess on his own." Josh's grin split a mile wide.

Hernandez gave Josh the middle finger.

"Hey, I resent that. It isn't *my* mess. It's Craig's, he started it all," I protested shrilly.

"Actually, Rick and I decided you might be in deeper than you let on, and we though Hernandez might need help. Seems like we were right." Josh continued to smirk down at me. "I heard you dragged poor Rodrigo into it also."

My face burned at the bald truth. I coughed and fiddled with my earring. "Yeah, I feel bad about that."

"Where is he?" Josh glanced around.

"In here," Rodrigo called, leaning over the back seat. "I'm keeping an eye on Craig. Hernandez told us to stay in the car."

While Josh and I had been chatting, Hernandez shook hands with the other men and started a conversation in Spanish. One of them, a medium height, slight fellow, had black hair and walnut skin. Another was brown-haired, average height, average weight, with chunky black glasses. His age could be anywhere from thirty-five to forty-five. The third stood out from the rest with his red hair, freckled face, and pale blue eyes. The men looked nothing alike, however, there remained a similarity between them. They each wore different colored chinos with button-down shirts and colored ties. None of them looked like any sort of librarian I'd run into. Like Craig, I too wondered how Historical Spanish Library Studies could help us. However, considering we'd pulled around back to a relatively enclosed parking area where at least four security cameras were trained on us, and the fact that Josh was here—I concluded we'd arrived at a CIA front.

"Who are your friends?" I asked Josh.

"Let me introduce you. Guys!" The men paused their conversation and turned toward us. "This is Karina. Karina, the red head is Julian, the guy with the glasses is Edgar, and that's Mateo over there." He indicated each man as he spoke.

"Hi, fellows." I gave a finger wave to the crew. "Thanks for helping out." I wondered if I should bother committing any of those names to memory, being fairly certain they were all cover identities.

Edgar smiled. His handshake was firm, and I could feel calluses on his palms. "Welcome to the research center. Joshua told us about you. It's nice to meet you in person." His English held no accent nor inflection of any kind.

"Hi, um, pleasure meeting you too. How long have you worked here?"

Edgar adjusted his glasses. "This will be my sixth year."

"And how did you get involved in, uh, Spanish Library Studies?"

He shoved his hands in his pockets and rocked back on his heels. "About nine years ago, I finished my doctorate in Anthropology with a concentration in ancient Mayan civilization. One thing led to another, and here I am."

Okay, I could buy that. I nodded. "Wow, a doctorate in anthropology. Cool. The Mayan civilization is fascinating." This guy seemed fairly normal. Perhaps my suspicious nature had jumped to conclusions.

"Well, Julian, let's see what we've got to work with," Josh declared, ending our conversation.

The redhead folded back the El Camino bed cover, revealing three black duffle bags, tactical vests, and half a dozen semi-automatic, military-style rifles. The stash washed away any sense of doubt regarding who these guys were. Not to say Edgar didn't have a doctorate in Mayan anthropology—he probably did. That doctorate was probably also paid for by the American government for him to use as his cover. Seeing the cache, both Rodrigo and Craig trundled out of the SUV and gathered around to goggle at the loot.

The men began talking tactical gear and the pros and cons of each rifle. Even though they were now conversing in English, they may as well have spoken in Spanish. I didn't speak gun. Josh or Hernandez would pick one up and evaluate each weapon before putting it down to check another one. I crossed my arms and watched the show.

"Any of you know how to use a gun?" Hernandez looked directly at Rodrigo and me.

"I do." Craig raised his hand like a schoolboy.

Rodrigo shook his head.

"I'm good with a taser," I volunteered.

Hernandez gave a frustrated frown, while Josh said to me, "I thought Rick worked with you last week."

I swallowed. "He did."

Josh curved his hands around the tailgate. "And how did it go?"

My gaze bounced between the two men. "Since you're staring expectantly at me, I can see that Rick didn't tell you about it?"

Hernandez shook his head, while Josh simply raised a brow.

I placed my hands on my hips and blew upward at my bangs. "I couldn't hit the broad side of a barn from ten paces."

Rodrigo snorted, but shut it down quickly when I delivered a death glare.

"That bad?" Josh's other brow rose to match the first.

"As much as I would love to say I'm just joking—I am not. I think Rick was genuinely perplexed by my ineptitude. My shots were erratic at best. If you've got someplace you can take me for target practice, I can certainly give it another go. But I'm afraid it might be more dangerous than helpful for you to arm me right now." I stepped forward to peer into the back of the El Camino. "Are you sure you don't have a stun gun or taser I could use?"

Hernandez and Josh shared a look and Josh shrugged. "It's better than nothing. Go ahead and give it to her."

Mateo dug into a duffle bag and pulled out a compact, camo-colored rectangular box, a little larger than a pack of cigarettes. "Here, stun gun." He tossed it across the bed.

I had my hands up to catch it, but Josh whipped his arm out

and caught it first. "Is it charged?"

"Charged it last night," Mateo replied.

Josh turned it on, pressed the button, and electricity sparked between the two prongs. He turned it off and handed it over. "Put it in your pocket and keep it there. If you need it, I don't want you rummaging around in that black hole of a bag you carry."

I didn't argue. If I put it in the backpack, it would likely fall beneath the death mask box.

"Hey, do you have another one of those?" Rodrigo asked.

Mateo tossed another to Rodrigo.

"What about me?" Craig whined, clearly disappointed that he'd been ignored.

Hernandez put out a hand to stop Mateo digging in the bag for a third. "We've got you covered." While I hadn't referred to Craig as a crap weasel when discussing him with Hernandez, it was clear the man had Craig's number and trusted him about as much as he would an adder. Hernandez said something in Spanish; Julian grabbed another duffle bag and passed it to him.

"Here," Hernandez said to Craig as he pulled out a small, black oval the size of a key fob. I recognized it immediately, because he'd already put one in my backpack and given me another to put in my pocket. "That's a GPS tracker. Rodrigo, you take one too. We'll be monitoring you the entire time."

Craig's face looked like he'd eaten a worm. "You know, I'm not quite sure why you're treating me like the bad guy here. It's *my* aunt they've got. I've done nothing but do what you told me to do. And I could help. Besides, I should be able to defend myself too. It's not like I'm going to taser everybody and run off."

We all stared at Craig, because that's exactly what worried all of us, or at least it worried me. Since I'd be carrying the item, I really had no interest in allowing Craig to have any sort of weapon he could use against me.

"You know, Craig, you're really getting on my nerves,"

Rodrigo snapped. *"You are the reason we're all here. In case* you've forgotten, Karina and I came to Mexico on vacation. And neither one of us has gotten any 'vacationing' done. We are in this mess because your shenanigans got Mrs. T. captured and turned into a hostage. These guys, in front of you, flew all the way down here to make sure nothing goes wrong and none of us gets hurt. Don't you dare play the innocent victim," he continued, cutting off Craig as he started to protest. "You're only here because the Italian Stallions are expecting you at the exchange, and because we need you to identify them. If it were up to me, I would have dropped you off on the side of the road and told you to lump it. Now shut up and do what you're told, or we'll say screw it and have these nice fellows from the historical library lock you in a closet for the rest of the day and do this deal without you. Got it?"

Craig closed his trap and put the tracker in his pocket. I put a hand to my mouth to keep from letting out a whoop of laughter. Rodrigo, in his perfectly pressed black shorts and royal blue polo, had just put our little crap weasel in his place like nobody's business. Unfortunately, Rodrigo's little tirade brought home just how much I owed him. I'd have to rack my brain to come up with a way to repay him.

Rodrigo turned his attention back to Julian. "Now, where were we?"

About three conversations started at once to fill the uncomfortable void. The Silverthorne boys finished retrieving the necessary materials, which included night vision goggles, a handful of weapons, a sniper rifle, and other tactical gear, and put everything in the back of the SUV. Handshakes went around, the weapons cache was covered up, and we piled back into the car. Only this time, I was relegated to sitting in the middle of the back seat with Craig and Rodrigo. Craig had showered and shaved, so he no longer smelled like a broken bottle of tequila, and he wore the new clothes he'd purchased last night. With the beard gone, he looked attractive and reputable. I had no doubt that boyish handsomeness helped his job as a con. I specifically left the backpack up front with the Silverthorne boys.

"Does Edgar really have a Ph.D. in anthropology?" I tossed out.

Both the men nodded, and Josh answered, "Yes, he does."

Chapter Fourteen

Evening finally arrived, and brought with it some relief from the blazing hot Mexican sun.

After such a long day—Rodrigo, Craig, and I had wandered aimlessly around the ruins, while Hernandez and Joshua went off on their own to conduct reconnaissance—I would be happy never to see *Chichén Itzá* again. I'd seen every ancient nook and cranny and heard every passing tour guide's story about the place. Rodrigo and I could probably set up a sign and make some *dinero* conducting our own tours. At four-thirty, we'd herded out of the site with the rest of the tourists. The place closed down until eight to set up the seating area and prepare for the nighttime show. At seven-thirty, Hernandez and Josh dropped the three of us at the front gate to get in line while they "got into position," as they'd explained.

Again, we wandered in and out among the temples with the rest of the tourists until, turning around, I beheld a vision. "Hey, guys, look at that." I tugged Rodrigo's hand.

"What? Oh, wow," he said with reverence.

We, along with dozens of other visitors paused as the summer sun waned, dropping behind the Castillo. The glimmering sunset turned the gray granite into a glowing golden temple fit for the gods. I was glad to have been able to witness this natural splendor. The simple sunset calmed my nerves, for they had become stretched to the breaking point throughout the day. Rodrigo too had become snappish and grouchy as our time drew near. Craig was the only one not exhibiting outward signs of concern. On the other hand, every time he'd opened his mouth, Rodrigo barked at him, and eventually, I think he gave up attempts at any conversation.

"Okay, *pequeña ave,* once that sun dips below the horizon, it's going to get dark real fast," Hernandez said in my ear. "The three of you need to make your way over to the Jaguar Temple and hide yourselves. When they announce it's time for the show to begin, foot traffic will move to the seating area."

The Silverthorne boys had outfitted all three of us with coms. Josh had presented the little earbud as if giving me a Christmas present. "Hey, Cardinal," he'd said with enthusiasm, "guess what you get today?" When I shook my head, he'd held out a small box in his open palm and announced, "Coms!"

"I guess you learned your lesson," I'd said drily. "You better show us how it works."

Rodrigo took my hand, and, with Craig trailing behind, we passed by the open seating area for the laser lightshow guests and trucked our way over to the Lower Jaguar Temple, along the east wall of the Ball Court. It wasn't quite as impressive as the Castillo, however, I felt the temple held its own charm. In between the columns sat a small stone Jaguar throne. When I was a child, we must have been able to go inside the small overhang, because my parents have a picture of my sister, my brother, and I sitting on it. Now, like the Castillo, the portico was roped off to tourists. An American family of four wandered around, taking photos with their phones.

"I have a visual on three blind mice," Hernandez said.

"Copy that. I have eyes on the south and west sides," Josh said.

"You know," I said, turning to Rodrigo with a smile as though we were having an enjoyable conversation, "I don't appreciate the fact that the code name for our group is three blind mice. Couldn't you have come up with something better, a little less offensive?"

Josh snorted. "What would you prefer, three Billy Goats Gruff?"

"Three little pigs?" Hernandez chimed in.

"Three little kittens who lost their mittens?"

"How about hear no evil, see no evil, speak no evil?"

"Oh, here's one you'll like—the three stooges." The pair continued to banter back and forth at our expense.

My smile turned into a teeth-gritting grimace, and I hissed, "Never mind."

Craig jammed his hands in his pockets and kicked a stone, which bounced over my shoe. "You know, it could be worse. At least your code name is 'little bird.'"

Rodrigo snorted and received a scowl from Craig.

"Point taken," I said quickly to avert another nasty exchange between the two. Craig had been saddled with crap weasel, only the boys had translated it into the Spanish version, *mierda comadreja,* which I think was a bit nastier. Rodrigo's code name was Sycamore. Josh had declared it as he stared at a Sycamore tree.

An announcement came on over the loudspeakers directing everyone to take their seats for the show. The family wandered off, and we were left alone.

"I have movement coming from the west. Looks like a staff member. Three blind mice, you need to hide, or you'll be shooed away," Josh said.

"We are in a fairly open area. Where do you suggest we go?" Rodrigo asked.

"Head toward the north side, that's it. On your left is a deep corner with dark shadows," Hernandez directed us. "Move in together."

We stepped over the cordons and jammed ourselves into a corner. Craig squeezed into my left shoulder, and Rodrigo to my right. The black box pressed through the backpack's canvas fabric into my spine.

"Sycamore," Hernandez's firm and steady voice commanded, "stand in front of *pequeña ave*, her white shirt is visible. That's better."

"You were the one who told me to wear light-colored clothes," I reminded Hernandez in a whisper.

Craig shushed me, and a moment later, I understood why. The pit-pat of a pair of boots on hard-packed earth walked past us. No one breathed. I skootched down a little more to hide behind Rodrigo's motionless back.

Finally, after what seemed like an hour but was probably no more than two minutes, Hernandez came back on. "All clear."

"Should we return to position?" I asked.

"Negative, remain in place until I tell you."

We spread out a little bit but stayed leaning against the rough stone wall.

Rodrigo checked his watch. "They're late."

"Relax. They may be hiding from the staff members too," I reassured him, but silently I fidgeted with my earring.

"I have movement. Coming from the south," Josh murmured.

"How many?" I asked.

"Three approaching."

"Those must be Adolfo's brothers," Craig whispered. "Is there a petite one with pink hair?"

"One is wearing a ball cap, slim, may be our target," Josh answered.

"Do you see any weapons?" Hernandez asked.

"Negative."

There was a grunt, then Hernandez came back on. "I'm moving to a better position. Three blind mice, move out."

"Roger that," Rodrigo responded and immediately walked

forward.

"Watch out for the—" I started to say, but immediately cut off in a stifled gasp. Rodrigo must have forgotten about the cordons because he ran into one, bounced off, and slammed into me, stepping on my shoe. Losing my balance, I windmilled my arms and began to fall to the side.

"I got you." Luckily, Craig caught my shoulder just as Rodrigo got off my shoe. I stumbled around a moment before righting myself with his help.

"Thanks," I muttered.

"What's going on down there—three blind mice?" Josh's voice held a silky tone, and I realized we'd just lived up to our moniker.

"Nothing. Three blind mice moving into position," Craig countered.

Once we were back in front of the Jaguar Temple, Josh said, "Mice have come into range, I have visual on all three."

"Copy that," Hernandez murmured. "Our visitors are heading directly to the location. I think this is it."

Rodrigo and I stood a few steps behind Craig as we waited for the three to approach. I wiped sweaty hands against my shorts. They appeared in silhouette first, then the laser show began, and our position brightened significantly. With the increased light we could identify one man, about five-eleven, rather beefy, leading the other two. A voice in Spanish bellowed over the loudspeakers, startling me. Already on edge, the noise sent my heart sprinting like a rabbit at a Greyhound race.

"The one in front is Nico Dinapoli," Craig murmured. "The fat one behind him is his brother Gaetan."

My heart sank as I identified the third in the trio as Adolfo, not Mrs. Thundermuffin. "They don't have her," I whispered for the boys on com. Josh grunted in response.

The brothers arrived at our position and spread out in a line, with Adolfo on the right of Nico, and Gaetan—a shorter and much rounder version of Nico—to his left. Gaetan must have really enjoyed the heavy Italian pasta dishes. It looked like he ate them three times a day. His breathing was heavy, almost to the point of asthmatic. I saw little resemblance between Adolfo and his half-brothers. Whereas Adolfo's features were very fine, almost feminine, his brothers were full-blooded Italian, with dark, hooded eyes, thick, pudgy fingers, and heavily-jowled countenances. All three of them wore dark pants and dark tops. Nico wore a black sweatshirt. The temperature hovered around seventy-eight, and perspiration gathered around Nico's hairline. One of the brothers must have bathed in his cologne. The scent permeated our group like mustard gas. I'd smelled that scent before and, as the men spoke, I searched my mind, trying to pinpoint where.

"Nico," Craig greeted him, stepping forward, "where is my aunt?"

"Nearby. We told you to come alone." Nico's gaze flicked between Rodrigo and I, assessing the situation.

"Plans changed." Craig straightened, sticking his chest out like a male buck trying to establish dominance. "I knew you wouldn't come alone. I didn't see any reason not to bring my own friends."

If his face was any indicator, Nico did not like the increase to the party, but Rodrigo and I must have looked harmless enough, because he didn't push the issue. "Where is the mask?"

"My aunt first," Craig replied firmly.

"Show us the mask first, then we'll bring out your aunt," Gaetan wheezed.

Craig glanced over his shoulder at me and jerked his head. I didn't move, waiting to hear what the Silverthorne guys had to say. I didn't like the fact that Nico had not brought Mrs. Thundermuffin with them. Then it hit me.

"My room!" All eyes turned to stare at me, and I coughed to cover my outburst. The cologne was the smell from my room at the hotel. The one that got trashed.

"I have no visual on the target," Josh whispered.

"Neither do I," Hernandez said quietly in my ear.

"Karina, show him the box," Craig bit out.

"Fine," I said through tight lips. I unhooked the backpack, pulled out the box, and opened it toward the group for inspection.

Nico said something in Italian to Adolfo, and his brother trotted across the invisible line in the sand separating our two groups. Craig didn't turn, keeping his attention on the brothers. The lasers shifted, illumination darkened, and Adolfo pulled out a small penlight to examine the death mask. At one point he removed it from its foam bedding. Rodrigo made a small jerking move. I sucked wind and my muscles tightened.

"Easy, easy," a voice cautioned over the coms.

Adolfo put the mask back in place and pivoted. "Yes, this is the one I made."

Quietly, I closed the lid and, ever so gently, stepped back. Adolfo's glance flicked at me, aware of my movements, but he didn't follow my retreat.

"See? We brought the mask." Craig indicated with his hand. "Now where is my aunt?"

"We'll take the mask now and tell you where you can pick up your aunt," Nico stated.

My grip tightened on the box.

"I don't think so," Rodrigo interjected, moving forward to flank Craig. "The deal was, the mask for his aunt. No aunt. No mask."

I stepped back further into the shadow of the Temple.

"The mask, now, and we tell you where to pick up your aunt," Nico said slowly and evenly, putting his hand behind his back.

Gaetan pulled out a shiny silver handgun. A .38, if I remembered correctly from Rick's lecture. I didn't doubt Nico's hand rested on a similar weapon.

"Whoa." Craig put his hands up and lurched backward, leaving Rodrigo to head our little troupe and face the brothers.

"I don't think so." Rodrigo's voice held no hint of unease, which surprised me because the gun caused a lightning bolt of fear to course down my spine, and the box shook in my hands. "Light 'em up, boys."

Two red laser dots appeared dead center on Gaetan and Nico's chests, easing my anxiety only minimally.

"Who the hell—" Nico started.

Adolfo spoke rapidly in Italian, and both the brothers looked down. Gaetan actually tried to wipe the dot away with his hand.

"It's not a stain. It doesn't come off, moron," Craig taunted, clearly feeling more impowered, though he remained behind Rodrigo.

"Don't antagonize him," I hissed.

"As you can see," Rodrigo said over the top of Craig and I, "we brought our own protection. Now, if you'd like to go fetch his aunt from wherever you left her, we can get back to the business at hand."

Nico did *not* look happy at this turn of events. "We will—"

I had no idea what Nico planned to say because, to our left, an explosion shook the ground. Flames licked up the side of an information kiosk sitting next to a closed-up food truck. The blast distracted everyone.

Everyone except Adolfo, who snatched the box out of my hands and took off, hollering, *"Correre! Correre!"*

Many things happened at once. Nico swiftly took to his heels and was soon lost into the darkness. Gaetan waddled after him at a surprising speed for such a rotund fellow.

"Shit!" I stared blindly at my hands for a precious few

seconds. "He took the box." Comprehension kicked in, and I bolted after him, shouting, "Adolfo took the box! Adolfo has the box! Get him!"

Craig pelted past me, throwing something to the ground. I didn't stop to see what it was as I followed in his wake. Adolfo, taking advantage of the chaos that erupted from the explosion, headed straight toward the mass of confused tourists. I kept a running monologue of their movements for Josh and Hernandez.

The laser show, frozen on an image of Quetzalcoatl, a.k.a. the "plumed serpent," splashed across the pyramid. Meanwhile, across the field, the brightly burning kiosk created a dance of macabre shadows, making Quetzalcoatl seem alive. Spanish, repeated in English, barked over the loudspeakers directing everyone to exit in an orderly manner.

KABOOM!

A second, larger explosion rocked us, and the taco truck flew five feet into the air. It was accompanied by an enormous fire column worthy of a Hollywood action movie. I faltered. Ahead, confusion turned into downright hysteria. Spectators began screaming and running in different directions. I lost sight of Craig and Adolfo in the melee.

"*Do not pursue! Do not pursue!*" I finally tuned into Josh yelling in my ear. "*Stand down, Karina! DAMN IT, WOMAN, STOP RUNNING!*"

I came to a halt, pressed a hand to my ear, and panted, "What? You want me to stop following? He took the box. Do you copy? Adolfo has the death mask. We do not know where Mrs. Thundermuffin is. *We have nothing.*"

"We copy you," Josh said. "Something else is happening."

"Wait." My eyes darted around. "The explosions weren't a diversion tactic you created?"

"Negative. We are looking at some sort of terror attack."

"Sycamore, retrieve *pequeña ave*. She is at your three o'clock.

Everyone return to the extraction point," Hernandez ordered.

"Karina!" Rodrigo, barely winded, grabbed my hand. "C'mon, we'll figure out Mrs. T. later. We have to leave. Now! Before the next explosion!" Initially, he pulled me along, but soon I was sprinting with him—my feet pounding and my breath puffing.

We ran parallel to a group of frightened visitors, when suddenly a high-pitched scream erupted. The crowd shifted like a school of minnows, and the wave of bodies headed straight at us. Rodrigo tried to course correct, but we'd been running too close, and there wasn't enough time. Our hands broke apart. Someone slammed into me, my right foot landed in a hole, causing my ankle to give way, and I went down to my hands and knees. In an instant, I was living one of my biggest nightmares. Someone else nailed my side and knocked me completely to the ground. Feet scrambled around, trying to dodge past me. Another person tripped over me. I put my hands to my head and rolled to my left, away from the cluster. The scent of earthy dust and dried grass filled my nostrils, and I knew that smell would forever cause a rush of fearful adrenaline.

Finally, the pounding feet receded, and I lowered my hands from my head. A new pain throbbed along the left side of my rib cage. Getting to my hands and knees, I took deep breaths to center myself. A gentle hand touched my shoulder.

"Karina, are you okay?"

I must have taken that hit to the head harder than I thought. That voice sounded like— "Mrs. Thundermuffin?" I asked dubiously. Her hair stood on end, and the firelight turned it a blazing orange shade, which reminded me of the Heat Miser from a Christmas movie I watched as a child. I squeezed my eyes shut for a moment. When I reopened them, she was still there. "Is that you?"

"Yes, dearie, in the flesh. Can you get up?"

"I think so." She helped me rise to my feet. I rotated my twisted ankle. There was a little soreness, but nothing to indicate a bad sprain

"Come on, your friend is searching for you." She pointed.

In the distance, I could see Rodrigo silhouetted by the firelight, waving his arms, and as we got closer, I heard him screaming my name, "KARINA!"

"Rodrigo!" I called.

He rotated spotting me. "Karina! Thank god! I found her. Wait, who is? Is that?"

"Mrs. Thundermuffin, this is my friend Rodrigo," I introduced them as if we'd just met up for a cup of coffee.

"We have located the target. Repeat, Karina has found our target, and she is in our custody. Copy that, moving directly to extraction. Come on you two, follow me." He turned and took off at a fast trot. Mrs. T. was able to keep up, and I tried to hobble quickly, but my knees were scraped raw and painful. Additionally, the pain along my side was making it difficult to run and breathe at the same time. Rodrigo noticed I was lagging and glanced back at me. "What's wrong? Geez, your legs are a mess." He pulled my arm across his shoulder to take some weight off the injury and headed into the woods past the pyramid of Venus.

"Wait, where are we going? The extraction location is that way." I pointed with my free hand in the direction of the entrance.

"Change of plans. Didn't you hear?"

"No." I realized Josh and Hernandez weren't yelling instructions in my ear. "I must have lost my earbud in the stampede."

"It's okay. I'm still plugged in." Rodrigo held up his hand for silence and led us deeper into the glade. "Um-hm. Yes. Turn right here? Okay. Copy that."

We came out onto a dirt track and Rodrigo halted.

"What next?" I asked.

"We wait."

In the distance, I heard the growl of an engine growing louder and louder. The SUV turned a corner and its headlights speared the three of us. Hernandez brought the car to a dusty and skidding halt. Both passenger side doors were thrown open.

"Get in!" Joshua and Hernandez barked in unison.

Rodrigo climbed in front, while Mrs. T. and I took the back. I found myself in the middle, again, and staring at Joshua. He wore black from head to toe. His face had been blackened with grease paint, and his golden crop of hair was covered with a dark knit cap. The blue eyes appeared startlingly bright in comparison to all the black.

"You've never looked more like a Navy SEAL to me than you do now," I commented.

His teeth gleamed in the darkness.

Hernandez pulled out, and we swayed back and forth as he made a U-turn.

"We better get you cleaned up. Rick is going to kill me if I send you home bloodied and bruised." Josh reached behind me into the cargo area and retrieved a first aid kit. "Can someone turn on the dome light? Thanks." He pushed my hand to my shoulder to assess the damage at my elbow. "You are filthy, Karina. What the hell happened?"

He was right. A thin layer of dust coated me from top to bottom. "I got trampled by the crowd." The light-colored shorts and shirt were grass, dirt, and blood-stained. They would never wash clean; I'd have to throw them away. Just one more clothing casualty on this trip.

"Christ," Josh whistled through his teeth.

While Josh disinfected and bandaged my wounds, I asked, "Anyone know what happened to Craig?"

Hernandez shook his head. "He switched off his tracker, and we haven't heard anything from him on coms."

"I think he threw them out. I'm afraid he might be in cahoots with his buddy Adolfo. Speaking of Craig" —I rotated to my seatmate— "I'm not a fan, Mrs. T."

She sighed and crossed one hand over the other in her lap. "I know, dear. Craig can be a little shit, but he's my sister's grandchild and I had to help him. Frankly, the boy is too smart for his own good."

"Ow!" I winced as Josh sprayed a stinging antiseptic on my elbow. "How on earth did you come to be at the site? Did they leave you locked in the car or something?"

"Oh, yes, they locked me in the trunk."

Rodrigo put his arm across the back of the bench seat and turned to face us. "How did you escape?"

"It wasn't that hard. They underestimated my skills. Usually, when I wasn't in sight, they would handcuff me, like during the night. They really didn't like doing it, though. Gaetan was always in charge of restraining me, and he would apologize profusely as he did it. I told them there was no way I could get out of the trunk and complained that the handcuffs were painful. Gaetan convinced Nico to tie my hands in front with rope. He left the knots rather loose, but it did take longer than I expected to get out. The car model is older and didn't have the interior auto-release latch," she explained.

"So how did you get out?" Rodrigo asked.

"With the help of a crowbar, I was able to push the back seat down."

Hernandez hit a particularly bad pothole, slamming me and Josh against the window.

"Oof," I gasped, pressing a hand to my bruised side.

"What's wrong?" Josh asked.

"Got kicked in the ribs."

"Let me see." Josh raised my left arm high and gently hiked up my top. "You've got a bruise the size of a baseball. Here, put this against it." He cracked an instant ice pack, wrapped some gauze around it, then pressed it against my side.

I sucked wind through my teeth as we bounced through another pothole. "Is there a reason we're traveling down this goat track?"

"We put a GPS locator in the case," Hernandez explained, wheeling around another particularly bad pothole.

"Of course you did," I mumbled under my breath. No wonder the boys didn't need me to chase Adolfo down. They'd already planned for this contingency.

"I'm trying to follow it, but I keep having to take my eyes off the, erm, road."

Rodrigo faced forward. "I can help. Tell me what to do."

Hernandez slowed to a crawl and handed Rodrigo a tablet. "The red dot is the mask, we are the green dot, here. This indicates the compass. Tell me north, south, east, or west."

"Got it. Head west."

Hernandez continued to jounce and bounce us down the bumpy trail while Rodrigo gave directions.

Josh pulled my left leg across his lap and tackled my knee.

"What were those explosions all about? I thought maybe you two had done something to cause a distraction," I asked him.

"That would be my fault," Mrs. Thundermuffin confessed. All eyes except Hernandez's turned her way. "Like I said, I'm afraid it took me awhile to get out of the trunk. I knew I was late to the meeting. I didn't trust those men not to hurt you, so I rigged a distraction."

"With what?" Rodrigo asked.

"They had a bottle of vodka in the glovebox and a case of bullets. I dumped some gun powder inside the bottle and used the car's cigarette lighter to light a rag I found in the trunk."

"Okay, but why did you rig the second explosion?" Josh asked, while taping gauze to my knee.

"I didn't. The first explosion was much too close to the food truck. A mistake. I didn't realize until too late. The second explosion was the propane tank." She grimaced. "I feel bad about that."

"What's that noise?" Hernandez asked as the theme song to *Grease* sang out.

"My phone. It's my sister calling," I replied.

"Is it important? Should you answer it?" Josh inquired.

I gave him the side-eye. "You mean more important than this? Let it go to voice mail."

"Wait, stop!" Rodrigo shouted. "He's turned north."

We jerked to a stop and Hernandez looked to his right. "North? Are you certain?"

"Yes, heading north."

The track continued west as far as the lights could illuminate. We followed Hernandez's gaze. To our right was nothing but woods and underbrush. The Latino wrenched the wheel.

Uh-oh.

Yup, into the forest we went.

Twigs and branches scraped and scratched the car, the radio antenna twanged as it brushed past a bough. Bumping along the track had been like riding on asphalt compared to the off-road adventure Hernandez embarked upon. It was so bad, Josh paused his ministrations to grip the "oh shit" handle. My fingers curled around the seat in front of me, and I clamped my teeth together to keep from biting my tongue as the car bucked through the forest. Rocks and debris cracked against the undercarriage. I feared, at minimum, we'd end up with a flat tire, a broken axle at worst. It went on for probably only five or six minutes, but seemed a lifetime to me. Finally, a break in the trees appeared and we pulled out onto another dirt road.

"Now where is he?" Hernandez asked.

"Turn left. No. wait." Rodrigo rotated the tablet. "Sorry, turn right. That's it." We drove about a mile down the dirt road. "Okay. Stop here." Rodrigo passed the tablet to Hernandez and pointed at something.

Hernandez grunted and turned off the lights, including the dome light. All went quiet.

"What are we doing?" I whispered.

"Waiting," Hernandez said in a normal tone, which sounded loud to my ears.

"Waiting for wh—"

Whap! A man smacked into the front quarter panel and pancaked across the hood of the car. Something went flying and slammed against the windshield. Hernandez turned on the lights.

"Craig?" Rodrigo rolled down the window. "Craig? Is that you?"

"Rodrigo? How did you find me?" Craig squinted. "Never mind, thank the stars you did. I got it. I got the funerary mask back!"

Hernandez opened his door and retrieved the black box. "Get in."

Rodrigo threw open the passenger side door and scooted to the center of the bench seat.

Craig clambered in, looking as disheveled as the first time we met—sweat stains around his pits, and a leaf sticking out of his hair. "See, I got it, now we have leverage to get Aunt Milly back."

"Hello, Craig," Mrs. Thundermuffin said.

Craig jerked his head, craning his neck to see over the headrest. "Aunt Milly?"

"The one and only," she replied drily.

"What happened to your GPS and earbud?" Rodrigo asked in an accusing tone.

He touched his left ear. "Uh, I must have lost it when I was chasing Adolfo. Here's my tracker." Craig dug into his pocket. When he didn't find it there, he dug in the other one. "Huh, I must have lost that too. Sorry, guys."

Lost it, my ass. I remembered Craig throwing something aside and realized it was probably the tracker and earbud, leading me to wonder—what the hell was he up to?

"How did you find me?" he asked.

"Tracker on the mask," Hernandez supplied.

"Oh." He digested that little tidbit for a moment, and I wished I could have seen his face. "Lucky for me, I guess. You know, this is great, we really duped them," he went on with enthusiasm. "We have the funerary mask. Nobody got hurt. Everything worked out fine."

I delivered Craig a glare so heated, I'm surprised his hair didn't burst into flames. Mrs. T. smacked him upside the head.

"Ow, what was that for?" He rubbed the area where she struck him.

"Because you're a moron," Rodrigo drawled. "Karina's back there bleeding all over the place. Your aunt had to escape out of the trunk of a car, and Hernandez just tore up the undercarriage of this vehicle to catch up with you."

Craig glanced back at me and grimaced. "What happened to you?" My eyes turned to slits, and Craig looked away, mumbling, "Jeez, sorry."

Mrs. T. smacked him again. Josh returned to his ministrations. Craig stared forward and remained blessedly silent the rest of the trip.

****

We stopped at the Historical Spanish Library Studies, aka, the CIA front, and returned the tactical gear and most of the weapons to the El Camino. Josh retained a handgun, and quietly told Rodrigo and I to keep our stun guns. I don't think anyone believed Craig "lost" his GPS, and our trust levels were low. Nobody came out to greet us this time, and we left Hernandez behind. Apparently, he was due to catch a midnight flight home.

Josh took over driving us back to the resort.

I'd love to say that we prepared some elaborate scheme to sneak Josh and Mrs. T. up to my suite, but I can't. We walked in the front door and went directly to the elevators, unmolested. Our motley group must have been quite a sight. Josh, who had wiped off most of the grease paint except for a few swipes around his ears, simply looked tough and unapproachable. The twig had fallen out of Craig's hair, but there were still remnants of his race through the jungle, including the sweat stains on his new shirt. Mrs. T., wearing dark slacks and a blue blouse, would have ranged on the normal scale, except for the pink hair standing on end, and the new gauze wrapped around her wrists. Bloody, bandaged, filthy, and walking stiff-legged like Frankenstein, I probably looked the most disreputable. Rodrigo was the only one who appeared normal. It didn't even look as though he'd broken a sweat.

When we got into the elevator, Craig gave me the once-over, taking in my sorry state, and opened his mouth to say something.

"Not a word." I held up a finger. "Not a fucking word."

Chapter Fifteen

I gave Rodrigo my spare keycard, and we agreed to meet in my room in half an hour, which gave me time to shower and change into a clean pair of shorts and a tank top. I gave Mrs. T. one of my beach cover-ups to put on after her bath.

Before getting in the shower, I listened to the phone message from Jillian. "Hey, Rina, just checking in to see how you're doing in Mexico. I'm bored. Tony is working tonight, Mom's asleep, and I finished reading the *People* magazine she brought home from the grocery store," she whined. There was a pause and then she sighed, "You're probably out at one of the bars with Rodrigo, whooping it up. Call me if you get home before midnight."

I let out a bark of laughter. *Yeah, that won't be happening.*

Unfortunately, showering soaked my bandages. Josh had me sit at the dining table to reapply fresh ones. He was working on my elbow when Rodrigo and Craig, clean and changed, let themselves in for our after-action report.

Craig, in khaki slacks and a white T-shirt with the resort's logo emblazoned across the front, sat at the piano. "Whew, what a night, eh?" He proceeded to quietly play "Moonlight Sonata."

"Don't you think Beethoven is a little dark for tonight?" I asked drily.

He paused. "You're correct. Tonight was a success. We need something a little more upbeat." Craig began pounding out "Flight of the Bumblebee" instead. His fingers flew across the keyboard at a dizzying pace, and, I'll admit, we all stopped to watch him play with astonishment. Which I'm fairly certain was his intention. The piece came to an end, and Craig spun around to face the room with a smug smile.

Without comment, Joshua and I returned our attention to my injuries.

Rodrigo stuck his head in the refrigerator. "Karina, have you got any booze in here?" he asked.

"Check the wet bar, over there." I pointed to the little sink tucked into a corner on the far side of the room. "I think there is a minifridge in that cabinet below, and glasses above."

Rodrigo strolled over, opened the cabinet, and revealed a minifridge stocked with mini-sized bottles of alcohol and cans of soda. "Jackpot. Okay, let's see what we've got. Who wants tequila?"

"I'll take the tequila," Craig called, raising his hand, and Rodrigo tossed the little bottle to him.

"You want a mixer?" Rodrigo asked.

Perhaps not getting the accolades he expected, Craig abandoned the piano in favor of the couch. "Is there any salt or lime?"

Rodrigo shook his head.

"Straight up, it is." Craig twisted the cap, took a swig, and made a sour face.

"What's this?" Rodrigo scrutinized another bottle. "It looks like brandy. Do we have a brandy drinker?"

"I'll take the brandy. In a glass, please." Mrs. T. exited the extra bedroom, wearing my flowered rayon cover-up. It came down past her knees. She drew on the hotel's complimentary, fluffy white robe over top. "Craig, was that you on the piano? It was lovely. You were always such a skilled player. I'll never understand why you didn't pursue the scholarship opportunity to Julliard."

Craig didn't respond to his aunt's comments.

Rodrigo took care of making Mrs. T. her drink, placing it on the coffee table in front of where she sat next to her grandnephew. "Okay, is anyone a bourbon drinker? Karina? Joshua?"

I shook my head.

"I can't drink. I'm on duty," Josh declined, taping the last bandage to my knee.

"On duty?" I laughed. "Forget that crap. C'mon, Josh, lighten up. Toss the bourbon over." Rodrigo lobbed it our way and I caught the little plastic bottle in my right hand. I placed it in front of him. "You want a mixer with that? Coke? Sprite? A glass?"

Josh studied me for a moment.

"Listen, I won't tell if you don't. What's that saying you military folks have? What goes TDY stays TDY?" I winked.

"A Coke and a glass would be nice," he replied.

"Here, catch," said Rodrigo. To my dismay, he tossed one of the cut crystal lowball glasses at Josh. I gasped, but needn't have worried. Josh caught it neatly with one hand. The soda arrived the same way.

"Karina, you're next. I've got another tequila, we've got some rum, vodka, beer. . . ." Rodrigo reeled off.

"Is there an orange *Jarrito* in there?" I asked.

"Yeah."

"I'll have a vodka screwdriver, then."

"Then I'll take the rum and the pineapple *Jarrito*," Rodrigo said. He fixed our drinks and we all took seats around the coffee table. He sat at the end of the couch and put his feet up. "Okay, boys and girls, what now?"

The question of the night, to be sure.

Nobody answered, and Rodrigo continued, "I don't think Nico and Gaetan will retreat with their tails tucked between their legs. They may have lost out tonight, but Adolfo knows you have the mask, Craig. I imagine they've returned to their lair to regroup."

"If they've managed to get a ride home," Mrs. T. added.

"What do you mean?" I asked.

"Oh, didn't I tell you? I removed the ignition fuse," she said as she sipped her brandy, with a self-satisfied smile.

"Whoa." Rodrigo peered at her. "Did they teach you that at the CIA camp? What is that? Spy School 101?"

Mrs. T. simply raised her brows and took another sip.

I let out a noisy snort, and everyone stared at me. "Can't you picture it? Fat old Gaetan and skinny Adolfo trying to push a jalopy down that excuse for a road, with Nico behind the wheel berating them. Because you sure as hell know, alpha dog Nico isn't getting out to push." By the time I finished, my snort had turned into a high-pitched giggle that must have been contagious, because Rodrigo and Mrs. T. caught it. Craig's shoulders bounced up and down in silent mirth. Josh was the only one who didn't deign to join in on our post-stress merriment. I gripped my injured side and wheezed, "It hurts. Oh, stop."

We wound down and Rodrigo sighed, "Oh, Mrs. T., you're a gem."

"So, I guess we're back to where we started. What the hell do we do now? Josh, you got any suggestions?" I turned to him.

He rubbed a hand through his hair. "Now that we have recovered everyone, I would suggest returning the piece to the artist, Adolfo. You said you haven't paid him yet. Make the deal. Give him the piece to leave you alone and his family can do with it as they will."

Craig began shaking his head the moment Josh mentioned returning the death mask.

"Craig, whatever crack-brained idea you've got about making money off that thing" —I pointed at the black case resting in the center of the coffee table, surrounded by all our drinks— "you can forget it. I had it analyzed by a collector who figured out it was a fake within moments of opening the box. Even if you successfully sold it on the black market, you'd be found out and could bring an even worse criminal enterprise down on your head."

"I don't want to sell it," Craig murmured.

"Bullshit!" Rodrigo retorted. "You told us on the first day that you wanted to get in on the sale. Always looking to make a buck. Always looking for the angles."

"You're mistaken. I didn't want to sell it—unless I was forced to do so by Nico," he defended.

"Whatever the case," I said, cutting off Rodrigo's rejoinder, "they won't leave you alone until we are rid of the damned thing. Josh, what would you suggest is the safest way to return the item?"

"Dead drop," he replied.

Hmm. A dead drop certainly had merit. I twisted my earring around. "But where? And how?"

Josh opened his mouth, but Rodrigo got there first with his suggestion. "In the Jaguar Temple."

I doused his enthusiasm with the stink eye. "I am *not* returning to *Chichén Itzá*. Ever again."

"Okay." He tried again. "We have to find a tree in the park downtown with a hole in it big enough to leave the case."

"While I like your enthusiasm, Rodrigo," Josh interjected, "the safest and easiest route to take would be a locker at a bus station or airport." Rodrigo's eagerness deflated as Josh continued, "We leave the key at a designated location. Tell them where to find it. Everyone walks away unharmed."

"Sounds simple enough. And nobody has to actually meet with them." I took a long drink and felt the gentle wash of alcoholic calm flooding my body.

"*I* think," Mrs. T. said as she stared at her nephew, "we should mail it to a contact at the Brazilian museum, as a gift—from Adolfo and his family."

The room went silent, contemplating the suggestion.

"That . . . is . . . freaking brilliant," I marveled. "The museum gets a fine-looking replica of the destroyed item. Adolfo and company get recognition for their generous donation, and there is nothing left for them to do but humbly receive the gracious thanks of grateful nation."

Rodrigo clapped his hands. "I love it."

Josh pinched his chin in thought. "It's certainly another option."

"Well . . ." Craig rose, stretching his arms above his head and yawning. "That's a lot to think about. It's getting late. I'm exhausted. I'm sure you're tired too, Aunt Milly. I can see the bags gathering beneath your eyes. Why don't we reconvene tomorrow morning? Say, nine-thirty? Ten? And make a decision when we are refreshed? In the meantime, Karina, stick that back in whatever hidey-hole you've been keeping it." His eyes darted over to the plant and away just as quickly. If I hadn't been watching, I wouldn't have noticed. "Sleep on it, and we'll take a vote in the morning. What do you say?"

Mrs. T. yawned, and I followed suit. "You're right," she said, "I could use eight hours of shut eye."

"But . . ." Rodrigo didn't look happy.

"We'll figure it out in the morning, dearie." She patted his knee. "Don't you worry."

Rodrigo slugged back the last of his drink and stood up. "Fine. C'mon, Craig, I guess you're with me . . . again."

"Don't sound so excited about it." Craig slapped him on the back. "I promise not to snore tonight."

Rodrigo peered over his shoulder at me with a pleading gaze. "Are you sure he can't stay here tonight? You've got loads of space."

Once again, I didn't trust Craig. At all. Like Rodrigo pointed out, he always seemed to be looking for the angles. Even with

Josh here, there was no way I wanted the crap weasel sleeping in the same room with the funerary mask. I ushered the pair to the foyer. "Forget it. I've got Josh and Mrs. T. Besides, Craig has all his new clothes down in your room."

Rodrigo closed my door a little harder than necessary.

When I returned, Mrs. T. was alone, clearing up the glasses and loading the dishwasher. "Oh, thanks, Mrs. T.—"

"Milly. Call me Milly."

"Uh, Milly . . . but you don't have to do that."

"It's done." She closed the dishwasher door. "Craig's right. We all need a good night's sleep." Yawning again, she shuffled toward her room. "I'll see you in the morning. Oh" —she paused in the doorway and snapped her fingers— "I've been terribly remiss. I haven't thanked you for all that you've done. I know I've put you and your friends through a rough couple of days. Although, I believe that Joshua fellow is used to it."

"Pshaw. Think nothing of it. Anyone would have done the same."

Her sunken blue gaze peered at me. "No, dearie. Anyone would *not* have done the same. You are quite something. You've got guts, mental fortitude, and just enough of a loose moral compass. . . ."

My face burned.

"Did you ever think about going into intelligence?" she asked.

I scrunched my nose. "Languages elude me, and I hate camping. I never would have made it out of the Farm," I said, referring to Camp Peary, where CIA agents were trained. "I'm also a terrible shot."

"Some of that comes with training." She tucked her hands into her robe's pockets.

"Uh . . . thanks, but it isn't for me. By the way, where is Josh?"

"He's taking a shower in your bathroom. I offered him my other bed, but he refused. I believe he plans to sleep on the couch.

I'll bring out pillows and a blanket for him."

Chapter Sixteen

I awoke, groggy and sore. Josh had provided me with an ibuprofen PM, which helped get me through the night, but was probably the reason for the cobwebs. The vodka probably didn't help either. Scratching my belly, I realized I'd never changed into pajamas and was still wearing the same tank top and shorts I'd put on after showering.

Something went *thunk* beyond my door, and I wondered if Josh had fallen off the couch. The clock read half past six in the morning. Considering we hadn't gone to bed until well past one in the morning, I rolled over, pulling the covers up to my chin, and closed my eyes, intent on getting another few hours of shut eye.

Crash!

Moving slower than planned, I staggered out of bed and opened the door. "Everything all right, J—"

Josh was on his knees with his hands laced behind his head, while a man pointed a gun at him. A woman, dressed in black like her partner, turned and pointed her gun at me. The man, of average height with a wide, crooked nose, kept blinking, and his right eye started purpling.

"Well, shit," I sighed. "Really, Josh, I expected more from you."

Josh grimaced, and I think if he could, he would have strangled me.

"You! Go sit by your friend." The woman indicated with her weapon.

I yawned. I should have been wigging out, but I just didn't have it in me. I think all my adrenaline got used up the previous night. Or the PM in the night-night pills were still at work, keeping the freak out at bay.

Across the living room, Mrs. T. opened her door. "Is everything okay? I heard . . ." She took in the tableau.

The woman whipped her gun back and forth between Mrs. T. and I, unsure at which person to point the deadly weapon. In the end, she must have decided I was the bigger threat. "Both of you. On your knees next to the big fella. And tell me where Craig is." Her enunciation held a slight European accent—Dutch or perhaps German.

I shuffled slowly toward Josh and noticed Mrs. T. staring hard at the side table, which held a pretty bronze figurine of a lizard, and a stun gun behind it. A knock at the door startled everyone. Mrs. T. moaned and promptly fainted to the floor, distracting both of our visitors. Josh moved more swiftly than I, disarming the man, but for once my aim flew true. The lizard sailed through the air and beaned the woman on her right temple. She went down like a felled tree, and there seemed to be no need to engage the stun gun.

"Nice job, dearie." Mrs. T. jumped up and snatched the gun from the woman's limp hand.

Josh held the man to the ground with his knee jammed into his spine and growled, "There are plasticuffs in my bag."

Of course there are.

While I scurried over and dug through Josh's duffle, dumping most of the contents on the floor, there was another knock at the door, accompanied by the doorbell. "I don't see them," I said.

"Check the outside pockets," Josh told me, never taking his eyes off the assailant.

"Found them." I tossed one pair to him and then went over to help Mrs. T. roll the woman over so we could zip tie her hands behind her back. A large red welt rose on her forehead. "She's still alive, right?"

Mrs. T. placed a pair of fingers to her neck. "Yes, her pulse is steady."

The woman groaned, and I breathed a sigh of relief. I couldn't imagine the red tape I'd have to go through if I'd been responsible for the death of a stranger . . . in my suite . . . in Mexico. Lord, that sounded bad.

The knocking turned into an incessant banging, and I jogged over to check through the peephole to see who was on the other side. Before he could knock again, I had the door open. "Mike? What are you doing here?"

"Surprise!" he said jubilantly, scooping me into his arms and swinging me in a circle. "The case closed quicker than we expected. I took a red eye here! *And* I can spend the rest of the week!" He showed me his wrist with a band that matched mine.

"Yay," I said faintly.

Putting me down, he stepped back. "What happened to you? What are all these bandages?" He turned my hands over. "Your palms are all scraped up."

"Karina, bring him in here," Josh called. "I need him to watch these two while I go check on Rodrigo and Craig."

Mike's brows knit together and he walked past me.

"Rodrigo!" I'd completely forgotten my coworker. At the mention of his name, the adrenaline spike I'd been waiting for finally kicked in. Slipping into a pair of flip-flops I'd left under the foyer table, I grabbed the keycards— one for my room and one for Rodrigo's—and bolted out the door.

One disadvantage of being on the upper floors—the elevator took forever. Like an impatient child, I kept pressing the button, as though it would bring the car faster. My suite door slammed shut, and Mike strode down the hall toward me.

"So I guess you won the coin toss," I remarked as we entered the car together.

He didn't respond to my quip. A chilly silence reigned as we watched the elevator floors count down. Once we hit the fifth floor, I didn't exactly run, but shuffled as quickly as my injuries would allow. The *thwacka-thwacka* of my sandals were the only sounds in the quiet hallway.

I stopped in front of Rodrigo's door and lifted my hand to knock, but Mike stayed me and shook his head. Reaching behind his back, he pulled out a gun.

"Where did you get that?" I whispered. "You didn't bring your service weapon to Mexico, did you?"

He shook his head. "It's being shipped back to the home office. Joshua gave me this. On the count of three, open the door, and stay behind me." He counted down with his fingers.

At three, I slipped the card into the slot. Mike pushed the handle down and entered first, his gun at the ready. Nothing moved in the darkness.

"Rodrigo? Craig?" I flicked on the lights.

Rodrigo blinked, covering his eyes, and rasped, "Karina? What's going on?"

Mike swiftly returned the gun from whence it came. "Are you two okay?"

Craig snored.

"We're fine. Mike, is that you?" Rodrigo asked through the slits of his fingers. "When did you get here?"

"He just arrived. Get dressed. We have visitors." I picked up Craig's shoe and beaned him with it. *Wow, twice in one day.*

"Hey," Craig grumbled, putting a hand to his head. "What's going on? What time is it?"

"Time to get up. We have visitors this morning, and they are asking for you. Get dressed. Quickly," I snapped. "Mike and I will wait outside."

They took no more than five minutes, but it was the most uncomfortable five minutes I've ever spent with Mike.

"So your case wrapped faster than expected. How did that happen?"

"Local police arrested our suspect during a routine traffic stop," he said without inflection. We both leaned against the wall next to Rodrigo's door. He wouldn't look at me.

"Well, it's a win for the good guys. Right?" I tried to infuse some enthusiasm into my voice.

"Yup."

That single syllable pretty much shut me down. I coughed, said no more, and silently thanked the heavens when Rodrigo opened the door. "Ready? Good. Let's go."

Once in the elevator, my colleague turned to Mike. "Hey, man, I thought you were working a big case. What happened?"

"We got an unexpected break and my services were no longer needed," Mike replied, then stuck his hand out toward Craig. "I'm Mike, by the way, I don't believe we've met."

"Craig." They shook.

"So, are you an innocent bystander that got dragged into one of K.C.'s messes?" he asked, and I sucked wind.

Craig coughed.

Rodrigo filled the awkward silence, clarifying, "No, he's not. Craig, the crap weasel here, is the reason for this mess. Aren't you?" Rodrigo slung his arm over Craig's shoulder. "Why don't you tell Karina's boyfriend all about your shenanigans? Oh, and did I mention, he's an FBI agent?"

Craig visibly blanched.

I couldn't stand it anymore. "All right, that's enough. Mike, we'll read you in as soon as we get back to the room. And, Craig, you better get ready because you've got some 'splaining to do." The elevator doors opened, and I stomped down the hall, leading the rest of the pack.

Mrs. Thundermuffin and Josh had gotten our intruders off the floor and were securing them to a pair of dining chairs with a roll of duct tape—another handy item from Josh's duffle bag. The woman was conscious again, and her eyes spit daggers at me as we entered the living room.

"Craig, meet Intruder A and Intruder B." I pointed to the man first, then the woman. "They jumped Josh this morning and seem to be intent on finding you."

Craig stuffed his hands in his pockets and shrugged. "I've never seen them before in my life."

"They aren't friends of Nico and crew?" I put my hands on my hips.

He shook his head. "Not that I know of."

I looked to Josh. "Did we get any names yet?"

"No, they aren't carrying any identification, and the serial numbers have been filed off their weapons." He pointed to the gun sitting on the dining table as he finished securing the man's bindings.

Mike went over to add his gun and check out the one Josh left there. Mrs. T. and Josh retreated to the kitchen area and started whispering, likely trying to decide upon our next move. Eventually, Mike joined them. Craig scrutinized the pair, as if searching his mind to figure out who they were. Rodrigo stood behind the couch, his arms crossed, observing the situation as it unfolded.

I trotted over to the woman and ripped the duct tape off her mouth. "Who are you? Who do you work for?" Subtlety was not in my bag of tricks this morning.

She was around my height, in excellent shape, with a dark brown pixie haircut, and she could deliver a whopper of hateful glare. Her cheekbones were so sharply honed, they looked like they could cut glass. And I had no doubt, if she weren't strapped to the chair, she'd be able to kick my ass in under ten seconds.

"Fuck you," she spat at me.

"Good talk." I replaced the tape and moved to her friend. "Ooo, that eye is not looking good. Though I doubt it's your first. You look like quite the brawler," I said, removing his muzzle. "What's your name?" I waited while he ignored me. "No? You two were looking for Craig. Well, here he is." I indicated our little crap weasel. "What do you have to say to him?" When more silence greeted me, I mused, "Hmm, maybe you're not the interrogators. Was your purpose to capture him?"

The corner of the man's mouth twitched.

"Capture. Okay. Alive or dead?" I prodded.

"Alive," the perp grunted.

"So, you *do* work for Nico and Gaetan."

"No." He gave a sharp head shake.

"Well, you went to an awful lot of trouble to get into my room. Which, by the way, how *did* they get in?" I directed at Josh, who had rejoined me in the living room, along with the whispering posse.

"They pinched one of the maid's keycards," he replied.

"Of course, so easy. Why my room? Craig wasn't staying here."

The pair looked at each other and the man scowled.

"They must have seen him enter your room at some point," Josh suggested.

"What do you want with Craig?" I waited for a response. "Nothing?"

Josh socked him. Out of the corner of my eye, I saw Mike take a jerking step forward. The guy moved his jaw around, but it wasn't bleeding or broken. Josh had pulled his punch.

"Is your employer going to be happy if you end up in a Mexican prison?" I tried again.

Nothing.

"Look," I said conversationally as I picked up the stun gun, pulled my favorite slipper chair forward, and took a seat in front of our guest, "why don't you just tell us what is going on—or I can have my big friend drag you into the bathroom for some waterboarding and shock therapy." I would *never* do that, but they didn't know it, and Josh looked particularly lethal this morning.

Our intruders remained mute, and I pressed the button on the stun gun, which, luckily for me, still had some juice in it. *Zzztt.* Frustrated, I zapped his shoulder, and he jerked. Overall, he took it in stride with his teeth clamped shut, but I noticed the woman's leg began to shake and her eyes darted around in their sockets. I changed tactics and moved the stun gun slowly toward his private parts. He watched with big eyes and pushed back against the chair as far as he could. The stun gun was within millimeters of the family jewels, and he cursed fearfully in a foreign language.

The woman made noises, and I paused to rip off her tape again. "You have something to add to the conversation?"

She licked her lips. "We work for Victor Schaffhausen."

That's a new one. I glanced over my shoulder to see Craig's reaction. He paled visibly, and blindly perched on the arm of the couch. "And what does Mr. Schaffhausen want with Craig?" I asked.

"To make sure the item he sold to Mr. Schaffhausen is genuine. There have been . . . rumors . . . the same item is available on the black market. Mr. Schaffhausen is not pleased. He does not like to be made the fool," she replied silkily.

Craig drew an audible breath, and a bad premonition washed over me. "Everyone into my room. You two, wait here." I muzzled our intruders and escorted everyone who wasn't currently tied to a chair into my darkened bedroom.

Mike closed the door behind us. Mrs. T. swept open the curtains, and the morning light poured in. Craig stood in a corner between the dresser and the wall, looking pale, with his arms crossed. Josh texted madly on his phone. Everyone else took up random stations around the room, but all eyes were turned to Craig.

"Care to explain, nephew?" Mrs. T. asked, perching on the dresser.

He shrugged and seemed to squeeze himself tighter into the corner.

"Come now, Craig, don't be shy." Rodrigo took him by the arm and dragged him into the middle of the room. "Tell us all about your dealings with Mr. Schaffhausen. I'm sure it's a fascinating story." Rodrigo's behavior throughout this trip continued to surprise me. Normally a man of happy and relatively passive nature, relying more on verbal persuasion, he'd shown himself to be quite forceful when necessary. Not a side I'd seen from him in the past. "If you don't tell us, Mike or our Silverthorne contact here can get the information they need."

Craig shoved Rodrigo away. "I don't know anyone by that name."

Josh's phone rang and our attention diverted away from Craig. He answered, staring down at the floor. "What have you got for me . . . ? I see . . . uh-huh . . . uh-huh . . . interesting. Text me that information." He hung up, and his gaze swept the room. "Schaffhausen is a Swiss national. He has business interests all over North and South America, including a hotel in Bolivia, a restaurant in San Diego, one in San Francisco, he owns a vineyard in Sonoma, and a handful of bodegas in Bolivia and Peru. He has homes in at least three different countries. He has an affinity for fine wines and . . . art." Everyone's gaze swung back to Craig. Josh delivered the cherry on top. "He is also suspected of laundering money for the Bolivian drug cartel. Are you familiar with him?" he directed at Mike.

Mike shook his head. "Never heard of him, but drugs aren't my wheelhouse."

A distinct thunk outside my room drew our attention.

"Someone needs to check on our guests," Mrs. T. suggested.

"I'm not sure I want to hear the rest of this. I'll go," Mike volunteered.

"I'll help him." As Rodrigo passed Craig, he shoved him hard enough to push the crap weasel onto my bed.

Josh closed the door behind them.

Craig righted himself. "Jeez, he sure woke up on the wrong side of the bed this morning."

"Oh, Craig, what have you done?" Mrs. Thundermuffin uttered faintly.

"Yeah, *Craig,*" I said rather nastily, "what did you do? Is there another fake Egyptian death mask out there? Did you have Adolfo make more than one, and that's what you sold to the man who sent the muscle that's in my sitting room?"

But Craig wasn't listening to me. His attention was riveted on his aunt, who had a hand to her mouth. "Oh, Craig, tell me you didn't."

He blinked but remained still as a statue.

"Didn't what?" My eyes bounced back and forth between the pair. "*Didn't what?*"

"But why did you keep the fake?" she whispered. "Are you responsible? Did you set the fire?"

"Fake? Fire? What are you—" I glanced back at Josh, who also watched the show with his brows drawn.

"God, no! I'm not responsible for that!" Craig thundered. "How could you think it? I have the utmost respect for those pieces. I certainly never wanted to see them burned."

The lightbulb finally turned on. "Wait a minute. Wait a minute." I held up my palm. "Do you mean to tell me—you actually stole the *original* Egyptian funerary mask from the Brazilian museum? And sold it to the drug cartel accountant?"

"Money launderer," Josh clarified, coming to stand behind

me.

Craig whipped his attention to me and drawled, "Welcome to the party, you dense halfwit. Yes, Schaffhausen hired me to retrieve the funerary mask."

"And what about the fire?" Mrs. T. asked in a steely tone.

He stared off into space with a faraway look. "I was there— that night in September. I waited until closing and hid myself in the drop ceiling of the men's room. When I realized there was a fire, I knew I couldn't wait until midnight, as I'd planned. The smolder turned into a conflagration in only minutes. I worked my way to the Egyptian exhibit. Smoke poured out of the ventilation system. I could barely breathe, and, at one point, I wondered if I'd make it out alive."

"Why didn't you just leave it? Flee? Run away?" I asked.

He shook his head and pressed a hand over his eyes as if trying to blot out the memory. "I'd gone too far to turn back. The smoke got so thick, I had to crawl along the floor to find my way out. I didn't leave the fake. There wasn't time. Besides, I figured the fire would cause enough of a distraction. I knew I'd be able to get the funerary mask, and myself, out of the country unnoticed." He pulled his hand away and met my gaze. "I know what you're thinking. I couldn't. I'd already spent Schaffhausen's deposit. I didn't have the money to repay him if I didn't retrieve the artifact. He's not the type of man one wants to owe a debt to."

"After your dirty deeds, you left the building to burn?" his aunt accused.

"The fire engines were already on the way. I had no idea the entire exhibit would go up in flames." His hands flew up in the air. "Had I known, I would have taken . . ." he tapered off.

Crack! Craig's head recoiled. I have to give Mrs. Thundermuffin props, she could deliver a hell of a smack for such a tiny little woman. "You will make this right, Craig Beaufort

Mettler, or the next time you see your mother, it will be behind bars. That I can promise!"

"What do you expect me to do, Aunt Milly? The man's house is an armed fortress, there is no way I can steal it back without getting killed," he whined, holding his cheek.

"Well, you're going to have to try," she declared.

"I'm telling you, Schaffhausen has his own private army, and better security than the museum I stole it from. Besides, the piece is clearly safer with Schaffhausen than it ever was with the Brazilians."

"What an arrogant assertion. That artifact belongs to the people of Brazil!" I declared.

Craig snorted and replied sarcastically, "Technically, it belongs to the Egyptians. And let's not ignore the fact, if I hadn't stolen it, the damn thing would have burned along with every other piece in there." A red welt in the shape of his aunt's hand spread across his face. "You've read the articles. That fire started because the air conditioning systems were so old. There wasn't appropriate fire suppression to save those treasures. If it weren't for me, that mask would be another pile of ash in the rubble left behind."

"I see, and now you're the artifact savior?" I snarled, realizing we were bickering like siblings, and I longed to give Craig a walloping. "Should we give you a medal?"

"Maybe you should." He stuck out his chest and delivered a snotty little smile.

"Why, you conceited ass—"

Josh grabbed my arm as I raised my fist to sock him. "Whoa, there, Karina. That's not going to help anyone."

"All right, that's enough," Mrs. Thundermuffin said in a tone sharp enough to cut through our spat. "Let's all take a breath."

I stopped fighting Josh's hold. He released me, and I paced away to cool off.

"Why the death mask?" Josh asked, with arms folded and feet shoulder width apart.

"Schaffhausen's got a hard-on for Egyptian artifacts, and the Ptolemaic period in particular. He believes he is a descendent of Cleopatra. The artifact is small and relatively easy to obtain."

"So, this little acquisition isn't the first piece of illegal artwork Schaffhausen has hiding in his fortress, is it?" I gave Craig the squint-eye, daring him to lie to me.

He didn't deny the accusation.

I paced in a small circle as the pistons in my head cranked up. I doubted this theft was Craig's first. Schaffhausen's collection likely held other "small" items acquired by Craig. I wondered how many museums held Adolfo's fakes. "Do you know where the artwork is kept? Does he display his dirty deeds out in the open? Or does he hide it?"

"He hides the stolen ones. He's built a vault for them. Fire resistant. Proper lighting, climate controlled to maintain appropriate humidity levels, and pressure plates beneath the art pieces. Not to mention the foot-thick vault door. That's *after* you've managed to get past the half a dozen armed guards, dogs, and surveillance cameras surrounding the place."

"Where is this fortress? In Bolivia or the US?" Josh asked.

Craig paused as if debating whether it would be in his best interests to answer; the little hamsters were running the wheels in his head. "Let's say I know where the vault is located . . . and I could be more helpful . . . if there was a deal on the table." Good old Craig—only concerned for himself.

"Fine. What's the plan, and what do we do about the Hansel and Gretel out there?" I pointed toward the door.

"I'm not sure. Let's have a conversation with them," Josh suggested.

Back into the living room we went. Mike and Rodrigo were whispering in the kitchen, while our guests were in the same place we'd left them.

"Any problems?" I asked.

Mike didn't respond, giving me the silent treatment.

Rodrigo looked over his shoulder. "The woman had fallen over. Probably an attempt to get loose. We took care of it. I was just bringing Mike up to speed on our vacation adventures."

"Great," I deadpanned.

Josh and Mrs. T. assessed our two guests. "I'd try the woman, she seems more willing to talk," she suggested.

Rip. Off came the tape. Josh loomed above the woman. "Why does your boss want Craig? Didn't he have the item properly assessed?"

She stretched her mouth for a moment before speaking, "He wants Craig to provide his personal assurance that the item is not a forgery."

"In other words, you plan to beat the crap out of him until he confesses, or until you feel as though he's telling the truth," I commented.

"Certainly not. Mr. Schaffhausen simply wishes to speak with Craig." Her denial wasn't very convincing, and I rolled my eyes.

"Let's say, there is a . . . reproduction floating around," Josh said.

"Not a very good one either," I added.

"What I can do is send the reproduction home with you," Josh asserted. "Mr. Schaffhausen can compare the two and be assured that he, indeed, possesses the original."

The woman glanced at her partner. He didn't make any sort of response. "You would let us go? And send us home with this . . . copy you speak of?"

Josh put his hands on his hips. "There are conditions."

"Such as . . . ?"

"Mr. Schaffhausen would be severing all ties with Craig, and we'd need assurances that no harm would come to him or his family."

"If he possesses the original, as you say, I think that is a reasonable request," she replied.

I glanced over to Mike, who stood like a statue, wearing the unreadable expression I'd come to know as his FBI interrogation face. He was letting this play out, but I didn't doubt if we crossed a line, he'd shut down this little drama.

"Okay." Josh replaced the tape. "Mike and Craig, would you please join me in the bedroom? Rodrigo, Mrs. Thundermuffin, stay out here and keep an eye on Frick and Frack. You know what to do if anyone gets feisty," he directed at Mrs. T.

I followed the men, but was stopped at the door by Josh. "I think you should stay out here with Rodrigo," he murmured.

"I don't think so," I whispered. "I'm a part of this mission too."

He drew in a breath. "I don't think Mike is happy with you right now. I'm walking a fine line, and I need his cooperation."

"I know he's not happy. He'll have to suck it up. After all, this *is my* hotel room." My whisper turned into an angry hiss.

"Fine. You can join us. But keep your mouth shut," he warned.

Chapter Seventeen

"I don't know what's going on, but I don't like it. We should call the authorities and turn them over." Mike frowned down at Craig and I where we sat on the edge of the bed, like crows on a wire, while he and Josh loomed above us.

"How much did Rodrigo tell you?" Josh asked.

"He got as far as dropping Hernandez at some CIA black site."

"It was a front. Not a black site," Josh clarified.

I snickered. Josh sent me a glare. My lips rolled inward.

"Hypothetically, let's say Craig knows where some priceless pieces of stolen artwork are being hidden," Josh explained.

"Why am I not surprised? Hypothetically, would it be our Mr. Schaffhausen?" Mike's lips pursed.

"Perhaps, and he would like to tell the FBI where they can find these items."

"Uh-huh. Don't tell me. In return, Craig" —he indicated Craig with a two-fingered point— "would like some sort of hypothetical immunity package."

"And anonymity. Schaffhausen had long fingers." Craig pinched Mike's two fingers for emphasis.

Mike whipped them away and sucked his teeth. "How much artwork are we talking about?"

"A twelve-by-twelve room filled with statues, paintings, and artifacts. I would estimate at least a dozen items," Craig replied. He leaned forward, rubbing his hands together, and his face held excitement, just thinking about all that loot.

"And the estimated value of this hypothetical room?" Mike prodded.

"Millions," Craig asserted.

"Where is it?"

Craig's head waggled back and forth. "Not until I've got a deal."

Mike pinched his lip. "I need to know if they are in the US. If they're in a foreign country, I can't help you."

Craig's foot bounced up and down, shaking the bed as he debated his options.

I elbowed Craig in the ribs. "Out with it."

"Oof. All right, all right. It's in the US. That's all I'm saying until there is a deal on the table." He crossed his arms.

Mike's brows continued to make a deep *V*.

I'd seen him look like this too many times, and I began to wonder if that wrinkle between them was my doing. "You could get in contact with your art crimes buddy, Bruce, isn't it?" I asked.

Josh glared at me, and I snapped my mouth shut.

Mike turned to Josh and hooked a thumb over his shoulder. "What's your plan for the two out there?"

"The mask has a GPS tracker on it. We put them on a plane with it. Wait for them to make contact with their boss," Josh explained.

Mike shook his head. "What happens if they don't go home to the States? What if they go to Bolivia?"

"I would imagine Schaffhausen is on someone's radar. If not FBI, then DEA. If the original *is* in the US as Craig claims—"

We all waited for Craig to confirm. Josh and Mike looked as though they could stand there all day. Craig finally gave a sharp nod.

"—then he'll want to compare the copy with the original," Josh said, completing his thought.

"Are we sure he'll be able to tell the difference between the two?" Mike addressed Craig.

Craig remained mute.

"Yes. If he knows anything about Egyptian antiquities," I supplied.

"And how would you know this?" Mike asked nastily, dropping the neutral, businesslike tone he'd been using with Josh.

Josh's head gave a nearly imperceptible side-to-side movement, but I refused to be silenced on this matter. Not when I could supply valuable information.

"First, the scent. Adolfo didn't use resin to shape the papyrus," I said, doing a reasonable impression of Jillian's schoolteacher tone. "It smells like garden dirt and coffee, rather than pine tree. While the gold leaf and paintwork on the front has been done beautifully, the back remains relatively unfinished. It is without a cartouche, and even reveals some of the modern-day glue."

Mike's brows rose and his jaw flexed, and he said in a honeyed tone, "And how do you know all of this?"

Umpf. A punch to the gut, that question. I *did not* want to confess that I'd met with Martin Dunne before leaving the US. Josh was right. I should have kept my mouth shut.

Craig spoke up, saving me. "What does it matter? She's right. The fake was made to be a short-term place keeper. Nothing more. It was never meant to stand up to a deeper inspection."

Mike glared at Craig. "If we are simply following the mask home, explain to me why I should make a deal with you. What is it you bring to the table?"

Craig sighed. "Fine. I know how to get into Schaffhausen's vault room."

Mike didn't look convinced. "I'm sure we can get in once we identify which of Schaffhausen's homes to raid."

"Not if you want the artwork undamaged," Craig replied with smugness.

"What do you mean?" Josh asked.

"He's rigged the entire collection to go up in flames. It goes poof" —Craig demonstrated with his hands— "if there is unauthorized access into the vault."

"Tell me more." Mike leaned back against the dresser crossing one ankle over the other.

"He is prepared for a raid. To get through the safe door, you need a ten-digit access code and thumbprint scan. If Schaffhausen enters the wrong code—poof. If you drill into the safe and set off the sensors—poof. Try to come in through the ventilation system—poof. If you trip an alarm—"

"Poof," Mike supplied.

"If you don't go in through the vault doors, there will be nothing left for the FBI to confiscate, and nothing to charge Schaffhausen with. You'll simply find charred carcasses of masterpieces," Craig said assuredly.

Stunned, I asked, "He's willing to ruin the entire collection to keep from getting caught?"

"Yes."

"And you have the ten-digit code," Mike stated.

Craig coughed. "I do."

Mike did not look happy. "Fine. Let's make a deal."

Chapter Eighteen

Mike kicked everyone out of my room except for Josh. The remaining four of us were left to cool our heels and keep an eye on our intruders. Craig took his place at the piano again and banged out a rousing version of "The Piano Man", by Billy Joel. After the first stanza, it got on my nerves, but I think it got on our intruder's nerves even more, so I didn't put a stop to it. To my relief, as Craig started in on Sinatra's "Fly Me to the Moon", Mike called him and Mrs. Thundermuffin back into the bedroom.

During Craig's mini-concert, Rodrigo made coffee. At the conclusion of the performance, he parked himself on the couch and turned on a Mexican news station. "Now they're saying last night's explosion at *Chichén Itzá* was due to rival drug cartels."

"Charming." I poured myself a cup of coffee and stared out the sliding door at the ocean waves while I sipped the strong brew. "Hey, why don't we sit out on the deck and get some fresh air?" I suggested.

"Better not," Rodrigo replied with his eyes glued to the screen. "We need to keep an eye on them. I don't trust the woman. She's a tricky one."

"We could drag them out with us," I suggested. "You all would enjoy some fresh air, wouldn't you?"

I didn't get a response from the captives, but Rodrigo finally pulled his attention away from the TV and laughed. "I don't think that would be a good idea. Two people strapped to chairs on your deck?" He returned to the news. "I'll watch them if you need to step out for a moment."

"Never mind." I paced around the apartment. Visited the bathroom. And finally, flopped on the couch next to Rodrigo. "Thanks for explaining things to Mike."

"He seemed rather perturbed," Rodrigo murmured.

I sighed. "Yeah. He is."

"It's not your fault." He absently patted my arm, still watching TV.

I chewed my lip. "I'm not sure he sees it that way."

"Yeah." He drew his attention away from the news. "It *is* strange how trouble seems to find you."

"Don't remind me. I'm sorry your vacation got messed up. I feel bad. You should have gone with Alfonse to the conference."

"Well, it may not have been relaxing, but it's sure been far more entertaining than going to a cooking conference," he said as he grinned at me.

The woman started making noises.

Rodrigo grunted as he pushed himself off the couch and pulled off the tape. "What is it?"

"I have to go to the bathroom," she replied.

"What do we do?" He glanced at me.

"Dunno, let me find out." I went over to the bedroom door and was about to knock, but then I realized it was my damn bedroom, and I wasn't going to knock like a guest in my own suite. Instead, I opened the door, and all eyes turned to me. "The chick out here says she has to pee."

"Tell her to hold it," Josh replied.

"If she pees on the chair, I'm going to be responsible for paying for the damage."

Josh strode out and got in the woman's face. "Hold it. If you piss on the chair, I'll reach out to my contacts with Mexican intelligence and have them find a hole to throw you in so deep you won't see the light of day for the next twenty years. *Comprende?*"

She delivered one of her magnificent glares.

"She doesn't need to go. It's a ploy to cut her loose," Josh stated, then returned to the bedroom, slamming the door.

Rodrigo shrugged, replaced the tape over her mouth, and went back to the TV. I was stymied, and debated storming into my *own* bedroom.

"Don't do it," Rodrigo said as I placed a hand on the knob. "Just let them finish."

Irritated, I stomped over to the slider and let myself onto the balcony. The warm salt air enveloped me, and the breeze blew a stray hair into my face. I curled up on the lounge chair, listening to the ocean waves break upon the sands at regular intervals. The consistent whoosh of the surf and the warmth soon calmed my irritation at being left out of the discussion.

"*Karina*, wake up." Josh shook my shoulder.

I rubbed my eyes and yawned. "Hey, I guess I fell asleep. What's going on?"

"We have a problem." He did not look happy. "The mask is missing from the plant. We found the case but it's empty."

Stretching, I rose. "Yes, I know. I moved it last night."

He jerked back. "You moved it? Why?"

"Craig. I think he figured out we'd been hiding it there. After Mrs. T. went to bed, while you were showering, I moved it to a new location." I brushed past him and entered the living room.

Our guests were no longer strapped to the chairs. Instead, they stood warily as Mrs. T. held them at gunpoint, while Rodrigo opened and closed various doors, mumbling angrily beneath his breath as he searched. Craig frantically tossed the cushions off the couch and got down on his hands and knees to check beneath it. Josh's bedding had been folded and lay on the coffee table. I heard Mike slamming drawers in my room.

"Whoa, whoa!" I held my arms out with palms up. "Everyone, relax! I know where it is. What time is it? How long have I been asleep?"

"Two hours," Rodrigo said, strolling in from the foyer.

I couldn't help the yawn that escaped. "What did I miss?"

"K.C., focus. Where is the mask?" Mike stood in the doorway, looking a little harried.

"It's here." I strode to the kitchen and pulled the microwave forward, revealing a perfect little cubby behind it that fit the mask perfectly.

"Is it damaged?" Craig ran over and cupped it in his hands as if it was an injured baby bird.

"I doubt it." I shoved the microwave back in place. "What does it matter? It's a forgery anyway."

"It's a beautiful piece of artwork, you uncouth nitwit," Craig snapped, gently placing it back in the case.

"Nitwit? That's a new one." I dusted off my hands, placing them at my hips. "So, what did I miss? What's the plan?"

Mrs. Thundermuffin was the first to speak up. "Joshua and his friend will be escorting this pair, along with the mask, to the airport. They have spoken to Mr. Schaffhausen, who has directed them to stand down until that mask is proven a forgery. They will fly home on a flight chartered by Mr. Schaffhausen. If it is as we say, then he will leave Craig alone."

"Okay, then why are you still holding them at gunpoint?" I asked.

"One can never be too careful, dear." Mrs. T. didn't take her eyes off the pair.

Josh's phone buzzed. "Our ride is here." He threw his duffle bag over his shoulder.

"I'll go with you." Mike stuck one of the guns sitting on the dining table into the back of his pants and pulled his shirt over top of it. "The rest of you, remain here until I return," he ordered as he and Josh escorted our intruders out.

The door slammed, leaving behind an awkward silence.

I straightened the cushions, kicked off my flip-flops, and curled up in a corner of the couch. "Okay, who wants to bring me up to speed? What did I miss?" I asked expectantly, glancing around.

"Where should I start?" Rodrigo mused.

"Why don't you start with Mr. and Mrs. Smith. Who is going with Josh? I thought Hernandez had a flight out last night."

"He did. Some of our friends from the *Estudios Históricos de Bibliotecas Españolas* offered to help get the pair on a plane back to the states," Mrs. Thundermuffin explained. Tightening her robe, she took a seat on one of the slipper chairs.

"Great. So that's taken care of. I assume the tracker is still hidden in the death mask case, and our friends aren't aware of it."

"Correct." Rodrigo joined me on the couch, while Craig anxiously paced around the kitchen.

"You guys were in quite a panic. Why didn't Josh check the tracker to find out where I hid it?" I asked.

"We don't want them to know we've placed one on it, dear," Mrs. T. said with a yawn. "Besides, it would have been difficult to pinpoint its exact location. The GPS is precise within a few yards. That would include the entire apartment."

"Oh, right." I looked over the back of the couch to see Craig open the fridge. "That's the third time you've looked in there. Food is not going to magically appear."

The door shut with a thump, and Craig moved to opening and closing the cabinets.

"Craig," I said sharply, "you're driving me nuts. Sit down!"

Begrudgingly, he condescended to join us.

"Tell me about your deal," I suggested.

"I will be getting my own FBI escort home," he said in a sour tone. "If my information doesn't yield stolen items, I will go to jail. If my code doesn't get them into the vault and fire breaks out, I go to jail. If I've provided false information regarding the funerary mask that just walked out the door—"

"You go to jail," I supplied.

"I think it's a very fair deal." Rodrigo surveyed his nails. "You're a thief. Basically, if you lie or try to weasel out of anything, you go to jail." He gave a Cheshire cat grin.

My gaze went to Mrs. Thundermuffin, who studied her grandnephew with an inscrutable expression. I couldn't tell if she was irritated with him or simply tired from her adventures. Thinking about it, she'd had a hell of a week—searching for Craig, making a deal with the brothers to be held hostage, escaping from the trunk of a car, and setting off an IED. She was a tough old bird. I couldn't imagine my mother, who was probably twenty years younger than Mrs. T., handling any of this with as much aplomb.

Something else occurred to me. "What are we doing about Adolfo and the Brothers Grimm?"

"We texted and told them the FBI had confiscated the mask. Which is . . . kind of true. A novelty for you, right, Craig?" Rodrigo threw a pillow at Craig.

Craig dashed the little gold throw pillow aside. "Piss off."

My stomach grumbled. "I suppose we're all hungry. Why don't I order up some breakfast?"

"I'm starving." Craig rose. "I'm not going to wait for room service. I want to go down and eat at the Green Gecko Cantina. They have an omelet bar."

"Sit down, Craig. Michael asked us to remain until he returns," his aunt said in a steely voice.

"And if I don't?" he replied in the manner of an insolent teen.

She sighed. "Joshua left half a roll of tape behind. If I have to, I will strap you to a chair until Michael returns."

"You wouldn't dare."

"Don't test me, nephew." The pair glared at each other.

"Knock it off, Craig. It's three against one." I tried to diffuse the situation. "I think we're all overtired and getting hangry. Take a load off. I'll go fetch some pastries from the VIP lounge that we can munch on until room service arrives. Rodrigo, the menu is on the kitchen counter by the fridge. Can you place the order while I go down the hall?"

"My pleasure." He brandished the menu booklet. "What do you want?"

"Get one of everything." I slid into my flip-flops.

Fifteen minutes later, Mike returned to find the four of us sitting at the dining table, wolfing down croissants and fruit.

"Hey, honey, we ordered some food, and Rodrigo put on a fresh pot of coffee. Are you hungry? Would you like a croissant or some melon? This cantaloupe is delicious." I held up a forked piece of the juicy fruit.

Mike surveyed our little crew.

Rodrigo swallowed a mouthful of pastry. "Did Josh get off okay with Mr. and Mrs. Smith?"

"Yes. K.C., may I speak with you in the other room?" he requested in a hard voice.

Uh-oh. The moment I've been dreading. "Sure." I scooted the chair back.

"Michael," Mrs. Thundermuffin said, rising to her feet, "I understand you're frustrated with Karina, but this isn't her fault."

"Maybe not, but I've no doubt she's thrown herself headfirst into danger without giving it a second thought. *And* without calling me for help. I came here expecting to find her drinking mojitos on the beach! Instead, I find two people duct taped to chairs, her neighbor, coworker, a thief" —he indicated each person— "and a questionable security specialist, hatching plots in her hotel room. Not to mention the mess of bandaged injuries she apparently received during a stampede from a bombing at a local tourist attraction. Which, by the way, is trending on international news."

Ah, I see now. Everything came into focus with that statement. Not only was he angry I'd gotten into mischief in Mexico, but I hadn't bothered to contact him when the shit hit the fan. Outrageous, considering he'd volunteered for a case, and getting in contact with him while he, was God knows where, was tenuous at best. I thought he'd thawed toward the Silverthorne guys, but maybe today's debacle pushed his limited patience too far.

"It wasn't a bomb, dear, it was an incendiary device. Really, people need to get their facts straight," Mrs. Thundermuffin said mildly as she sank back down into her chair.

I'm not sure the explanation made anything better. "C'mon, Mike." I took his hand. "Let's go to my room where you can yell at me in private."

He followed me, shutting the door gently behind us. I released his hand and went to sit on the spindle-back chair by the window. Crossing my ankles, I primly placed my hands on my lap and gave Mike my "interested neutrality" look. "You wished to say something?"

"What the—how did—can you . . ." He ran a hand through his dark locks in frustration. "I don't know where to start."

"Which question is bothering you the most? Begin there," I suggested helpfully.

"What the hell is going on between you and Joshua?"

I couldn't help it. I burst out laughing because it was the furthest thing from what I'd expected.

"Damn it, K.C., I think I deserve an answer!"

I sobered with a sigh. "What on earth do you think is going on? Josh is like a big brother. He has saved my ass on more than one occasion. You must be out of your mind if you think there is anything remotely romantic going on. With Josh?" I rolled my eyes. "No."

Mike's stiff posture deflated, and he muttered, "Why the devil didn't you call me?"

I rubbed my temple. "Ah, hell, Mike, you're so unreachable when you're on one of those cases. And frankly, we found ourselves in a world of shit so quickly, I didn't have time to wait until you got around to checking your messages. Moreover, I didn't want to leave another freaky voice mail—I've done it too many times, and I know how much you hate it. I called Silverthorne for advice about swapping Mrs. T. for the mask. Rick sent Josh and Hernandez out here on his own. I didn't ask them to come." I tilted my head in thought. "However, considering what happened at *Chichén Itzá*, I'll be the first to admit we were lucky to have them. Josh's medical experience came in handy patching me up." I stared ruefully at my bandaged knees. "Now tell me, what are we doing about Craig?"

He sat on the edge of the bed. "I have a pair of agents arriving to take custody of him."

"Good. Because he's getting antsy, and I think if he gets a chance, he'll bolt."

Mike nodded in agreement.

"Is he being taken into custody?"

"Yes. The paperwork is completed for his deal, but until the Schaffhausen issue comes to a satisfactory conclusion, he will remain a guest of the FBI."

"Do you have to leave with Craig and the other agents?" My fingers played with a fraying hem on my shorts.

"No. Once I turn him over, I'm on vacation."

I stopped playing with the hem and eyed him. "So you plan to stay here? With me?"

His head tilted. "Unless that's a problem."

"No, it's not a problem. However, you're not welcome to stay if you plan to berate me about this . . . uh . . . situation. If you can let it go, I think we'll have a lovely vacation together. Although, with this sunburn, I might have to spend more time under cover or inside."

Mike got a look in his eyes, one I knew well. "I bet I can think of a few things we can do inside." He wiggled his brows.

I allowed a smile to break through my reserve. "Well, alrighty then."

Our snogging session came to an abrupt end when Rodrigo banged on the door. "Hey, you two, the food has arrived. If you want something, you better get out here now before Craig eats it all."

Chapter Nineteen

The bright sun shone high overhead as Craig rode out of sight in the rear seat of a black sedan, cuffed and escorted by an FBI agent and an envoy from the American Consulate. Law enforcement was now in charge of him, and relief spread across my shoulders. Even though he'd never shown violence toward me during this misadventure, there was something about Craig that made my skin crawl.

Mrs. T., who had changed back into her clothes from the previous night, shared a tearful goodbye with her grandnephew, hugging him tightly as she whispered something in his ear. The agents gently parted her from Craig. To my surprise, he hadn't quibbled when it came to the handcuffs or going with the FBI. It might have helped that his aunt kept assuring him to go quietly, and "everything would be okay."

Even though Craig hadn't made a fuss, we'd still managed to gather a small crowd of gawkers.

Rodrigo waved his hands and said, "Nothing to see here folks. Off with you." He repeated the directions in Spanish, and the crowd dispersed.

The four of us retired to an empty covered lounge area on the second floor overlooking the pool. A waiter appeared from nowhere and took our drink orders—Mike and Rodrigo ordered beers, I requested a mojito, and Mrs. T. got a scotch on the rocks. Craig had given her his wristband, so she ordered a top shelf scotch. I didn't begrudge her the booze. She'd certainly been through hell this past week; she deserved the best.

"Here." Rodrigo tossed a small white box at me.

"What is it?" I caught the paper box with two hands and examined it. "Oh, Band-Aids. Thanks."

"I figured you'd want to downsize your big bandages in a day or two."

"Yes, I will." I waved it in the air, then put the box on the little round table between Mike's chair and mine.

The waiter arrived with our drinks.

"To sunny skies, ocean breezes, and a completely boring end to our vacation." Rodrigo held up his glass.

"I'll drink to that." I grinned.

"Here, here," Mrs. T. and Mike echoed, and we all tapped our glasses together.

The minty sweet combination went down the hatch. "So, what's next for you, Mrs. . . . uh, Milly?" I asked.

"My ride should be here within the hour." She rolled the glass between her hands.

I cocked my head. "Oh? Who? Where are you going?"

"Marcellus is on his way. My belongings are in Mérida. I'll spend a few days visiting Marcellus and his family before flying home."

"That sounds nice." I nodded.

She sipped her whiskey. "What about the three of you?"

"I fly out on Friday. So I have a little more than forty-eight hours of fun in the sun to enjoy," Rodrigo replied.

"My flight home is Monday." I turned to my FBI agent. "I don't know about Mike. Hon, when do you go home?"

"I got on your flight home Monday." He winked and took a pull on his beer.

"Nice." I wondered if I'd be sitting in first class again.

We chatted about this and that. Mrs. Thundermuffin told us a story about her cat, Mr. Tibbs. Mike regaled us with the herculean efforts it took to get him to Mexico this morning—

which included a thunderstorm in a helicopter, a missed commercial flight, and a harrowing flight on a small Cessna. As we talked, I realized Rodrigo offered less and less to the conversation. I spied him enviously watching the antics of a group of young twenty-somethings playing water polo in the pool below.

"Rodrigo," I said, giving his knee a pat to get his attention, "go change into your swimsuit and join them."

He glanced away from the crowd. "What? Oh. I couldn't leave you."

I gave a short laugh. "Yes. You can and you will. I order you to go have some fun. This vacation has turned into a disaster for you. Enjoy your last forty-eight hours to the fullest. Go. Now."

"Well . . ." he said hesitantly.

"I insist."

"If none of you mind . . ."

"Don't stay on my account, young man." Mrs. Thundermuffin made a shooing motion with her hands.

Rodrigo needed no more urging and speed-walked his way to the elevators.

"And then there were three," Mrs. T. said with amusement, watching his retreat.

Mike's phone buzzed with a text. Reading it, he muttered, "What the—"

"What's wrong?"

"The agent in charge texted. Craig just escaped custody. He picked his handcuffs with a paperclip and exited the vehicle at a busy intersection." Standing up, he dialed. "Excuse me. I have to make a call."

I turned to Mrs. Thundermuffin, who watched Mike's exit with the slightest hint of a smile hovering around her mouth. I remembered how she'd clutched Craig, showing him affection in a manner I hadn't seen since the two were put together last night.

Even after we'd recovered him, she'd shown no physical maternal instincts, instead whapping him on the head.

"Oh, Milly, you didn't."

Her forthright blue eyes turned to me, and in an offended tone, she said, "I beg your pardon."

Blushing, I turned away from her gaze. "N-nothing. Never mind. I-I . . . nothing—"

A squawking ring interrupted my embarrassment. Mrs. Thundermuffin pulled an old-fashioned flip phone out of her pants pocket. "Marcellus will be here in fifteen minutes. Do you mind if we return to your room, so I can brush my hair and use the bathroom?"

"Yes, of course." We walked past Mike, who stood with the phone to his ear not far from the elevators. "We are going upstairs," I mouthed, and pointed up.

He nodded and held up five fingers, indicating he'd join us in a few minutes.

After Mrs. T. cleaned up, I accompanied her back down to the front entrance, where we found Marcellus waiting by the passenger door.

"*Tia!*" His arms opened wide and she entered the bear hug. They greeted each other in Spanish.

She laughed.

He grinned widely before turning to me. "Thank you for finding her."

Before I knew it, those thick arms wrapped themselves around me, and I winced as they squeezed my bruised side. "Oof, you're welcome, Marcellus."

"Marcellus, ease up. She's been injured," Mrs. Thundermuffin gently chastised.

He immediately released me with profuse apologies.

"It's fine," I assured him, relieved to be released. "I'm glad you're here to take her back to Mérida."

"Of course," he said, as if he had nothing else to do today.

Mrs. T. came over and took my hands in hers. "I can't thank you enough." She stood on tiptoe and kissed both of my cheeks.

"You're welcome. I'll see you back in D.C."

"Until then, dearie."

Marcellus held the door open for her and she climbed in. Before returning to the driver's side, he took my right hand in both of his, pressing something into it. "Here is my business card. If you need anything while you are in Mexico. Anything. You call me. I am here to help." Like his *tía,* he kissed my blushing cheeks. "Take care, *señorita.*"

"You too, Marcellus."

As he lumbered around the front of the car, my neighbor rolled down her window. I leaned down to hear what she was saying. "Don't think too harshly of my nephew. I had to help him. After all, he is my sister's grandson." The window slid upward, and the car drove away before I could think of a response.

I reentered the lobby, chewing my lip, and tried to decide if she meant helping him with the mask, or if I'd been correct in my original assessment—that she'd provided the means of his escape from the FBI.

"There you are!" Glancing to my right, I found Mike striding toward me. "I went to the room, but you'd already gone. Did I miss saying goodbye to your neighbor?"

"Yes, she's headed out with Marcellus. What's the situation with Craig?"

"It's out of my hands." He shrugged. "The agents who had custody of him are organizing a search with local police."

I cocked my head. "Does that mean you're free?"

"It does." He placed a gentle hand on my lower back. "What shall we do for the rest of the afternoon?"

It only took a few seconds for me to decide. "I need to feel the sand between my toes."

Hand-in-hand, we walked through the hotel, past the pool area, and down onto the beach. Mike spotted a couple vacating a cabana-style lounger for two. We curled up on it together, pulling the sunshade around us. My head lay on his chest, while one of his arms tucked behind his head, and the other curved around my shoulder.

I heard his breaths exiting and entering his lungs beneath my ear. Up and down. "Mike, I've been wondering . . ."

"Yes?"

"What did Craig do with the money that Schaffhausen paid him?"

The breathing stopped for a moment. "He gave us a numbered account in the Bahamas."

"Is the FBI going to confiscate it?"

"We were only going to do so if the Schaffhausen raid goes wrong. Now that he's on the run, the Bureau will be making efforts to freeze and watch the money should he try to access it."

I sat up. "You mean, if the Schaffhausen deal goes as planned, he was supposed to keep his dirty money?"

Mike's mouth twisted. "It's not a perfect world, Karina."

"How much money is in there?"

"Craig told us there was over a hundred thousand. The FBI is making arrangements to verify and freeze the assets now."

"Did he give you the codes to get into the safe?"

"He did."

"Well, I guess *that is* something." I yawned and returned to my comfy spot on his chest. As I watched a gray-haired gentleman in red trunks wade in the shallow waters, I debated telling Mike my rather far out theory regarding Mrs. Thundermuffin providing Craig the means to escape. I had absolutely no evidence. Even her final comments weren't a clear admission and could be interpreted in a variety of manners. The gray-haired man bent down to pick up a shell. I yawned again, feeling the fatigue from the past few days catching up. "I'm going to close my eyes for just a moment."

"Okay. Me too."

Chapter Twenty

After a brief nap, Mike changed into his swim trunks and spent time boogie boarding in the ocean. I stayed behind underneath the sunshade, reading my book and occasionally wading in the shallows to cool off. By the time he returned, I was sitting crisscross applesauce, with a nice little collection of flat white scallop shells and a few small pink conchs spread around me. Dripping wet, he shook all over me like a dog.

"Mike!" I squealed, turning my face away from the flying water.

He laughed, grabbing a towel. "Whatcha got there?"

I removed my sunglasses and wiped off the drops with the tail of my T-shirt. "Just a few mementos from the sea. How was your swim?"

"Fabulous. Maybe by tomorrow your injuries will be doing better and you can go in."

"I hope so. Your phone has been binging and buzzing for the past few minutes. You'd better check it out."

I held the phone out to him. As he read through the assortment of texts, a frown settled on his face.

"Now what?" I asked.

"It seems that Craig is a rather smart young man. He managed to elude our efforts at the airports, train, and bus stations by renting a motorboat."

"A boat! Well—but weren't you watching the marinas?"

He gave a snort. "Do you have any idea how many marinas there are between here and Playa del Carmen?"

"Lots?"

"Lots and lots. We've been watching his credit cards."

"Well, he can't be that smart if he used a credit card," I scoffed.

"To the contrary, he stole a wallet off of a very inebriated young man who looks rather similar to our friend Craig. The man reported the theft to local police half an hour ago, and we got a hit on one of his credit cards."

"At the marina where Craig rented the boat?"

"Yes."

"I suppose that's good. How long ago did he rent the boat?" Mike glared at me. "Three hours."

"Oh? Do you think he's taking the boat to the Bahamas?"

"That is the hope." His gaze returned to the phone.

"Well, you'll either catch him when he gasses up at the next stop, or when he gets to the Bahamas to get his money out of the bank," I reasoned. "What? What's that look for?"

"The FBI froze the account."

"In the Bahamas? Wasn't that the plan?"

"There's only five thousand dollars in it."

I sucked wind. "What happened to the rest? Did he already access the account before you were able to lock it down?"

Mike shook his head. "There haven't been any transactions on the account since it was opened a year ago, when the original five thousand was deposited."

"So . . . Craig lied about the amount? I don't get it."

His jaw flexed.

"Mike?"

"Either he never had a hundred thousand, or this is an account he opened with plans to use it at a later date," he said with frustration.

"Like the next time he got paid for a theft."

"Precisely."

"So, the question now becomes—does he actually have a bunch of money stashed away and, if so, where is it?" When Mike didn't respond, I continued, "There are an awful lot of little islands in the Caribbean with banks where he could have left it."

He grimaced and stared hard at me. "It's almost uncanny how you speak the exact words I'm thinking."

"Can he get to any of those islands without stopping for gas?"

"Surveillance video showed Craig loading extra tanks of gas aboard before shipping out."

"Oh, boy." I grimaced. "How far can he get on those tanks?"

"Further than I'd like."

Mike tossed the phone down on the lounger in disgust.

"Does this mean your vacation is over? Do you have to go to work?"

He let out a puff of air and scratched his chin. "No. There are other agents working on it now. They are keeping me informed as a courtesy."

I drummed my fingers against my leg. "Are you going to be able to relax if you're not a part of it?"

"It's probably better if I *do* stay out of it." He slid onto the lounger next to my array of seashells and distractedly fidgeted with one of the conchs.

"Hmm," I said as I licked my lips. "I can probably think of some things to do that would take your mind off of it." Interested, he looked up from the shells. "But we have to leave the beach. I wouldn't want to get arrested for indecent exposure. It probably wouldn't look good on your resume either." I winked.

In a quick movement, Mike swept the shells into my beach bag and tossed the rest of our items in after them willy-nilly.

"Mike! My shells!" I cried, reaching for the bag.

He held the bag away and gave me a hard kiss. "I'll get you more tomorrow. C'mon."

I laughingly gave in and allowed him to pull me off the lounger.

Chapter Twenty-One

"Rodrigo, I'm so glad you enjoyed your day." I sipped the last of my white wine.

Rodrigo agreed to join Mike and me for dinner at the seafood restaurant on the top floor. He'd just finished telling us about the group of people from Kansas that he'd hung out with all day. They'd spent the afternoon on a snorkeling excursion, which Rodrigo loved. It made my heart lighten, knowing he'd gotten something good out of today. I didn't want to bog him down with Craig's escape. Before dinner, Mike and I agreed not to discuss the latest developments on the case in front of him. Sometimes ignorance was indeed bliss.

I sat between the two men in my new green sundress. I'd removed the bulky gauze pads and downsized to the flexible Band-Aids Rodrigo had provided me. There were two each on my knees and one on my elbow. They did a better job blending into my newly tanned skin tones. Mike had kind of freaked out when he saw the bruise on my side. It looked even worse today, and I knew I'd be wearing my one-piece bathing suit instead of my bikinis for the rest of the trip.

"What time are you meeting up with your new crew tonight?" Mike asked, picking through the lobster carcass on his plate, searching for any missed pieces of meat.

"We're meeting in the lobby at ten and heading to Coco Bongo. Do you two want to come?"

"Um, I'm not sure. Mike, I think you ate everything that lobster had to give," I said with a small laugh, and he looked longingly to my plate. "No luck here, pal. I know how to strip a lobster down to the bare shell. Do you want to go to Coco Bongo?"

With a sad sigh, Mike gave up on the lobster. "Where is it?"

"Downtown. Not far from the shopping area. We plan to take a taxi," Rodrigo replied. "You know, it's all inclusive, you can order another lobster if you want."

Tilting his head, Mike gave the suggestion some thought. "No," he said, shaking his head, "I'll have dessert instead. Did you see the cart when we came in?"

"I did. I've been thinking about that chocolate torte since we sat down. But after the lobster, I'm not sure I can do it," I said sadly, holding a hand to my full stomach.

The waiter came to remove our plates. "Would you like some dessert?"

"I'll have the flan," Rodrigo ordered without a second thought. "It's my favorite. Oh, and a cup of coffee."

Mike looked expectantly at me, but I shook my head and moaned, "There is no way I'll finish it."

"I'll have the chocolate torte and the fruit tart." Mike winked at me. "You can have a bite of mine."

The waiter nodded and walked away.

I rolled my eyes. "Okay, maybe one bite." I held up my pointer finger.

"So, Coco Bongo? Are you two lovebirds in?" Rodrigo asked, slugging back the last of his beer.

"Well . . ." The long days, short nights, and stressful adventures had worn on me. Even today's nap did little to dispel the fatigue. Not to mention, the lovely mellow feeling the two glasses of wine I'd polished off over dinner were having on me. However, if Mike was up for it, I'd order a coffee and head out on the town. After all, I was wearing an awesome party dress. "I suppose . . . if you want to go out, Mike, I'm on board."

Mike let out an enormous yawn. The yawn was contagious, and I mimicked it while he spoke, "Not to be a party pooper, but I've had a hell of a day. Even though we got in a nap, I barely slept last night trying to get here. There's a sign in the lobby that said they are having live music in the second-floor lounge. I'd rather do something more low-key . . . if you don't mind."

"No, I'm fine with that." I turned to my coworker. "Sorry, Rodrigo. Are you going to be all right with your new friends?"

"Karina, you know me," he said with a grin, "I've never met a stranger."

"Too true. Go out and have fun. You only have a few more nights to par-tay. Oh, that reminds me, your hat got crushed the other day when all hell broke loose at *Chichén Itzá*." I leaned down and pulled a brown bag from beneath the table. "You tried this one on when we were getting clothes for Craig, and I thought it would make a nice replacement."

He pulled the straw boater hat with a green and navy band out of the bag. "Aw, thanks, Karina. This is great." He plopped it on his head. "How does it look?"

It made me grin. "Very dapper, indeed."

Mike nodded in approval. "That's a nice-looking hat. Did they have more? I only have a baseball cap. I could use a straw hat."

I took his hand. "They have many to choose from. We'll find something for you tomorrow morning, before we sign up to go snorkeling."

"Are you going to be up for snorkeling tomorrow?" Mike asked skeptically.

"Once I get a decent night's sleep, I'll be up for anything."

Mike's phone jingled and I tensed. It was the ringtone he used for his work contacts. He glanced at the screen and excused himself.

Rodrigo watched as he exited the restaurant. "What do you suppose that is about?"

I frowned. "It's work."

"Hm, I wonder if the Schaffhausen plan has gone into action."

"I wonder," I replied faintly.

"Ah, here's our dessert." He rubbed his hands together with delight.

By the time Mike returned, Rodrigo and I had taken tastes from each dish, and he was polishing off his flan.

"Mike, do you like flan? There is one bite left. No? Okay, then." Rodrigo popped the last bite in his mouth. "Mmm, so creamy, it's sinful." He smacked his lips.

"Nah, my money is on this chocolate thingy. Oh. My. Gawd. Mike." I held out a forkful. "You've got to get in on this. It's practically orgasmic."

Smiling, Mike sat down and spread the napkin across his lap. "Seeing as it's *my* dessert, I suppose I should give it a try," he teased, and took the bite I held out. "Wow, that is rich." After wiping his mouth, he continued, "While you two were devouring my desserts, I was getting the good news."

I paused with a forkful of cake mid-air. "What news?"

"Schaffhausen and his two associates have been arrested and a few hundred million dollars' worth of stolen artwork has been recovered." The hint of a smile hovered around his mouth.

"The sting? It worked?" Rodrigo pushed his empty plate away.

"It did indeed." The hint turned into a full-on beam.

I grabbed Mike's hand. "The original mask that Craig stole, was it in there?"

"It was." He squeezed my fingers.

"How exciting. What a win for the Brazilian Museum to get an artifact returned that they thought had burned in the fire. When will the FBI return it?"

Mike's hand slid out of mine and he picked up his fork.

"Um . . . I'm not sure."

"It's evidence in a case. *Will* the FBI return it?" Rodrigo asked. "Will they return any of it?"

Of course, I'd gotten ahead of myself. The artwork would be tied up in the FBI's case for possibly years.

"Eventually, all of the stolen items will be returned to their former owners."

"But you don't know when," I clarified with censure in my tone.

Mike gave me a hard stare. "Not at this time, K.C." I harrumphed and he frowned. "The case is out of my hands. There are protocols that will be followed. Chain of evidence is vital for a case like this. Don't worry, once word gets out, museums and private collectors who have been defrauded will be banging on the FBI's door to get their items returned. It will all work out in the end. It will simply take time."

Mildly mollified, I took another bite of the torte. "Was it where Craig said it would be?"

"Yes. The DEA has been surveilling the villa for the past three months. They almost messed up our raid, but cooler heads prevailed, and, after some high-level posturing, it turned into a joint taskforce. Schaffhausen's computer seems to be a goldmine of information, and since we're playing nice, the DEA and FBI are sharing the information. Schaffhausen will be out of the money laundering business for good."

"What's the problem with DEA?" Rodrigo forked a strawberry off the fruit tart. "I thought FBI and DEA worked together."

Mike delivered the side-eye. "There is a saying in the business that the only thing the CIA and FBI can agree upon is that they all hate the DEA."

"I don't get it. Why the animosity? Aren't you all on the same team? You all fall under Homeland Security," I replied naïvely.

Mike sighed, "It's an ingrained habit that goes back far, and includes politics and cross agendas. Agents work fine with one another. The 'agencies' are another matter."

Rodrigo sipped his coffee. "Whatever the case, it sounds like everyone got what they wanted. The information Craig supplied *was* true."

Mike delivered a rueful smile. "It was."

"That should make his Aunt Milly happy. It turns out Craig wasn't a complete crap weasel. All's well that ends well." Mike and I exchanged a look that Rodrigo missed as he raised his hand to flag down a passing waiter. "A bottle of champagne, *por favor*."

****

The Mariachi Band in the lounge was top notch, and very loud. However, I couldn't keep my eyes open any longer. As a matter of fact, I dozed off and fell against Mike's shoulder. At the end of the set, Mike made a unilateral decision to call it a night. His arm curved around me as I contentedly leaned against him on our ride up the elevator.

"Wait a minute." Exiting the elevator, I turned right, rather than left toward my room. "The VIP lounge has these chocolate chip cookies to *die* for. Let me get a few." I tugged Mike into the salon and waved at the concierge manning the room. "Hi."

"May I help you?" The uniformed man rose from behind the desk.

"I wanted to get some of the cookies," I said, pointing to the sideboard, which held a coffee carafe and a platter of sweets.

"Of course, allow me." He pulled out a small white baggie and loaded half a dozen cookies inside, then handed it over. "Enjoy your evening." He smiled and gave us a slight bow.

"Thanks."

I listed against Mike, carrying our treats as we trekked down the hall to the Lady of Tikal suite. After handing him my little purse to search for the keycard, I reclined sleepily against the wall.

"You sure can shove a lot of crap in this tiny bag. What is this?"

I opened my eyes. "Some sort of Mexican breath spray. Do I need it?" I breathed out, sniffed, and stiffened. There was a scent that sent my pulse racing.

"Your breath is fine. It smells like wine. Mine probably does too." He continued to search the bag, finally locating the keycard. "Ah, here we are."

Sobered and wide awake, I pushed upright. "Mike! Wait!" I stayed his hand before he could put the card in the slot. I took another whiff. "Do you smell that?"

Mike drew in a deep breath. "Very faintly. Perfume?"

"Men's cologne."

"What about it?"

"It's the same cologne the Dinapoli brothers wore at the exchange. The question is, which one?" I tapped my temple.

"Or . . . it could just be one of your neighbors." Mike quirked a brow at me and pointed to the doors across the hall and the one at the end.

"You think I'm being paranoid?"

"I think you've had a hell of a week. Your senses are over heightened and looking for trouble around every corner. Think. Are you positive that is the *exact* same cologne?"

"Um . . . ninety—" Mike frowned at me and my confidence dropped. "—eighty percent positive?"

He took a beat and his jaw flexed. "I'll tell you what, I will enter first and make sure the apartment is clear. Will that make you feel better?"

"Here." I took my purse back and dug my hand straight to the bottom. "You better take this with you. It's a stun gun."

His mouth twisted. "I thought Joshua took all his toys."

"I might have kept this behind." I shrugged. "You never know."

"I suppose when it comes to your world, that is the truth." Mike took the weapon and entered. "Your lights are on. Did you leave them on?"

"Turn down service leaves some of the lamps burning. It's a nice touch, don't you think?" I asked, peering over his shoulder. The lamp on the foyer table let off a soft glow.

Mike crept further into the apartment, checking left and right.

"Do you see anything?" I whispered.

"Not yet," he replied in low tones. "Everything looks normal in the living room. I'll check the spare bedroom. Wait there."

I allowed the door to close gently behind me and placed my handbag and cookies on the table. "Anything?"

"Not yet." I heard him open the bathroom door.

Sniffing, I could still smell the weak scent of the cologne, but I couldn't tell if that's because it was in my suite, or if it was stuck in my nostrils from the hallway. A faint click had my attention turning to my right. The light didn't throw far, and the closet remained in the shadows. I squinted.

Is the door moving? "Mi-ike . . ." I whimpered.

The door burst open. A man erupted out of the closet like a rabid dog, and, with an unintelligible yell, he charged me. I stepped to my left, grabbed his outstretched right hand with both of mine, and pushed his fingers and wrist backward. He went down to his knees. I took that hand around front and wrapped him in a choke hold. Mike rushed out of the bedroom at the commotion, but it all happened in an instant, and I had the intruder under control by the time he entered the foyer.

"Who the hell is this joker?"

"This" —I tugged the chokehold a little tighter, and he gagged— "is Adolfo. *Not* the brother I was expecting. Quick, search the rest of the apartment. His other two brothers won't be as easy to subdue."

While I held Adolfo in a viselike grip, Mike rushed through

the rest of the suite—stun gun at the ready—checking closets, bathrooms, behind furniture, and any other nooks where a human being might hide.

"Jesus, did you bathe in that cologne? I thought your brother was the one who wore it." I turned my head aside from the onslaught of odor.

"He . . . is," Adolfo gasped out, and I loosened my grip slightly. "The bottle spilled," he let out in a whoosh.

I tsked. "You should have washed. The scent gave you away."

Mike returned and forced Adolfo to lay flat on the floor. "Josh left the duct tape behind." He held up the half-used silver roll.

"Don't move." I placed my high heel against our intruder's neck while Mike trussed him up. Adolfo went limp in defeat.

"How on earth did he get in here? I'm supposed to be on the safest floor of this building," I cried, throwing up my hands. "For that matter, how is *everyone* getting up here, much less into my room? Hernandez, Mr. and Mrs. Smith, hell, even you got onto my floor." I listed off. "How did you know what room I was in? I didn't tell you—did I?"

Mike turned Adolfo onto his back and rummaged through his pockets. For the first time, I realized he wore the top half of the resort's bellhop uniform. It didn't surprise me when Mike pulled a plain white keycard from one of the pockets and passed it to me. A small black alphanumeric code was etched at the bottom.

"Another hotel passkey?"

"Looks like it. Up with you." Mike pulled Adolfo to his feet.

"Cripes, I might as well post an 'Open for Business' sign on my door." I flipped the key onto the foyer table.

"Where do you want him?"

"Put him in the dining room."

Mike shoved him onto a chair at the foot of the table. Adolfo did not look happy. As a matter of fact, his crumpled face looked as though he was about to cry.

"Should we expect more company? Will your brothers be joining us, Adolfo?" I leaned over his shoulder.

He shook his head and whispered, "What did you do with it? Did Craig take it?"

I sat to his right. "The death mask? It's not here." My gaze scanned the room, and I noticed small things out of place. One of the kitchen cabinets remained slightly open. The ficus plant had been moved to the right and the baby grand piano lid, which had been closed during my stay, was now propped open. "Which I'm sure you've figured out, since you've already searched the place."

"Craig promised. He *promised* me."

"What did Craig promise you?" Mike sat on the other side of our prisoner.

Adolfo sniffed. "He promised to pay me. All I had to do was keep it out of my brothers' hands. I had it at the ruins and he took it from me."

"Adolfo," I said kindly, "why didn't Craig pay you sooner? He'd already sold the original and received payment."

Adolfo's pitiful eyes, brimming with unshed tears, squinted up at me. "He wasn't paid in cash. He said he had to liquidate the assets."

Mike leaned forward. "Assets? What kind? Diamonds? Jewels? Drugs?"

"Not drugs. He assured me of that." Adolfo shook his head. "I don't know if it was diamonds. He wouldn't explain. He just said that he needed to be back in the states before the end of August — when he'd be able to liquidate them."

"Liquidate how? At an auction?" Mike pressed.

Adolfo shrugged. "Auction? Expo? Fence to a buyer? I don't know. Craig wasn't very forthcoming."

I tried a different tactic. "Adolfo, where are your brothers?"

"They were called back to Italy."

"Called back? By whom?"

"My father. They work for his import business. Once you texted them the FBI was involved, they figured Craig got pinched and gave up on the escapade. Only . . . my debt still needs to be paid."

"I see. And you were hoping . . . what? To find Craig? The mask?" I shifted, crossing my legs.

"Any of those things." He stared miserably at the tabletop.

I waited for Mike to say something, but when he didn't, I continued, "What's your relationship with Craig? How did the two of you meet?"

"We met at the Royal College of Art, in London. I was working on my graduate diploma in art and design. Craig was on summer holiday from Oxford, where he was studying archeology and anthropology. He was taking a curating course at the Royal College." Adolfo threw back his head, and his long hair hung down behind the chair as he glared at the ceiling. "Our professor asked graduate students to teach a few classes while he traveled to Copenhagen. In the biggest mistake of my life, I befriended Craig."

I bit my lip to keep from laughing at the poor boy's dramatics. "How many 'jobs' have you done with Craig?"

Adolfo didn't answer, simply shaking his head.

"Was this the first time?" Mike asked.

His eyes scrunched shut. "This was the first time. Craig had gotten me a couple of commissions replicating other artifacts for legitimate buyers. The work paid the bills while I waited for my own art to take off. I thought my copy of the funerary mask was supposed to go to the buyer." He opened his eyes wide and faced forward. "It wasn't until later . . . I found out the truth."

I couldn't decide if I believed him. "You'd best give it up. The FBI has the mask, and Craig . . ." I glanced up at Mike.

". . . is in custody," he finished for me.

Adolfo's features crumpled.

Mike folded his hands together. "Adolfo, do you know where Craig keeps his monetary holdings? His bank accounts?"

The kid lifted his shoulders. My fingers tapped out an irritated drumbeat, but then he perked up and said, "I remember that he spent a Christmas in Grand Cayman with his mother."

"When?" Mike rested his chin in his palm.

Adolfo searched his mind. "I would say 2012, maybe 2013."

Pulling the phone from his pocket, Mike excused himself and departed to the balcony.

Once the door closed, Adolfo returned his attention to me. "What will you do?"

My brows rose. "Do? About what?"

His face returned to misery, and those big brown eyes sheened over. "With me? Turn me over to the police?"

I gazed at Adolfo. The damn fool had allowed himself to be led on a merry chase by Craig. I swore, if I ever saw Craig again, I would slap the shiznit out of him. Too many lives had been disrupted by his tricks. Sighing, I answered, "I'm not sure. You see, that man out on my balcony is an FBI agent. And it's going to be up to him to determine your fate. I'm afraid there's not much I can do."

Speaking of the devil, Mike reentered the suite. "There is a team en route to take custody of Adolfo."

"Is that really necessary?" I asked.

Mike's eyes bugged out at me.

"What? He didn't hurt me. He's taken nothing from the suite." I spread my hand open, palm up.

"How about kidnapping? Conspiracy? Breaking and entering?" he listed off. "Not to mention INTERPOL has a Red Notice on him. K.C., he attacked you!"

I grimaced with embarrassment over allowing this twerp to

con me with his sad pound puppy eyes. He *did* lie to me. Steal the mask from me. Attack me. The wine must have gone to my head. I stiffened my spine. "Right. Sorry, kid. Nothing I can do."

The misery turned to anger faster than the flip of a dime. *"Vaffenculo!"*

"Watch your language," Mike reprimanded.

I wasn't sure what that meant, but I had a fair idea. All my pity dissolved in the face of his hatred. "Temper, temper." I shook a finger at him.

Adolfo, much like Craig, left the resort in custody. Only this time, since Adolfo wasn't an American citizen, he left under the hands of some very nice INTERPOL agents and local police.

****

Mike and I lay on the balcony lounge chairs, admiring the twinkling stars overhead while eating the most sinful chocolate chip cookies I've ever tasted.

"How many fakes do you think he's really designed for Craig?" I asked.

"More than one. I don't believe for a minute this was his first."

"No?"

"As a matter of fact," Mike mused, "I'm wondering if we'll find more of Craig and Adolfo's handiwork among Schaffhausen's stash."

I rolled on my side to face Mike. "Do you think he knows how to find Craig?"

"He likely has some sort of information that could be valuable. We have contacts in the Caymans on alert. I expect INTERPOL will share any information they get out of him."

"You're sure INTERPOL will share?"

He sighed, "No."

I waited for Mike to elaborate. When he didn't, I changed the subject. "You never did explain how you found out my room number."

He slowly chewed a cookie and swallowed.

"Mike?"

"I. . . uh . . . hacked the hotel's database."

I rolled my eyes. "*Mike!* Really! Wouldn't it have been easier to text and ask me?"

"I had some time on my hands during the flight. And I wanted to surprise you," he cried in a defensive tone.

I snorted with derision. "I'm not sure who was more surprised, you or me."

"Touché." He held up a half-eaten cookie.

"Okay, so you knew the floor. How did you get up to the tenth floor without a keycard? Or did you steal one?"

"I rode up with a nice couple staying in room 1021. They are celebrating their fortieth anniversary."

"Was it just luck?"

He rolled his head back and forth on the lounge pillow. "No, I overheard the wife tell the front desk to bring up a package they were expecting."

"You were eavesdropping!"

"I wouldn't say that. She spoke rather loudly. I'm fairly certain anyone within a hundred-yard radius heard her room number. I . . . uh . . . rode up with them."

"Cripes. Is there *any* security on this floor?"

"If I were you, I'd be more worried about the nefarious characters you've been gathering in your wake."

"True." I tapped a finger against my chin. "I wonder if Adolfo's brothers actually left Mexico as he claimed."

"According to my sources, they boarded a flight this morning on Air Italia, stopping over in Madrid. Look!" Mike pointed to the sky. "A shooting star."

I ignored his attempted diversion. "Then I won't be having anymore unexpected guests drop by?"

Turning away from the heavens, he sent me a stern glance. "You tell me."

"You're right. Let's go through the list. I'm assuming the FBI picked up Mr. and Mrs. Smith during their raid of Schaffhausen's place."

"Correct."

"Adolfo walked out with your friends from INTERPOL, and I assume their agents will be a little more diligent in retaining the suspect in custody than the FBI's efforts."

Mike winced, acknowledging the hit.

"You said Adolfo's brothers have left the country." I ticked off each suspect. "And, while I don't trust Craig, there is no benefit for him to return here. Especially with you in residence. So, I do believe we are out of nefarious characters who might leave their calling card."

"What about your Silverthorne pals?"

"Josh? Hernandez? Pft. No, they decamped upon your arrival. Probably glad to wash their hands of me. Hmm, now that I think about it, it's probably a good thing Josh and Hernandez weren't here to deal with Adolfo." My mind recalled our harrowing ride through the Mexican jungle.

"Oh?"

"I don't think they were too pleased with any of the Dinapoli crew. Adolfo might not have left with his face intact."

Mike didn't respond for a few minutes and I wondered if I would be getting another lecture about Silverthorne's questionable tactics. "Speaking of Silverthorne—"

"And here it comes," I muttered.

"—who taught you those moves?"

Taken by surprise, I gaped for a moment before regrouping. "You mean, the one I used on Adolfo?"

Mike nodded.

"I believe it was Jin. He's taught me some very good self-defense tricks to use against an attacker. Although, Adolfo is clearly inexperienced when it comes to hand-to-hand combat. A ten-year-old could have taken him down." I popped the final bit of cookie into my piehole and chewed. "No, it isn't the move that I am proud of. It's my quick thinking. He came at me like the Tasmanian devil. I guess Josh was right, if I don't allow the fear to take over, the training will kick in when I need it." I yawned. "What time is it?"

Mike checked his phone. "Half past midnight."

"I do believe the adrenaline has finally worn off. I'm hitting an energy low." I reached across and took his hand as another yawn escaped.

He tugged me to my feet. "Come on. Time for bed, Rip Van Winkle."

Chapter Twenty-Two

My eyes flew open, and I gasped as the nightmare retreated. Mike slept peacefully, curled on his side, his back toward me, and I had the sudden urge to whack him over the head with my pillow. Did you ever wake from a dream angry at someone, and even though you know it was a dream, you're still pissed? I'd been back at *Chichén Itzá,* running through ruins, which kept shifting into different maze patterns, searching for my sister and Mike, who'd been carrying on an affair behind my back. I blinked and checked the clock, which read 8:43. As the cobwebs of the dream dissipated, so did my irrational anger, and I snuggled deeper under the covers to get more rest.

My eyes opened again at the bing-bong-bing of the doorbell, and I wondered if it was the reason for my original awakening. Mike didn't move. His breathing remained steady and even. The bell rang again. I sighed and flung off the covers. The cool air conditioning blew against my naked skin, causing goose bumps, and I dragged my beach cover-up over my head for modesty's sake, before trudging to the front door. The peephole revealed the hotel security director, David Ortiz-Marin, on the other side.

Oh, boy.

"Hello, can I help you?" I pushed a hank of hair aside.

"I apologize, did I wake you?"

"Yes, but it's fine. What can I do for you?" It wasn't fine, and I don't know why I said it was. Deeply ingrained social convention, I presumed.

"I wanted to make sure you had no more issues with your new room."

I took a beat, trying to decide whether to answer or laugh. "You mean any problems . . . like, so far today?" I shook my head. "Not yet, but the day is still early. Why?"

He cleared his throat and puffed up his chest. "We've been reviewing security footage and are hearing about . . . strange activity on this floor. Men have been escorted out by law enforcement."

I'll bet you have. So many people had come in and out of this room in the past few days, I could field a baseball team. Crossing my arms, I affixed "interested neutrality" on my face and waited for him to elaborate.

He fidgeted with the clipboard he carried. "Perhaps you can provide an explanation?"

Yawning, I shook my head. "The men who broke into my room were captured. Otherwise, I think we're good." I began to close the door, then paused. "Wait, I would recommend that your staff do a better job keeping track of their keycards." I swept the keycard Adolfo had stolen off the foyer table and slapped it into the security director's hand.

His mouth dropped, but whatever he was about to say got cut off when I shut the door in his face.

I climbed back into bed, and Mike rolled over to spoon around me. "Who was at the door?"

"Why, you stinker, you *were* awake." I pushed my cold feet against his shins, and he shifted them away.

"I woke when you opened the bedroom door." He nuzzled my neck. "Who was it?"

"Hotel security, wondering if everything was all right with my room."

It took a moment for that to sink in. The bed shook with Mike's silent laughter.

"He was expecting an explanation for my revolving door of freak shows. I told him to talk to the staff about keeping better track of their keycards. It's not yet nine. I want to get another hour of sleep before we get up."

"Fine with me."

It was well after ten before we finally rolled out of bed, and there hadn't been much sleeping going on in that hour. For the first time in days, I felt refreshed and ready for some fun. We put on our swimsuits and cover-ups and headed down to get some *huevos rancheros* and coffee at the Oasis, an open-air restaurant located at the far end of one of the pools. I texted Rodrigo where we were eating and invited him to meet us if he was awake and functional. He shuffled up wearing wrinkled shorts, sunglasses, and bed head as the waitress laid our plates in front of us.

"Well, this is a surprise," I said.

"*Café, por favor*," he croaked, and plopped into the chair on my left. "You texted me to join you. Right?"

"Yes, of course, but I didn't actually expect you to be coherent yet. I suspect you were out late partying."

"We got back around three in the morning." He thanked the waitress as she placed a steaming cup of dark brew in front of him. "Only one day left. I didn't want to sleep it away."

"About that." I chewed my lip. "I do have an extra bedroom in my suite. You're welcome to stay longer, if you want to change your flight."

Rodrigo sipped and shook his head. "No thanks, don't want to horn in on your little romantic vacation."

"Oh, we don't mind, do we, honey?" I hadn't run my proposal past Mike and felt bad sideswiping him with it. Having Rodrigo around might curtail some of our extracurricular activities, like the one that happened on the kitchen counter yesterday. However, I felt worse about ruining Rodrigo's vacation.

Mike took my cue and said with mild enthusiasm, "No, it's fine. K.C.'s suite is big enough for all of us."

Rodrigo ruminated for a moment, then shook his head. "Nah, I'm fine. Besides, Alfonse is returning on Sunday. Getting home on Friday gives me time to unpack, start laundry, and relax a bit before he does. What are your plans today? I plan to get some windsurfing lessons today. You want to join me?"

Mike perked up. "They have windsurfing?"

"We'd talked about going snorkeling," I reminded him. Mike deflated at my comment, and I laughed. "But we can do that tomorrow. What time is your lesson?"

"Dunno." Rodrigo put down his empty mug. "I figured I'd trot on over after breakfast and sign up."

"Do you want to try it, K.C.? Or are your ribs too sore?"

Mike looked so excited, I couldn't let him down. "What the hell? I'll give it a go. Sign me up."

****

Friday morning, Rodrigo stuck his hand out of the window of the hotel airport shuttle and held up the peace sign. I waved until the van reached the end of the driveway and pulled onto the main road.

"I feel bad so much of his vacation got wrapped up in this death mask mess."

Mike stood next to me with his arm wrapped around my shoulders. "You did offer to let him use the spare room in our suite."

"I did. And you didn't even flinch. What a good boyfriend you are." I stood on tiptoe and kissed him.

We broke apart, all smiles.

"Come on, let's get into our kit. The snorkeling excursion leaves in an hour." He swung me around and through the revolving door.

"I expect it will be more successful than our windsurfing adventure," I said ruefully.

Mike laughed. "Windsurfing is perhaps not for you."

"That's an understatement. I spent the whole damn time trying to pull the sail up, then promptly falling off the board once I got it up. I couldn't get the hang of it."

"I don't think your bruised side helped the situation."

"It didn't. I favored the other side. My right arm is twice as sore as my left today."

"Well, when it comes to shell collecting, you beat us all, hands down." Mike squeezed my shoulder.

"Ha ha," I said drily. "I've got a feeling that the rest of this vacation is going to be what it should have been from the start. And no more surprises."

"I certainly hope so."

"By the way, has there been any news on the Craig front?"

"Nothing. We are watching a number of banks in the Bahamas and the Caymans." He paused at a rack of sunglasses outside one of the shops and slid on a black pair. "So far, zilch. How do these look? To replace the pair I lost in the ocean yesterday?"

I handed him a different pair. "Here, try these silver ones on. They wrap around a little more. Technically, Craig lived up to his end of the bargain. Right? He gave you the access codes to Schaffhausen's super-secret safe room. You have both the real and the fake mask."

Mike frowned down at me. "It doesn't work like that."

"I know, but I think the FBI should consider this a win. You need to get that pair. They look good on you."

"It is a win. However, Craig is a loose end." He dug out his wallet to pay.

Back in the suite, I ransacked my backpack, tossing odds and ends onto the bed. We'd changed into our suits and slathered up with sunscreen.

"What are you searching for in there?" Mike passed me on his way to the bathroom.

"A hair tie. I brought three of them and now I can't find a one. I need to pull my hair into a ponytail, or it gets in my face when I swim." I turned the pack upside down and shook hard. A lone piece of gum, a roll of mints, a brown hair tie, and an envelope clanked onto the bed. I straightened out the bent corner of the envelope and turned it over. *To Aunt Milly for your stamp collection.* "So that's where it went," I murmured.

"Where what went?" Mike jutted his head over my shoulder, causing me to jump.

"Jeez!" I put a hand to my chest. "I didn't hear you come back into the room. This envelope of stamps that Craig sent to his aunt along with the mask."

"She collects stamps?"

"Apparently so." I tossed the envelope back on the bed.

"I'm not surprised. She seems the type. I heard something jingle. What else is in there?"

"Just some coins from Brazil."

Mike stiffened. "What kind of coins?"

"Brazilian coins. Why?"

"The American Numismatic Association's annual auction is happening in Chicago next week," he said thoughtfully.

I raised a single brow. "The American what-huh? You totally made that up. Didn't you?"

"I didn't." He rubbed his chin. "It's one of the oldest coin collector's associations in the world. And the upcoming auction is known for selling ancient coins for hundreds of thousands of dollars."

My head rotated side-to-side. "I know what you're thinking. Craig told me the coins weren't worth more than five or six dollars."

The chin rubbing paused. "And you believed him?"

"Not particularly, but I looked up Brazilian money online and they look like modern day coins. I'll open the envelope if you want to see them."

Mike didn't hesitate. "Yes, I would."

I unhooked the brad and allowed the Reals to slide onto Mike's hand. He picked up a silver fifty centavo and took it over to the window to examine it—flipping it back and forth and scratching it with a thumbnail. I joined him at the window and waited for the verdict. He went through each coin the same way, placing them, one-by-one, in my hand. Once each coin had been examined, he shrugged and said with a tinge of dissatisfaction, "They look normal to me."

"Me too." I slid the pieces back into the envelope. "I don't know what he had to liquidate, but I don't think it's these coins."

"You're probably right."

"So how do you know about this pneumatic coin collector's society?"

"American Numismatic Association." He gave a wry smile. "My grandfather on my mom's side used to collect coins. He went to a few auctions over the years."

"Was he buying or selling?"

"A bit of both. When he died, he left his children a little over one hundred thousand dollars' worth of coins."

"Holy crap, that's a lot of coins. What happened to the collection?"

Mike's mouth curved south. "We sold some of them to pay estate taxes, and the rest were split up between his three children."

"What did your parents do with their cut?"

"My mom had them framed. They're hanging in my father's study."

"That sounds cool."

Mike stared past me into the middle distance and replied contemplatively, "I used to love looking through Pop's coins when I was a kid. We'd spend hours at it. He died when I was in middle school, and it was horrible to see the collection split up. I'd gotten it into my head that he would leave the collection to me. Imagine the crushing disappointment when I found out that the collection was split up without my knowledge. I yelled and pitched a terrible fit. It wasn't until my senior year in high school that Mom told me the collection's total worth. I finally understood why it was part of his estate to be split among his children. I'd been angry at my aunt and uncles for years, thinking they'd shafted me out of *my* inheritance." He gave an embarrassed half-shrug. "The arrogance of a self-involved teenager."

"Hmm. There are hidden depths to you, Michael Finnegan. I'm sorry about your grandfather." I stroked his wrinkled brow with my finger. "You were in mourning, and probably felt the coin collection was your connection to him. When you weren't allowed to keep it, it was painful, and made mourning him that much harder."

He nodded. "The fact that I was going through puberty, at the time, didn't help either."

I laughed and shoved the envelope into the outside zipper pocket of my suitcase for safe keeping. "Ain't that the truth. Ugh, I'd never want to relive my middle school years. Braces, acne, and gangly limbs." The clock caught my eye. "We'd better hurry or we'll miss the boat for our snorkeling excursion. Here, toss those towels and the bottle of sunscreen in my bag while I brush my hair into a ponytail."

Chapter Twenty-Three

I stared dispassionately at the pile of clothes I'd left littered on the floor of the closet and thrown over the chair. Sighing, I reached down and, with two fingers, picked up the blood-stained shorts from my little *Chichén Itzá* adventure and threw them in the wastebasket. Once started, I turned into a whirlwind of organization. Dirty clothes went into a plastic laundry bag, clean clothes were hung up or refolded and put in a drawer, and the filthy, grass and dirt-stained T-shirt joined the shorts in the trash.

As I sorted through the clothes, I found the missing hair ties, and some postcards that were shoved in the back pocket of my black shorts. I'd purchased them on my first day in Cancun—the calm before the storm. There were two cards with Cancun beach vistas, one of Cozumel, and one of the Castillo at *Chichén Itzá*. I debated ripping the latter one up and leaving it in the bin with the ruined clothes. However, I'd purchased it for my mother in remembrance of our first trip when we were kids and couldn't bring myself to destroy such a pretty picture. Instead, I tucked all four into the zipper pocket on the outside of my suitcase, where my hand encountered Mrs. Thundermuffin's manila envelope. I pulled it out again, fingering the coins through the thick paper.

A vague recollection whispered around the edge of my brainbox—a book, or was it a movie? The idea was so nebulous, the harder I tried to bring it to the surface, the further it seemed to recede into the recesses of the deep storage memory cabinets. I allowed the coins to clank onto the desk. After a brief inspection of each one, I pushed them aside and shook the envelope to extract the plastic package of stamps. They were stuck on something, but with a tug, the baggie slid into my hand. There was a strip of five stamps with the Brazilian flag on it and the word *Brasil* along the bottom. Behind the strip, there was a half sheet of commemorative 2016 Rio Olympics stamps in striking greens, bold blues, and orange. Each stamp showed a sport—such as rowing, wrestling, and cycling. They were beautiful stamps, and I could find nothing out of the ordinary. I flipped the plastic bag over and found three individual stamps—a lilac stamp with the words *Correio* and 100 *Reis* written across it; a bronze stamp with laurel leaves surrounding a tree, a crown at the top, and the words *Correo Interior* at the top and *3 Cuatros* at the bottom; finally, a rose-colored stamp with a plane flying across the Atlantic Ocean.

Before I could get a closer look at the tiny writing, Mike's voice jerked me back to the present. "K.C., the shower is available; you better get moving if we want to eat dinner tonight," he called from the bathroom.

I hadn't heard the water turn off and realized how far my attention had strayed into the beautiful stamps. I could understand why Mrs. Thundermuffin collected them. With care, so I didn't bend them, I pushed the plastic bag back in the envelope, dropped the coins in after, and sealed the brad closed.

"Coming!"

****

The rest of the vacation skipped along swimmingly. The ocean's saltwater helped heal my scrapes, and my sunburn deepened into a lovely tan. Mike and I probably gained five pounds each from all the eating and drinking we did. And, best of all, there were no further intruders into my room. It seemed that the case of the forged death mask had come to a close—well, at least it did for me.

Craig never showed up on the FBI's radar, and I began to wonder if he'd stashed something in Brazil and was making his way back there on the illegally rented boat. I had a feeling Mike was thinking the same thing, but neither one of us talked about it. As a matter of fact, for the rest of our trip, we ignored real life. I didn't think about home, work, Craig, or the stupid masks for three days straight. I lived in a little bubble of relaxation and happiness—eating, drinking, swimming, sunning, and makin' bacon with Mike.

Chapter Twenty-Four

Except for the woman who spent twenty minutes trying to argue her way onboard with her unkenneled, unvaccinated emotional support chicken, and some gut-bubbling turbulence over Texas, the flight home was uneventful. Mike didn't have the miles to upgrade us to first class on the flight home, but we were able to be seated together. However, as the plane brought us closer and closer to our destination, I found my anxiety levels increasing. Work issues invaded my thoughts, as did my sister, and even my relationship with Mike. We'd had a lovely vacation, but what would happen when we returned from paradise and real life once again intruded? When the drink cart was brought out, I decided to settle my nerves and spinning thoughts with a vodka and tonic.

Unfortunately, the post-vacation blues reared their ugly head during the ride home from the airport, and, as we entered the elevator of my apartment complex, I was definitely feeling a bit down in the dumps. I carried my backpack and my beach bag, which had been stuffed to overflowing with gifts, while Mike chivalrously wheeled my suitcase and wore the large, floppy sombrero I'd purchased for my brother. The sombrero itself was rather funny, but Mike had also purchased a straw fedora and placed it on top of the sombrero. I couldn't help the giggling that started on the way up to my condo.

Mike grinned down at me. "My hat has a hat. I know, you're jealous."

"I don't know if jealous is the word." The elevator opened, and I turned left toward my apartment, when a thump stopped me in my tracks. "Did you hear that? I think it came from Mrs. T.'s apartment." Mike and I both cocked an ear, but we heard nothing else. However, I was afraid she might have fallen. I glanced at Mike, whose face was also drawn with concern. "She's old, I think we should go check on her."

"Agreed. Do you want to drop your stuff in your—" His question was interrupted by another crash, and, saying no more, he turned to jog down the hall toward Mrs. T.'s apartment, pulling my suitcase behind.

I chased after him, and we rounded the corner to find her door slightly ajar. People were talking, but the voices were muffled and conversation indistinguishable, until a male voice barked out the distinct phrase, "Where is it?" There followed another crash.

Dropping my baggage, I put a hand on Mike's arm and whispered, "I think that's Craig's voice."

He nodded, removing the hats, and shoved my suitcase aside. "Wait here, I'm going to get my gun. I'll be right back."

"Wait." I grabbed his arm and hissed, "You don't have your service weapon. You said it was being shipped back to the office."

"I have a personal weapon in a lockbox in my car." He disappeared around the corner at a quick pace.

Hmm, learn something new every day.

Leaning forward, I placed my ear against the crack of the opening to hear better. The voices were muted again, and I couldn't make out what they were saying. I pushed the door open a tad bit further and heard Craig say, "She told me she left it on the counter!" There was a slapping sound. I didn't really believe Craig would hurt his aunt, but desperate men do desperate things, and I couldn't stand by if he was going to smack her around.

My entrance could wait no longer.

Tentatively, I stepped over the threshold. "Mrs. T.? Milly? Are you all right? I thought I heard a crash."

Entering the living room, I stumbled onto a disturbing sight—a sight I'd seen all too recently. The room had been tossed. Couch cushions were thrown willy-nilly around the room. The collection of framed photos on the mantel lay broken across the hearth and looked as if they had been brushed off in one swipe. Dozens of books, pulled from the bookcase, rested in a random pile on a gray bergère chair, some opened with their spines broken. Other knickknacks from the coffee table had been flung to the floor.

However, it wasn't the mess that gave me pause. "Craig? What the hell?"

Craig held his aunt at gunpoint. His skin had darkened during his trip, and there were white tan lines around his eyes from his sunglasses. He wore a pair of jeans and a yellow polo. His aunt had also gotten some sun during the rest of her visit in Mexico. She wore a pink-and-red striped maxi dress, a pair of lime-green sandals, and a blue pashmina draped across her shoulders. However, she wasn't holding her cheek or nose as I expected. She stood half a dozen feet across the kitchen from Craig.

Instead of shaking or looking frightened by the weapon pointed at her, she seemed calm and cool. "Karina, dear, I think it best if you leave. This is a family matter." She continued watching Craig as she spoke to me.

"Actually—" Craig's weapon turned to me. "Karina is just the person I've been wanting to see."

Oh, great.

"Just home from your little vacation, are we?" He wiggled the gun at me as he spoke. "Perfect."

"Craig, is that any way to greet a guest? Put the gun away, this has nothing to do with her," Milly insisted.

This was the second time in a week a gun was leveled my way, and I wasn't happy about it. Even though my heart leapt into my throat when Craig turned the black revolver on me, I knew I needed to maintain my cool and keep him talking while Mike returned to his car to get his weapon and call for backup. At least, I hoped he would call for backup.

"It has everything to do with her. Now, one of you is going to tell me. Where. Are. The. Stamps?"

"I told you, they are around here somewhere. Just give me some time to remember where I put them," Mrs. T. pleaded.

The gears clicked into place, and the nebulous memory that had played around the edges of my mind in Mexico clarified. Unbidden, the words popped out of my mouth. "Oh my lord, it's *Charade!*"

Craig's face split with a smug smile. "Very good."

"I beg your pardon? What's a charade?" Mrs. T. asked.

"Why don't you explain?" Craig waggled the gun back and forth between his aunt and me.

I swallowed. "The old movie. You know—Cary Grant and Audrey Hepburn . . . *Charade*. Five men steal $250,000 worth of gold during a World War II mission, and uh . . . Audrey Hepburn's husband—I can't remember his name—double-crosses his partners and takes the money." I purposely stumbled and dragged out my words to buy time. "Uh, you know . . . he is murdered before the . . . uh . . . surviving three men can find out where he hid it. And, you know . . . she's chased around by the three men, along with Cary Grant, whose name changes three or four times through the film. In the end . . . we find out that Audrey's husband put the money into purchasing rare and valuable stamps."

Mrs. Thundermuffin's gaze sharpened on her grandnephew.

"Guess who showed me that movie?" His head rotated as he met her stare with self-satisfaction, although he kept the gun trained on me. "Why, *you* did, Aunt Milly. Remember that Christmas, when Mom and I came to stay, and instead of taking me to the movies, you insisted *you* had a perfectly good movie on DVD that we could watch. I was twelve and wanted to see the latest *Fast and Furious*. Instead, we watched *Charade*. A movie for old ladies. I don't believe I thanked you at the time."

"No, you didn't. If I recall, when the movie came to an end, you said, 'that was stupid,' and stomped off to bed," Mrs. T. intoned.

"My apologies." Craig gave an exaggerated bow while retaining the gun's position. "I shall remedy that right now. *Thank you, my dearest Auntie*, for introducing me to the masterful film, *Charade*," he derided. "I'll be honest, it might have been the gateway to my . . . extracurricular activities."

"Oh, Craig, you were always too smart for your own good. Why couldn't you be happy curating for that private museum or managing the online auction house?" she asked in a defeated voice.

"Because, it's bo-ring. And once I met Schaffhausen—well, the world became my oyster."

"How much of Schaffhausen's dirty art collection did you acquire for him?" I asked.

"I can't claim them all, but a few of the finer pieces," he boasted.

"Which ones?" I pressed.

"A few. Now . . ." Craig seemed to have come to the end of his little braggart session, but Mike had yet to return. At least, I hadn't heard him in the hallway.

"How much are the stamps worth?" I asked nonchalantly, picking up a discarded book, thinking I could wing it at him, if I got the chance.

"Around seventy-five thousand. And you'd best drop that book, right now." He waggled the gun at me. "I'm an excellent marksman."

My gaze shot to Mrs. T.

"Auntie should know, she's the one who taught me," he taunted.

She gave an ever-so-slight nod.

The book hit the floor. "Did you buy the stamps? Or is that how Schaffhausen paid you?"

"It's how he paid me. I knew he had a collection, and I knew it would be an easy way to get the money out of Bolivia. No need for bank accounts or a bag of cash. I thought about diamonds, but he didn't have access to them in Bolivia. Then" —he tapped his forehead with his free hand— "I remembered Auntie's *favorite* movie."

"What's happening this month?" I continued, "Some sort of stamp collecting con?"

"As a matter of fact, it's in Denver. The show opens on Wednesday, and I've set up private meetings with three different dealers. If I play my cards right, my payday could earn me over a hundred thousand. More than my agreed upon price with Schaffhausen. So you can see why I need them. Now, you said you put them on the kitchen counter, but Auntie here can't seem to remember what she did with them. Are you sure you put them on the counter?"

"Uh—" Luckily, I didn't have to finish that thought.

"Put the weapon down." Mike stood next to me, pointing a .9mm Sig Saur at Craig.

"Tsk. Tsk." Craig clicked his tongue. "A foolish move on your part, Mr. FBI." Quick as a leopard, he pounced on his aunt. He wrapped his arm under her breastbone, using her as a shield, and put the gun to her head.

I sucked wind and expected to see panic or fear on Mrs. T.'s face. Instead, she gave the slightest grin, moaned, and went limp. Craig, not quite knowing what to do, tried to hoist up her dead weight to keep his shield in place.

"Take the shot," I murmured out of the side of my mouth.

"Get down." Mike put a hand on my shoulder and pushed me.

Realizing he wanted me out of Craig's line of fire, I dropped to my knees. As I did so, Mrs. T. came back to life. With her right hand, she reached back and pushed Craig's right elbow forward, and grabbed the barrel of the gun with the other hand. Before I knew what was happening, she'd twisted his hand backward, and the weapon was now pointed at her grandnephew. Craig cried out while she continued pushing the hand and wrist backward, forcing him to drop to his knees. She disarmed him as he went down.

Mike jumped into action with handcuffs at the ready. "Lie on the floor, with your hands above your head. Now!"

"Whoa." I got to my feet. "That was badass, Mrs. T. I need you to show me how to do it sometime."

She placed the gun out of reach and put her hands on her hips. "It's easy, once you know the motions, and when your attacker is discombobulated. Really, Craig, the number one gun safety rule I taught you was to be aware of your surroundings at all times. And don't allow your gun within arm's length of another person. What were you thinking?" she chastised.

I bit my lips to keep from sniggering.

After Mike got Craig cuffed, he pulled him to his knees and reeled off the Miranda Rights. "Do you understand these rights as I've explained them?"

"Yes," Craig scowled.

I crossed my arms and tilted my head. "So, Craig, you mentioned that you'd stolen other items for Schaffhausen. Care to elaborate?"

He glared at me. "I want a lawyer."

"Okey doke." I gave a shrug. "But you should know that your buddy, Adolfo, is in custody."

"Ha! I don't believe you," he spat.

"Oh, but you should," I replied in velvet tones. "You see, he paid me a visit in Mexico."

Craig's cocky glare shifted ever-so-slightly toward uncertainty.

"That's right, he came back to find you and the mask." I smiled confidently. "He knew you'd been paid and was still looking for his cut. Poor boy. I wonder if he's realized that you never meant to give him any of the money."

Craig glanced over his shoulder at Mike. "I have immunity. You found Schaffhausen's stash, didn't you? I held up *my* end of the bargain."

Mike's brows rose. "Your immunity deal went belly-up when you escaped custody. Now there are new charges. Credit card and identity theft. Grand larceny for the stolen boat." His gaze surfed the room. "Not to mention the vandalism and the felony you'll be charged with for holding your aunt and Karina at gunpoint. Is the gun stolen too?"

"No, it's mine," Mrs. T. sighed. "He took it from my bedside table. I won't press charges. He's already neck-deep in his own pile of poop."

"Craig, you might want to squeal while you have the chance. Before Adolfo does it for you," I coaxed. "He's so delicate, he doesn't seem the type who will do well in jail."

He gave a knowing look. "Forget it. Adolfo will keep his mouth shut if he knows what's good for him."

"Is that a threat?" Mike growled.

"Not from me," Craig replied snidely.

"Schaffhausen's in custody too," I clarified.

Craig gave me a scornful glance and shut his lips tight.

During our conversation, Mrs. T. moved into the living room and gathered broken bric-a-brac off the floor.

"Here, let me help you with that." I picked up a black and white photo of two young children wearing pinafores with ribbons in their hair, holding hands. The glass was split down the middle, but the old photo undamaged. "I think you just need to replace the glass. Is this you and your sister?"

She glanced at the frame in my hand. "Yes. We were six and eight at the time."

"Ladies, please leave the things alone," Mike said gently. "This is a crime scene; they need to photograph it."

"But, honey, her possessions are broken and strewn across the floor," I bemoaned, indicating the mess.

His face turned to chagrin. "I know, K.C.—"

"It's okay, dear." Mrs. T. laid a delicate hand on my shoulder. "Leave it. It will get cleaned soon enough."

I couldn't bring myself to put the delightful picture back on the floor, so I placed it on the mantel. The calvary arrived soon after. FBI agents swooped in, filling the small apartment. While Mike got busy directing the crime scene, Mrs. T. sat down at the dining table with one of the agents.

Everyone seemed to have a job but me. At loose ends, I rescued my luggage from the hallway and retreated to my own condo while Mike did his thing. I finished unpacking, changed out of my travel clothes, and started a load of laundry. As I stuffed the outfit I'd worn on the plane into the washing machine, my nose crunched in disgust. I always hated the smell of airplane—jet fuel and burnt coffee—that would attach itself to anything within a ten-yard radius.

Someone knocked at my door as I pressed the start button on the washer.

Mike waited on the other side, and I waved him in. "Are they done processing the crime scene?"

He followed me into the kitchen. "Almost. We're going to need a statement from you."

"Sure." I opened the fridge and leaned in. "Would you like something? It's a little like Old Mother Hubbard's cupboard. I've got one diet soda, a bottle of champagne, a six-pack of water, and a questionable package of cheese. I really need to hit the grocery store."

"I'll have a water," he replied.

I handed him a bottle and popped open the soda for myself.

He didn't open his drink. "K.C., where are the stamps?"

I swallowed and pointed at the manila envelope on my dining table. "Stamps and the coins are in there. I still don't think the coins are worth anything. I noticed three singular stamps in the plastic bag. I have a feeling those are the ones you're looking for."

Picking up the package, he gave a rueful smile. "I never thought about the stamps. Did you?"

"There was something . . . unformulated . . . that had me looking at them while you were in the shower the other day. I don't know a damn thing about stamps. I never thought they'd be worth a hundred thousand." I slid onto one of the kitchen stools. "Has Craig spilled anything?"

"No. He's lawyering up."

"What about Adolfo?"

"INTERPOL's got more on him than we suspected. Craig may not be the only one who he's produced forgeries for." Mike joined me and slid the stamps onto the counter.

"Really? I'm surprised to hear that. So that sad sap story he fed me back in Mexico was just a bunch of cow hockey?" I flipped the package over and pointed to the three I thought might be the collector items.

Mike held the package up to the light to examine the ones I'd pointed out. He shrugged and slipped the plastic bag back into the envelope. "Apparently, Adolfo is quite the con man."

"Huh. I'm usually not such a sucker."

Mike eyed me.

"What? I'm a very good judge of people. I was onto Craig the crap weasel from the first," I asserted.

"You may be able to read people, but you get suckered into trouble all the time. Remember how this entire thing started. Your neighbor asked you to bring a fake Egyptian funerary mask into a foreign country."

"That's beside the point."

"No, I believe that *is* the point. Listen, I don't have time to argue." He tapped the manila envelope. "I've got to pass this up the chain. I'm going to send Agent Jones over to take your statement. Are you okay with that?"

"Yes. Send him on over. Just let him know that my cupboards are bare. I've got nothing to offer him but water, champagne, and moldy cheese."

Mike wrinkled his nose and headed to the foyer. "I wouldn't worry about it."

Ten minutes later, there was another knock at my door.

"Hello, you must be Agent Jones." I smiled at a tall fellow with horn-rimmed glasses and a receding hairline as he held up his credentials. "Can I offer you something to drink? I have water or champagne."

"Champagne, of course," he deadpanned.

"Agent Jones, I think we are going to get along like gangbusters."

Chapter Twenty-Five

"Nice move, jackass!" I yelled at the idiot who cut me off, almost taking my front bumper with him. I laid on my horn, and he replied in the usual, friendly D.C. fashion by flipping me the bird. Ah, the joys of being back home in rush hour traffic. My phone rang, and I pressed my Bluetooth to answer. "Hello."

"Morning. How is your return to the real world?" Mike asked.

"Just grand. I'll tell you what, I did *not* miss this traffic. I got your text. How late were you at the office?"

"I left around ten. I'm sorry I didn't get back over to your place."

"Don't worry about it. I figured you'd be late, and you also had to unpack." I heard heavy breathing. "What are you doing? Jogging?"

"More like a fast-walk. I'm running late for a morning meeting and the Metro got held up for ten minutes in one of the tunnels. What are you doing tonight?"

I paused. Rick's open invitation to attend Silverthorne's support group was on my mind. While I didn't feel as run down as I did when I left for Mexico, there was still . . . something—a sadness that came over me last night. I'd spoken to Jillian and Mom, telling them nothing about the mask fiasco—keeping things upbeat. When I hung up, I realized I didn't really tell anyone about how I'd been feeling. Not Mike. Not my mom. Not Jilly. Maybe it was time I did.

"K.C., hello? Are you still there?"

"What? Oh, I'm still here. Sorry, I was paying attention to traffic. I'm not sure what I'm doing," I hedged.

"It's Tuesday. Are you going to take Rick up on his offer?"

Wow, did Mike read my mind? "Yes, I was thinking about it."

Considering all the crazy crap that went down in Mexico and Silverthorne's part in it, I wondered if Mike would now be against my going.

"I think you should give it a try."

Will wonders never cease. "Okay. I'll do that."

"Great. How about dinner tomorrow night?"

"I've got yoga at six. If you want to meet afterward, I can do that." I halted at a red light. "There's an Indian restaurant across the street from the gym."

"Text me a time and address. I'll meet you there. I'm heading into the building. We'll talk later."

****

I pulled up to the callbox and waved to the camera. "Hi, it's Karina, I'm here to . . . uh . . . attend a group meeting. Um . . . Rick said I could come."

With a clackety-clack, the metal gate rolled back, and I drove through.

Rick opened the front door as I stepped out of the car. He wore a navy polo with the Silverthorne logo on it, and jeans. "You look" —his gaze narrowed as he surveyed me— "tan. And rested."

The fresh scent of Irish Spring soap teased me as I walked past him. "How are Josh and Hernandez? Recovered from our Mexico escapade?"

"They're fine. Josh is here, you can ask him yourself. What about you? Josh said you got pretty banged up. Said you broke a rib?" He frowned.

"It's just a bruise. Dulled now to a very unattractive boiled-egg-yolk green."

"That's descriptive."

I waited in the reception area for him to lead the way.

Rick continued to look me up and down. "How was the trip?"

I crossed my arms. "Well, the ending was much more relaxing than the beginning."

"Josh told me Mike showed up."

"He did." I waited for that zing that I'd felt before I left for the trip. So far, nothing.

"I heard Craig escaped custody."

"Wow, you really are plugged in." I waited for Rick to explain how he'd gotten his information. He didn't satisfy my curiosity. I sighed and dropped my protective stance. "Well, you're correct. He did escape custody in Mexico, but he was kind enough to be waiting here when we arrived home."

Those dark brows furrowed deeper. "Waiting where?"

"In my building. He stopped to pay his aunt a visit. Apparently, he'd sent her some valuable stamps and wanted them back."

Rick's mouth pinched.

"Luckily, Mike was on hand to . . . ah . . . apprehend our fugitive."

"Then it's finished?"

"I believe so," I replied with a sharp nod.

He didn't say anything more but continued to study me. I chewed my lip and fiddled with my earring. I didn't understand what he was waiting for. Did he want to say something else? Was this a power play? Did he realize my attraction to him at our last meeting? My face blazed at the thought.

Finally, I checked my watch. "Isn't the meeting starting?"

"C'mon." He went through the motions to call the elevator and we went up to the second floor. I trotted down the long, gray-carpeted hallway behind Rick, getting more and more nervous as we went. Rick stopped at a door labeled Conference Room D and waited for me to catch up. He paused with his hand on the knob. "Have you ever been to a support group meeting?"

I shook my head.

"You don't have to talk if you don't want to. Be respectful of those who are speaking."

I nodded, and he opened the door.

Four men sat around a large wooden conference table with chairs enough for ten and a handful of water bottles in the center.

Joshua sat at the foot of the table and greeted me with a wave. "Karina, nice to see you."

Rick pulled out a chair for me in the center of the table. "Everyone, this is Karina. You know Jin." Jin, on Joshua's left, nodded at me. "That guy across the table is Radhesh."

He pointed to a dark-skinned man missing an arm and with scarring along the left side of his face that looked as if he'd met with an industrial-grade cheese grater. Mentally, I cringed, wondering what happened to have created such an injury. Outwardly, I gave Radhesh a finger wave, which he acknowledged with a nod.

"And the guy at the other end of the table is Terry." Joshua indicated a black man with a bald head that gleamed beneath the fluorescent light. He had a diamond earring in one ear and wore an Army sweatshirt.

I indicated Terry's sweatshirt. "Army ranger?"

"Delta Force. Welcome to the group," Terry replied.

"Thanks for having me."

Rick took the seat next to me and reached out to grab one of the bottles. "Water?"

I nodded.

Terry leaned on his forearms. "I heard some bad stuff went down in Mexico."

"I suppose you could say that." I gripped the bottle in both hands.

Terry's head bounced up and down. "Josh said you took a beating. He patched you up?"

Josh pinched the bridge of his nose and scrunched his eyes shut.

"Um . . . yeah . . ." I stared at my water bottle, twisting and untwisting the cap, kind of hoping someone else would start talking. When no one did, I blurted out in a rush, "I was trampled by a stampede of frightened tourists."

"Jesus. That's messed up," Terry said.

He was right. I looked up from the bottle, straight at Terry, and said, "Yeah. It was."

"Want to talk about it?" His golden-brown eyes regarded me.

I didn't know this man at all. There was interest and sympathy on his face, but no censure. If I replied in the negative, I had a feeling he'd simply move on to someone else. It would be so easy for me to decline. But . . . I came to talk about my feelings. If I refused now, wouldn't it be harder to say something the next time? If I wasn't going to talk, what the hell was I doing here?

"The smell of grass and dirt used to hold childhood memories. Good memories. Now it holds fear," I admitted. "I'd like to get past that."

Author's Note

On September 2, 2018, around seven-thirty in the evening, fire broke out at the Brazilian National Museum, in Rio de Janeiro. The museum, which opened in 1818, housed over two hundred million artifacts. In 1892, the museum was relocated to the beautiful neoclassical São Cristóvão Palace, which sits upon a sizeable park in the northern part of the city. The palace was built in 1803 for the Portuguese royal family, and the building held as much important cultural significance to the city as the artifacts lost in the fire. It was a treasure-trove of human history. According to the *New York Times,* notable items from the museum included:

- Bendego, a five-ton meteorite, one of the world's largest, found in 1784.
- Luzia, an 11,500-year-old skull, one of the oldest human fossils to be found in the Americas.
- A vast Egyptian collection, which included an 11th century coffin and a mummified cat.
- Seven hundred pieces of a Greco-Roman collection, acquired in the 1850s.
- The largest collection of indigenous Brazilian artifacts, including dolls, baskets, pots, pendants, and other jewelry.

Faulty air conditioning units were the cause of the fire. The trio of air conditioners failed to meet manufacturer recommendations regarding the use of separate circuit breakers and grounding devices, according to an *Agence France-Press* report. The *Associated Press* adds that the units received a stronger electrical current than they were made to conduct, creating a powder keg situation poised for disaster. However, the building also lacked hoses, water sprinklers, and fire door suppression systems, which, had they been installed, may have limited the damage to the museum. Many Brazilians lay the blame for the fire at the feet of the government and president, Michel Temer, for the systemic decay of cultural and scientific institutions, due to a consistent decrease in federal funding.

Whoever is to blame, there are a few glimmers of hope to this tragedy. On the night of the fire, staff members, scholars, firemen, and military ran in and out of the building, at great risk to themselves, to rescue as many artifacts as they could. Meanwhile, the fire brigade fought the blaze, which burned for over six hours, reaching temperatures of more than eighteen hundred degrees Fahrenheit. As of March 2019, around two thousand artifacts have been recovered, including Bendego and Luzia. Additionally, back in 2016, Google Arts & Culture had begun working with the museum to bring the collections online. Google Arts & Culture digitized enough material to create a virtual experience, so the cultural heritage of the Museu Nacional will not be lost to human memory. Thanks to Google Arts & Culture, the inspiration for the funerary mask referenced in *Pharaoh's Forgery* can be seen on the Brazilian National website at *museunacional.ufrj.br*. Unfortunately, the funerary mask and most of the Egyptian exhibit did not survive the fire.

According to *Smithsonian Magazine*, governments and cultural organizations across the world have pledged to offer financial backing for rebuilding efforts. Finally, the Brazilian government released emergency funds of R$15 million for an ambitious restoration plan.

Acknowledgments

As usual, this latest Karina Cardinal mystery couldn't have happened without the help of many people and hours of online research. When I heard about the museum fire in the news, I was working on *Diamonds & Deception*. As a research junky, I paused my writing to find out everything I could on the tragedy. After spending time on the museum's website, I realized I wanted to incorporate it into the next Karina Cardinal storyline. I'd like to thank Google Arts & Culture and the Brazilian National Museum for working so diligently to digitize these artifacts so I, and others, can still view the valuable relics online. Thanks to Elizabeth Atalay, with *National Geographic Magazine,* for taking the time to send me her research, and for connecting me with Dr. Tasha Dobbin-Bennett, at Oxford College of Emory. Martin's knowledge about the false artifact came from Dr. Dobbin-Bennett's vast knowledge of forgeries and fakes. I could spend hours listening to her tell me stories, which are probably far more outlandish than Karina's own adventure. Thanks to Matt Fine for his usual tidbits and insights on FBI life, which I use to develop the storyline.

Finally, I'd like to thank my awesome team, Emily, Rebekah, and Carolan, who help me make Karina's stories better. Also, to my friends and family who read Karina Cardinal and continue to support my writing.

About the Author

Ellen Butler is a bestselling novelist writing critically acclaimed suspense thrillers, and award-winning romance. Ellen holds a master's degree in Public Administration and Policy, and her history includes a long list of writing for dry, but illuminating, professional newsletters and windy papers on public policy. She is a member of International Thriller Writers, Sisters in Crime, and the OSS Society. She lives in the Virginia suburbs of Washington, D.C. with her husband and two children.

You can find Ellen at:
Website ~ *www.EllenButler.net*
Facebook ~ *www.facebook.com/EllenButlerBooks*
Twitter ~ *@EButlerBooks*
Instagram ~ *@ebutlerbooks*
Goodreads ~ *www.goodreads.com/EllenButlerBooks*

Guided Reading Questions for Book Clubs

Available on Ellen's Website
EllenButler.net

Novels by Ellen Butler
Suspense/Thriller
Isabella's Painting (Karina Cardinal Mystery Book 1)
Fatal Legislation (Karina Cardinal Mystery Book 2)
Diamonds & Deception (Karina Cardinal Mystery Book 3)
The Brass Compass
Poplar Place

Contemporary Romance
Heart of Design (Love, California Style Book 1)
Planning for Love (Love, California Style Book 2)
Art of Affection (Love California Style Book 3)
Second Chance Christmas

Karina's next adventure will be hitting bookshelves in 2021. If you are interested in learning about upcoming Karina Cardinal mysteries, join Ellen's newsletter at *ellenbutler.net*.

www.ingramcontent.com/pod-product-compliance
Lightning Source LLC
Chambersburg PA
CBHW050417260626
47156CB00003B/1045